A DANGEROUS HOMECOMING

The long shudders were easing now. I concentrated on trying to forget the deathly cold, the evil presence in the dream, the man who towered, laughing . . . Why was I sure it was a man?

But even as I gathered the warming quilt about me, I knew the nightmare was not over. In that cold dawn, I was finally face-to-face with the chilling, whispering doubt that had brought me here. Face-to-face with the terrifying suspicion that I scarcely dared to breathe aloud in the silence of my room. . . .

I didn't believe that my grandmother's death was an accident. And if it was not an accident, there was only one alternative.

Murder.

DEADLY INHERITANCE

FIONNUALA REEVES

AVON BOOKS OF CANADA
PUBLISHERS OF BARD, CAMELOT, DISCUS AND FLARE BOOKS

DEADLY INHERITANCE is an original publication of Avon Books. This work has never before appeared in book form.

AVON BOOKS
A division of
The Hearst Corporation
959 Eighth Avenue
New York, New York 10019

First Avon Printing, August, 1983

AVON TRADEMARK REG. U. S. PAT. OFF. AND IN OTHER COUNTRIES, MARCA REGISTRADA, HECHO EN U. S. A.

Printed in the U. S. A.

WFH 10 9 8 7 6 5 4 3 2 1

To my father
and in memory of my mother

AUTHOR'S NOTE

Kilcollery does not exist, but all along the southern and western coasts of Ireland are many little towns and villages which match my Kilcollery for superb natural beauty and which could have stood as its model.

The people are fictitious; any resemblance to persons, living or dead, is purely coincidental.

CHAPTER 1

The letters started it all.

They were beside me in my bag, as I sat in the little yellow Ford on the steep West Cork road in the early May sunshine. I lit a cigarette and drew on it gratefully. I had come a long way in a hurry; a few moments' respite would be good. High atop the last rise of the narrow, winding, mountain road, about a mile before my destination, I had felt an urgent need to pull over to sort my thoughts out. I had to come to grips with the reason why I was here in Ireland instead of in my usual Monday morning history classes at the London boarding school where I had taught now for two years.

Yesterday, when I arrived back at the school after an Easter camping trip, there they were, two letters, propped up on the mantelpiece of my old-fashioned sitting room. Two simple, innocuous white envelopes. My name and the school address neatly typed. Each envelope bore an Irish stamp but no return address. My heart lurched as I deciphered the Gaelic postmark: Cill Coll an Righe—Kilcollery, County Cork. The home of my Irish grandmother, Elizabeth Wentworth.

Suddenly uneasy, I ripped the envelopes open, but neither letter was from Grandmother. I started to read. At first I was puzzled, even mystified. The impersonal typescript from Fred Moone, my grandmother's lawyer in the village of Kilcollery, informed me without preamble that he was forwarding details of the generous offer a client had made for Mainstay.

Now, as the heir and my grandmother's only living close relative, I might be assumed to take more than a passing interest in any proposal to dispose of Mainstay, the beautiful old house by the sea where my father's family had lived for five generations before me. But Fred gave no clue why

1

he had addressed his letter to me. Grandmother, though in her late seventies, was still very much the mistress of Mainstay. And if her health remained in any way comparable to her forceful, even domineering, nature, it was not likely that I would inherit the old place for some time.

Then I realized that, in my hurry, I had accidentally started on the second, and much later, of the two letters, both from Fred. Mechanically I reached for the first. Postmarked some days after Easter, two whole weeks ago, it was stark and brutal, and I read the message with disbelieving eyes.

Dear Joanna,

I regret to inform you that late on the Thursday evening before Easter, while walking on the cliff path near Mainstay, your grandmother somehow slipped and fell over the edge to the rocks below. Unfortunately, the tide being high at the time, her body was swept out to sea. It was recovered three days later. It might be of some comfort to know that the doctor was certain that death was instantaneous on her fall.

I am sorry to have to send you such news. There is no easy way to deal with such a tragic accident.

Several attempts were made to contact you, but, as I was informed by the school caretaker that you are away and cannot be reached, I have, reluctantly, been obliged to proceed with funeral arrangements.

Numbly, I read the stiff phrases of condolence that followed and, in a daze, recognized the familiar flourish of Fred's signature. In the last few years I had seen that signature, or that of his sister Nita, at the bottom of terse, periodic communications that "all was much as ever at Mainstay" or that my grandmother was "in good health but quite unchanged."

I had known what the words meant. Grandmother and I had not spoken in nearly five years.

And now she was gone. An old woman, dead on the rocks below the house she had lived in and cherished with obsessive pride for almost half a century.

I sat thunderstruck; I don't know for how long.

Then I reached for the other letter and read it, this time all the way through.

Fred did not refer at all to my grandmother but plunged immediately into details of what he described as a most generous and providential offer for Mainstay. It certainly seemed huge to me, even staggering.

The terms [Fred wrote] are cash—immediately and in full; possession also to be without delay, naturally. An annuity apiece provides adequately for the servants, Peggy and Joe. The furnishings and effects, except for those in the servants' rooms, are yours and my client wishes to make an additional offer for all ordinary household effects, with the stipulation that you should specify any particular items you would like to retain. These will be carefully packed and sent to your London home. Personal possessions will be forwarded without question, of course. My client is prepared to bear all legal and removal costs.

Hmm, I found myself thinking, not only a generous but an unusual offer—highly unusual.

Having already vacated his own house [Fred went on smoothly, as though anticipating my skeptical reaction], my client is anxious to close the sale and move in as soon as possible. Accordingly, the terms are rather more generous than you could have expected.

I am, of course, aware that your real home has always been in England and that Kilcollery holds only sad memories for you. And since you are financially well circumstanced in having inherited your late mother's house in London and in having secured a permanent teaching post at Lady Windermere School, I am sure that you will wish to have the Kilcollery property off your hands with the least trouble and as soon as possible.

In the circumstances, this cash offer is so opportune as to warrant no delay in acceptance. I have therefore drawn up the necessary papers which have been dispatched to you under separate cover. They require only your notarized signature in the places indicated.

No doubt your own or your aunt's solicitor will be glad
to look over the documents on your behalf.

At this high-handedness, I stiffened. All too clearly, my
grandmother was scarcely in her grave when Fred prepared the full legal papers to transfer Mainstay to this
unnamed "client." After all, my grandmother, too, had
been his client. Something better than this callous formality, this indecent haste, was owed to her memory.

The heavily legalese stiffness of the letter waned somewhat as Fred continued, merely to warm further to his
theme of persuasion.

I need hardly point out, Joanna, that with such a
good offer for the house, time is of the essence.

In the meantime, you know that you can rely on
Nita and me to comply, upon receipt, with your instructions about the consignment of personal effects
and other items. It can all be expedited as if you were
here yourself, but without interrupting your school
term. Indeed, there is no need for you to put yourself to
the trouble and upset of visiting Kilcollery, no need at
all. As soon as I receive the signed papers, I'll hurry
the proceedings and have the cash deposited in your
bank in no time. You can safely leave matters in my
hands, as safely as if you were here yourself; no need
to worry yourself about coming over at all.

Finally, adjuring me to be sure to include with the documents the name of my bank and the appropriate account
number, he remained my old friend, etc., etc.

As safely as if I were there myself. No need to come over
at all. . . .

I sat back and thought for a long time.

Then I rose and went downstairs to ask the headmistress
for immediate compassionate leave. Miss Ainsworth was
horrified at my news and sympathized with my wish to fly
over to Ireland to see personally to such important family
matters. Even though the funeral was over long since, it
would, she agreed, be quite improper to leave everything,
including the settling of the estate and the fate of my

grandmother's longtime servants, in the hands of a lawyer, however efficient.

What I didn't mention to Miss Ainsworth was that I had a vague but nonetheless unsettling apprehension that something was wrong. Somewhere in the back of my mind, a faint warning bell was sounding, slightly out of tune with the smooth pitch of Fred's letters.

Oh, his account of the "client's" offer for the house could be plausible; perhaps the client was rich and eccentric. What disturbed me was Fred's reiteration of words like "hurry" and "expedite." I couldn't help wondering why the urgency, why the emphasis on a quick sale. But his repetition that there was "no need" for me to come over to Ireland "at all" really unsettled me.

True, I hadn't shown the slightest interest in Mainstay in recent years, but Fred should know that that was because of the rift between Grandmother and me. I had never said that I would be glad to "have the property off my hands" as soon as possible. Or even that I wanted it off my hands at all.

So what was Fred up to?

Suddenly I was struck by something about the first letter. Something that, had I not been distracted by the pressing offer to purchase Mainstay, should have riveted my attention instantly. The circumstances of my grandmother's death.

The *unexplained* circumstances . . .

She was old. Though very healthy for her age, she had suffered for years from arthritic pain in her legs and was normally unadventurous. She had liked to walk along the cliff at Mainstay at times, but she had also known every dangerous inch of the path for over fifty years. And yet, alone, late on an April evening, she had gone out, walked down that path, and fallen to her death. How? Why?

A possibility, admittedly slim, occurred to me. Though I knew in my heart that it wasn't likely, I grabbed at it anyway. Quickly, I crossed the room to the telephone.

It took fifteen minutes and two calls before I got through to the person I wanted. Inevitably, he asked why I wanted the information. I invented a swift tale of settling a bet with a friend.

When I replaced the receiver, the remote possibility had

been dashed. The information I had got was quite definite and I didn't like the implications one bit.

With a deepening uneasiness, I hauled out my suitcase and began to pack it for the journey back to Mainstay.

I had never been able to separate the house itself from the demanding, domineering presence of my grandmother. I had watched my parents before me try not to be alienated by her. Each summer, we spent at Mainstay what seemed to me endless weeks of wrangling and arguing. How they endured her interminable nagging, her scarcely veiled resentment of my English mother, I don't know. I only know that I blamed her for their deaths, that summer when I was sixteen.

It was after another of their confrontations, not noisy but all the more bitter for that (about our year-round residence in London), that Grandmother had given fluent vent to her hatred of England and her corrosive jealousy of my mother. The only Wentworth son, Grandmother insisted obstinately, should know and accept that his "place" was at Mainstay.

Angrily, he reminded her yet again that the Wentworths had cheerfully mixed Irish and English lives and careers for generations and that in any case his job, with a chemical research firm, was in London. Then he stalked out to go fishing, accompanied by my mother. I stayed behind to finish a book I had borrowed from Dr. O'Brien in the village. There would be other chances to go fishing.

An hour or so later, a sudden squall that quickly became a raging, blinding storm caught and overturned their currach as they made hastily for the narrow rocky cove below Mainstay.

I was only seconds behind Joe as we stumbled down the cliff path in a vain effort to reach them. My father, holding my mother up in mountainous waves, battled fruitlessly against the undertow. Again and again he struggled toward the rocks, weakening visibly. A moment later they were gone.

My mother's only sister came from London that night. Despite Grandmother's opposition, she quietly enlisted Dr. O'Brien's support and, shortly after the funeral, took me home to London to pick up the pieces of my life.

For a long, miserable time after that, living simply with
Aunt Christine in my dead parents' too quiet London
house, I stonily held that Grandmother had caused their
deaths, that but for their upset they might have noticed
the squall signs sooner. . . . But though life was pitifully
reduced, my pain and bitterness dulled and ebbed slowly.

I even went to visit Grandmother—once only, almost
five years ago now. I had a naïve notion of restoring some
semblance of family feeling. Over the previous two years
she and I had exchanged the merest of formal communications.

My visit was a mistake. Worse, it was a disaster.

I came, prompted by pity. I had begun to visualize
Grandmother as lonely and desolate. I realize now that I
assumed the tragedy would have changed her, softened
her.

I was wrong.

I had scarcely arrived when she started in on plans for
me to shake the dust of England off my shoes once and for
all, to come "home," last of the Wentworths, to take my
place at Mainstay for good.

"I live in London, Grandmother," I said carefully. "I
even have a house there." Despite my best intentions, my
fists were clenching already.

"Yes, your late mother's home. Well, it must be sold, of
course. London property fetches a good price. That is something, at least."

I was astounded. "Sell my house? I don't want to sell my
house. Why would I do that? And what about Aunt Christine? She lives there, too, as you know."

At the mention of my aunt, a steely look of enmity closed
Grandmother's small face into a tight little knot.

"Besides, I'm all set for college. It's all arranged."

The tiny black figure sat straight-backed and unsmil-
ing. "Then it must be unarranged, child. Your place is
here." Her tone was unmistakably final.

She shifted briskly in her chair. "Now, that's settled,
dear. We won't speak of it again. We must think now about
paying some calls. And you'd like some new clothes. Yes,
definitely, now that I look at you, oh dear me, yes, indeed.
Don't get up and walk about when I am speaking to you,
child. Really, you are much too old to be so gauche. Per-

haps we should consider a finishing school, for a short
while. Would you like that, dear?"

Head on one side, she appraised me possessively.

It was the little smile that did it. The encouraging,
smug, triumphant little smile. In an instant it wiped from
my mind the tentative concern that had brought me back
to visit her, and I understood all too well the heated quarrels between my grandmother and my parents. Then, the
resentment I had tried to bottle up, the blame I was sure
she deserved for their deaths, the ache of irretrievable loss,
all roared to the boil again and I could no longer endure
her.

I shouted it all out at her. She sat, seemingly unmoved
by my childish outburst. No doubt she was waiting for
"sanity and good manners" to return to me; I had all too
often heard her use such phrases to my father. Somehow
the thought of him gave me courage and my rage cooled instantly to a new, stiff determination. As she opened her
mouth to speak, I forestalled her swiftly.

"Perhaps," I said coldly, "perhaps my father could not
bring himself to sever his connection with you and this
damned house, Grandmother, but I can. I intend to go on
living in London, to go to college, to live my own life. I
shall leave Mainstay as soon as I have repacked my suitcase. I am going home, home to London, by the next flight.
The day you accept me as I am, not as some puppet to be
manipulated, or some sort of doll exemplifying the latest of
the Wentworth line, that's the day you and I may have
something to say to each other, Grandmother. But not till
then."

Her face drained of color, she sat speechless and motion-
less.

I waited. She said nothing.

"Obviously, it was a mistake to come at all," I finished
icily. "That's a mistake I won't make again."

With that I turned on my heel and left her stiffly silent
in the library.

I remember Peggy's dismayed face appearing in the
hall. She had heard it all. She followed me upstairs and
while, stony-faced, I flung my possessions back into my
case, she tried to stop me, pleading with me to stay.

I put Peggy from me gently and walked out of Mainstay into the cold, starry night.

It was too late to leave for England that evening so I stayed overnight with the Moones, Nita and Fred. I blundered in on them as they were discussing their plans to expand the small Promenade Hotel they had inherited from their long-widowed father. Nita also had a rapidly growing local crafts and knitwear business supplying a major dress house in Dublin.

We had never been the closest of friends but, right now, they were just what I needed, people who knew my family and could guess fairly accurately what had happened. They asked few questions, sat me down as if I had been an expected guest and, over a light supper, told me of their expansion plans.

Such plans! New front steps and terraces, two huge porches, a new wing with lots of extra bedrooms. They would be very expensive. Nita admitted to some concern about the extent of capital borrowing involved. But Fred, her junior by ten years and brought up by his indulgent sister, flashed her a coaxing smile and reassured her. With her cooking and flair for management, the hotel would be a great success and they'd be rich in no time. His sharp dark face softened by the firelight, he poured himself another whiskey and spoke of the fast sports car on which he had his eye. Nita's smile was affectionate and tolerant and she was soon chuckling at Fred's projection of himself as host in the newly decorated hotel.

"Getting paid to ape the country squire and wow the ladies," he said, eyes alight as he postured and bowed at the fireplace.

Thus the evening passed pleasantly, soothing my edgy nerves. It was with gratitude that I said goodbye to Nita next day. Fred tried to persuade me to stay a few days, promising me a good time unspecified in words but all too clear in his dancing eyes as they roved freely over me. I extricated myself from his parting embrace with more haste than good manners.

As I got into the doctor's car—providentially, he was going to Cork, saving me a bumpy trip by the one daily bus—Nita added quickly that she would "keep an eye on things at Mainstay" and would "scribble a line" now and then. This unexpected extra kindness was too much for me and it was through an unaccustomed blur that I saw the last of Kilcollery.

Until today.

It was getting uncomfortably warm with the sunshine beating on the car windows. As I opened the door, I caught sight of my reflection in the mirror. Short dark curls framed a normally pale, oval face, now flushed slightly with the springtime warmth. I tilted my head and decided that my nose, a Wentworth nose, wasn't bad; reasonably nice and straight, in fact. And even if my mouth was a little large, my eyebrows were naturally dark and well shaped, setting off the wide-apart blue eyes generously fringed with the dark lashes I had inherited from my mother.

I smiled wryly at my reflection, remembering that I had come here to seek the answers to two nagging questions: the first, why Fred Moone wanted to sell Mainstay so quickly, and the second and far more troubling, what my grandmother had been doing on the dangerous cliff path on that particular evening.

I hadn't told Miss Ainsworth, but I smelled a rat.

I hadn't said anything more to her, not even when she called me to her office early on Monday morning to give me the legal-sized package which had just arrived by special delivery.

I didn't tell her about the phone calls I'd made, about the man in the weather office at Cork Airport who had told me that for seven hours on the Thursday evening before Easter, Holy Thursday, the entire southwest coast of Ireland was battered by wind and rain. Gale force, he said, a raging storm that left a lot of damage in its wake, particularly along the coast. Ruefully, he added that I had therefore won my bet that on a day picked at random it would, more often than not, have been "raining in County Cork."

Not even to Miss Ainsworth did I speak again of my grandmother, whose evening walk down the cliff path to her death was, to me, because of that storm, finally inexplicable. Grandmother had always, for as long as I could remember, hated storms.

On the plane, in the early hours of Monday morning, I examined the package of legal papers very carefully.

We landed at Cork in a damp, warm mist. It cleared as I rented the Ford and drove through the bustle and quaint chatter of Cork, listening with one ear to the lilt of these English-speaking, though very different, people.

On the long drive through the greening, burgeoning countryside to this high mountain pass, I had time to think, to wonder whether the rat I smelled was called Fred Moone.

A tragic accident and a hasty, "providential" cash offer? There was more to it than that. There had to be. I was distinctly uneasy about the whole thing. I had to know what it was all about. I couldn't simply shut my eyes and take the money.

Yet now that I was almost within sight of Mainstay I wanted to hold everything for just a moment. So I got out of the car and stretched in the clean, sharp, spring air. My five feet eight inches had been a little cramped, but the stiffness left me easily.

The fragrance of heather mingled with the faint, piquant tang of salt air drifting up from the shimmering bay far below. It was just after midday. The sound of the car door closing echoed harshly in this high seclusion. Nothing stirred. The country road had, for some miles, seemed completely deserted. On either side of it, the sharp limestone crags rose steeply, their obliquely angled strata edged with greenish moss and gray-white lichens, and splashed here and there with golden gorse, spiky dark green thornbushes, tiny blue wild flowers, and crimson valerian.

A short climb to a narrow, jutting outcrop was easy enough as I had chosen, for once wisely, to travel in a comfortable blue denim pantsuit and well-used walking shoes. I lit another cigarette, settled myself on the sunny parapet, my back against the dry gray rock face, and began to try to put things into perspective.

Whatever Grandmother had been in life, I thought heavily, no one deserved to die in such a grim way. I became aware of a queer, totally unexpected, numbing sense of loss. Envisaging her as clearly as I could, I found that a strange thing had happened. I could see the straight little figure and hard expression without difficulty but, curiously, without emotion either. Although I tried to summon the fierce resentment I thought I had so long nursed against her, I could not seem to feel anything. There was only the dawning realization that my deliberately active college years and teaching career had unconsciously healed old wounds and loneliness.

I realized now that I had never really known Grandmother at all, and that I had, all along, subconsciously expected something to break the deadlock between us and revive my connection with Ireland. At that moment, dimly, I understood my parents who, despite the quarrels, generously kept the contact alive; Grandmother was family and their regard for her transcended their exasperation.

Now, no longer concentrating on my own bereavement, I perceived for the first time the magnitude of what Grandmother had lost—for my father had been her only child. She had fought him at every turn, losing everything as a result of her blind obsession. And when I stormed out five years ago, she simply severed the connection, finally conceding defeat in her ill-fated crusade to have a Wentworth continue at Mainstay.

And now I, the last Wentworth, the sixth generation, was being pressured toward the act that would end the matter and, in effect, close an era. Such a simple act. But could I so easily hand over the family home to a client whom Fred named only as Heritage Trust Limited?

All I had to do was sign the papers.

I sighed. Even the buyer's name was an unconscious irony.

"I don't know," I said wonderingly to myself, "I just don't know."

A nearby gorse bobbed slightly, ruffled its golden flowers in a light breeze, and was still again.

"True," I said more strongly, addressing the gorse bush, "but I do feel that the matter shouldn't end quite so lightly. Nor in haste. And I know I don't trust Fred Moone as far as I could throw him. Oh, Lord . . . I've only just realized that! . . . Am I right? Is he really trying in that letter to keep me away, or am I imagining things? No. Somebody is trying to hide something. But what? Embezzlement? Theft of antiques? There is a lot of valuable stuff just lying around all over Mainstay. . . . Surely not! Peggy would have noticed. Unless she, too . . . oh, Lord, now I *am* imagining things. . . ." I trailed off, shocked at my own thoughts.

The gorse dipped and swayed again. The sun slid behind one of those fluffy clouds that are never far away even on the sunniest day in Ireland. The breeze was not cold, but I shivered. I stubbed out my cigarette vigorously and stood up.

Time to gather myself up and go down the last mile.

I swung my shoulder bag up and was starting down toward the road when a cheerful Irish male voice hailed me from a point somewhere above and behind me.

I turned quickly and there, coming toward me down the rocky incline, was a very tall man, a friendly grin on his sun-tanned face. Youngish, late twenties perhaps, untidy light-brown hair, well-marked eyebrows now raised inquiringly above keen gray eyes. He was clad in faded jeans and a fisherman-knit sweater, sleeves loosely pushed up to his elbows. A khaki knapsack and not one but two expensive but used-looking camera cases hung from powerfully built shoulders. A light meter dangled with a lens case from his neck.

Moving with an easy grace that spoke solid strength and physical conditioning, he plunged headlong down the scree toward me, with a rush of loose pebbles underfoot. Slowing his pace, he sauntered forward the last few yards with a lighthearted greeting.

"And what's a nice-looking girl like you doing in this place?"

CHAPTER 2

I had to smile. In mangling the overworked cliché he managed at the same time to give it a subtle twist and I was feminine enough to appreciate the casual compliment.

"That your car?" The newcomer jerked his head toward the road and, jabbing his thumbs into his jeans pockets, surveyed my car with interest. "You wouldn't think it was broken down, parked carefully like that."

"My car's fine, but thank you for inquiring."

"Ah, you're English." His own accent was not local; Dublin or thereabouts, I surmised, recalling accents from long ago. He went on idly, "A bit early for summer visitors, I'd have thought."

I smiled again, this time at his neatly roundabout way of finding out about me, yet offering me the opportunity to ignore the gambit should I so wish. Oddly, I didn't wish to do so. "A holiday in May would be delightful," I said, "but I'm really here on family business."

His rejoinder astonished me. "English and on family business? Then you must be Miss Wentworth, granddaughter of the poor old lady of that old house on the cliff!" Seeing confirmation in my surprised face, his tone grew sober. "I'm sorry about your gran. That was a hell of a thing to happen. It must have been an awful shock for you."

I nodded, reflecting wryly that the homely, affectionate diminutive "gran" was so unsuited to the authoritarian woman who had been my father's mother. Aloud I said, "Yes, it was a shock, in more ways than one," then bit my lip at the unthinking answer that elicited an immediate lift of those strongly marked eyebrows. But he merely went on conversationally.

"So you came from England today?"

"Yes, that's right."

"Drove from Cork, did you? You must be pretty tired, all

14

that twisting and turning of the wheel on our narrow, unfamiliar mountain road."

"Oh, I like driving. I do a fair bit of it on English country roads and they're quite as demanding as this one, I assure you."

He grinned. "Sorry. Didn't mean to sound like a male chauvinist."

"Apology accepted. But how did you know I had driven from Cork?"

"That's easy. The car has Irish plates and I know you came from London. So the car has to be either rented or borrowed. A rental from the airport seemed logical enough." He waited for my reaction to this masterly piece of deduction and typically Irish display of interest.

"I'm glad I'm not a wanted criminal or something," I said dryly. "Seems I would have little chance of melting into the landscape as a mere tourist if your countrymen are all so observant."

"You'd not melt into the crowd anywhere, girl," he rejoined cheerfully. "Anyway, sure, aren't all the Irish just curious. Like kids. And dogs." He added the latter impishly, cocking his head to one side.

I happen to like dogs and friendly people, though not necessarily in that order.

"Besides," he went on disarmingly, "I'm stayin' with Dr. O'Brien in Kilcollery. Since the accident, I've heard a fair bit about you and your family. I think people hereabouts wondered why you didn't come over before now."

I had to admire his neatly oblique, expertly indirect, Irish way of extracting information. "I was away in Scotland until yesterday. Incommunicado, so to speak." Even as I uttered the words, I was wondering why I was beginning to feel an almost irresistible compulsion to confide my suspicions to this large, friendly man. Firmly I resisted the impulse, asking instead, "How is the doctor? We're old friends, you know."

"The doc? Oh, well enough." He answered almost absently. Then he shot an appraising look at me and added nonchalantly, "I daresay you haven't had lunch yet? I haven't either." Even as he spoke, he was unhitching his various pieces of photographic equipment and the knapsack. Indicating my sunny rock perch behind us, he said comfortably, "That looks like a good place."

"Is that an invitation?" I asked happily. "I've just realized I'm starving."

"Come on, then, I've got lots of food. Cheese-and-tomato sandwiches to start with. Plenty of ginger ale, too. I don't usually drink the stuff, but the pub was still closed when I left this morning so I couldn't get my hands on any beer." All the while talking, he was unpacking an enormous amount of food. He looked up, grinned suddenly, and held out a large, sun-bronzed hand to me.

"Strikes me that an English lady probably requires a proper introduction before accepting an invitation to lunch," he remarked teasingly. "The absent doctor bein' deemed to guarantee my character, eh? The name's McCarthy, Colum. I was in college with Dr. O'Brien's son, Kevin, and I'm down here on an assignment. Photographic." Unnecessarily, he jerked a thumb toward the cameras.

I took his hand. It was big and warm. Unaccountably, something joyous deep inside me leaped quickly in response to the friendly ease of the man. Travel-tiredness ebbed.

"How do you do, Mr. McCarthy," I replied in solemn tones, but my eyes were bubbling with enjoyment of the small ritual attendant on first acquaintance, for I had the irrepressible feeling that he and I had, in some unspoken way, already progressed well beyond mere acquaintance and its commonplaces.

"Make it Colum, for God's sake, girl." He gave a happy chuckle and released my hand. "Nobody's called me *Mr.* McCarthy since a Latin teacher who was far from impressed by my efforts and it's much too nice a day, in all respects, to be thinkin' of that ould fossil."

I laughed merrily. "Reminds me of my young pupils. I suppose I seem like an ancient hag to them."

"Not you!" Colum grinned. "Though you never know with kids."

"Thank you, sir." I sketched a mock bow and sat down again on the warm rock. "My name's Joanna, by the way," I said, and accepted some ginger ale.

"No glasses, sorry, don't carry them," Colum said. "Have a sandwich."

We sat in the sunshine in a companionable silence. I sipped at my ginger ale and tried to remember where I had heard his name before. But I had so much to think about; Fred's letters, Grandmother's sudden and none too well explained death . . .

" 'Twill all work out, you'll see." Colum's voice was gentle.

I turned a startled face to him. How could he have known my thoughts?

"You said earlier that your gran's death was a shock in more ways than one," he reminded me, adding quietly, "It's not just curiosity this time. Would it help to talk about it?" His brown face expressed concern.

I hesitated only a moment. Then I was talking, slowly, and then with greater assurance, picking my words with care. I suppose I was really attempting to explain, as much to myself as to him, why I felt so uneasy. Yet, even as I spoke of the tone of Fred's second letter, of wondering what could have taken my grandmother out onto the dangerous cliff path, and of the storm on Holy Thursday evening, I became more and more aware of how vague and circumstantial my misgivings must sound.

Resigning myself to hear him proffer all the reasonable, plausible explanations that had begun to occur to me, I waited, as the silence hung heavily. After all, Colum was acquainted with the place, the house, the Moones, and might even have known Grandmother herself. But he sat, strangely still, not speaking, his face frowning and preoccupied.

His first words surprised me.

"So you haven't been back here in nearly five years," he said very slowly, turning those searching gray eyes on me. "You've had no direct contact with Mainstay for all of that time?"

For a long moment I returned his stare, mystified by the question. Around us there was a stillness as though the very rocks awaited my answer.

"Only brief notes from Nita and Fred, as I told you. Grandmother refused to reply to my letters and there's no telephone at Mainstay. Grandmother always characterized the phone as an uncivilized, intrusive, noisy invention," I added reminiscently. Then I wondered sharply why Colum was exhaling as though in relief. I was certain, too, that I saw him relax. What I didn't know was why the question held such importance, why I felt I had just passed some sort of test. But, had I unwittingly relieved him of a sudden anxiety, or confirmed a pre-existing suspicion of his own?

"So! I'm not imagining things? There seems to you, too, to be something odd about the whole business?" I asked swiftly.

Colum shrugged elaborately. "It's possible, but it is somewhat vague, you must admit." His tone was neutral but he frowned for a long moment. "Have you told anyone else, police or anyone, about all this?"

"Hardly. Haven't had time and in any case, what could I say to the police? I'm the stranger here, don't forget. Fred and Nita are solid citizens, he with his law practice and she with her craft business and the hotel. What motive could either of them have, other than the simple wish to buy Mainstay and to close the sale before I had time to decide to keep the house?"

"What's the house worth? Any idea?"

"I don't know. And there was no appraisal done, in recent years at least, that I'm aware of, and no figure, not even an educated guess, enclosed with the papers Fred sent. But I can't believe that he might be trying to cheat me. Wouldn't a surveyor's report be normal?"

"For the buyer, yes. Still, I wonder . . ."

"It is quite a marvelous old place. Fred's client is probably a rich American, someone who has the wherewithal to keep it up in the style the Old Boy intended when he built it. The first Captain Wentworth, a naval captain with Nelson," I added by way of explanation.

"A late eighteenth-century house, isn't it?" Colum said.

"Generally speaking, with modern modifications, that is. The captain does seem to have been a very decided, independent sort of fellow. I think he probably bossed his architects and carpenters mercilessly in the best Bligh of the *Bounty* style to get the house just the way he wanted it, regardless of niceties or rules." I smiled. "He retired in 1806, just after Trafalgar, and married a County Cork girl, a minor heiress. Their miniatures are still in the hall at Mainstay. They seem to have lived pretty high even for that time. My father always said that the Old Boy must have had more than a passing interest in maintaining free enterprise, so to speak; particularly in brandies, laces, silks, all that sort of thing. I don't doubt that after the Napoleonic Wars he found Kilcollery and its gentry a little too peaceful at times, but he probably knew well enough how to disturb that peace."

"And turn a tidy profit besides? I'll bet. Man after my own heart." Colum sighed. "Ah, those were the days—when a fellow wasn't hemmed in by government regulations if he didn't want to be. Paper-pushers!" he added with disgust, "they're everywhere these days! Bless your English law-abiding soul, Joanna, don't look at me like that! Landing at a quiet cove with a keg of French or Spanish brandy isn't so dreadful. 'Tis just a harmless and common feature of coastal life; adds spice to the act and taste to the brew, even now. It's been goin' on since time immemorial, on your own coasts, too. What about the Romney Marsh crowd?"

But my thoughts had shifted back again and I was more preoccupied by the immediate situation, trying to decide how to go about getting answers to my questions rather than worrying about peculiar brands of individual ethics and the law.

Colum's voice broke in. "Don't worry, Joanna. Things have a way of sorting themselves out." His tone was easy and the trite phrase sounded oddly reassuring. "And I'll be around, if you need someone. . . . The doc will, too. You're not alone," he finished cryptically.

It is only now that I realize that Colum, while listening intently to my story and my suspicions, had not at this point actually replied with anything other than the vaguest and most conventional of reassurances. Yet, in a strange and inexplicable way, I was already strengthened and even cheered by his air of solidity and reliability.

"Mmmm, delicious fruitcake," Colum remarked, somewhat indistinctly. "Great housekeeper the doc has. Grand cook. Keeps threatening to fatten me up. I have half a mind to string this assignment out and take her up on her offer."

"The O'Briens have a housekeeper?" This was news to me. "Is Mrs. O'Brien ill?"

"She died well over a year ago! It was a long business. The doc nearly went out of his mind." Colum shot a sharp look at me. "You *have* been out of touch, haven't you? Then you didn't know, I suppose, that Nita Moone had moved in to help look after your grandmother?"

I had been rooting in my bag for a handkerchief to wipe my fingers. I looked up, amazed.

"Into Mainstay? No, she never said anything. But why? I mean, Grandmother had Peggy and Joe . . ." I was more perturbed than ever by this piece of news.

"Hmm. Odd. From what I've heard, your grandmother was quite ill." Colum was again watching my face closely. "You didn't know? Nor that she wouldn't see anyone? Took against everyone for some reason. Kept herself very much to herself, never going out. Was that unusual?"

I had to turn away from that uncomfortable stare.

"I don't know. I just don't know. She was getting old, but—oh, I don't know . . ."

I sat stunned, thoughts whirling dizzily. Colum was asking me a lot of questions and I couldn't answer. He seemed to know a great deal that was new to me and I was unhappily aware that his friendly manner was now accompanied by a discreet scrutiny of my reactions. He was clearly wondering why I knew so little.

And I was wondering why the Moones' notes had been so uninformative and laconic.

Then I felt a sudden rush of guilt. I had never troubled to ask for any details, had I? As Grandmother's silence went on and on, I had, in my pride and bitterness, hardened my heart. Reluctantly now, I faced the truth: I hadn't wanted to know anything about her. The Moones hadn't said, and I hadn't asked.

I spoke slowly. "Perhaps Grandmother didn't wish me to know she was ill in case the news would bring me back to Mainstay. Or"—another thought struck with sickening clarity—"perhaps she was afraid to discover that even the knowledge of her illness would *not* bring me back . . ." I stopped short, realizing that I was more like her than I had known, and I felt a sharp wrench at the thought of the proud old lady who could not bring herself to reply to my letters.

"Oh, God," I said, sick at heart, "I should have ignored her silence and come over anyway. If only I had persisted . . . and it's too late now. . . ." I trailed off dully.

"Hey, Joanna, don't look like that!" Colum put a warm hand on my arm. "You couldn't have known. After all, your gran was pretty old and they take funny fancies. . . . Oh, God, girl, don't cry. Don't cry like that, Joanna!"

It was no use. The soft greens and grays of the mountains blurred and swam before me. Colum's reiteration of the soft, loving, diminutive "gran" was the last straw. One after another, large tears rolled down my cheeks. I was powerless to check them.

After one helpless look around, Colum simply pulled me to him and held me quietly. The years of pent-up bitterness and grieving, this latest bereavement and the horrible circumstances of it, all crowded in on me in a confused whirl of shock and hopeless defeat. A large crumpled handkerchief pushed its way into my hands. I dabbed at my eyes and tried, with aching lungs, to catch my breath.

Colum patted gently at my shoulder. The wool of his sweater smelled faintly of tobacco and heather. A strand of the wool tickled my nose and I sneezed. The sneeze jerked me upright and almost out of Colum's encircling arm. His face wore a serious expression and I was suddenly, embarrassingly aware of the situation.

"Oh, Lord, I'm sorry." I muttered the apology quickly. "I don't usually do this sort of thing." I pushed my hair back and blew my nose vigorously.

Colum released me and stretched back against the warm rock face.

"Ah sure, the stiff-upper-lip nonsense your countrymen have advocated for so long probably kills more people than it helps, you know," he remarked conversationally. "Better to get grief and pain and the whole damn thing out of your system. Bottlin' up anxiety and stress has been clinically proven to be very bad for people. Did you know that? 'Tis only good for the surgeons, keeps 'em in business slicin' out ulcers and things. Just glad I was around to provide the handkerchief for moppin'-up operations." He spoke solemnly, but the quick, twinkling smile that crinkled the corners of his eyes belied the serious tone and I smiled back, if somewhat damply.

"The Irish are my countrymen, too," I remarked after a while. "I'm half-Irish, after all."

"Best of both possible worlds. Or worst, dependin' on your point of view," Colum said whimsically and we both laughed, any awkwardness between us completely dissipated again. There was a moment's easy silence.

Then Colum said slowly, "I have a friend who'd be very interested in this. Comin' for a spot of fishin'. Should be here tomorrow. Lookin' into things in an unobtrusive sort of way is just his line of country. I could talk to him, if you wouldn't mind my shovin' my oar in. I think you'll like Mike. Mike Fanning. Nice guy. Just remember, I met you first, huh?"

A little puzzled but content, I nodded. In retrospect, it seems apparent that the turn our encounter took so quickly was quite extraordinary. But the extraordinary seemed quite natural then. Perhaps nothing about instant liking would seem odd in this easygoing, warmhearted country with its colorful speech, its infinite patience, its never-failing interest in and concern for the other person. A long-forgotten, yet sweetly familiar, feeling of belonging came over me. This green, soft, welcoming land was already weaving its timeless magic.

"Maybe there is really nothing to worry about . . ." Colum was saying. His tone held encouragement, but I caught the "maybe" and, despite myself, I was uneasy again. Could it be that Colum *knew* there was ground for my dreadful suspicions? He had already given evidence of knowing a lot more than I did about the situation at Mainstay. Had he told me all he knew?

Everything was still as I pondered this latest, and oddly more disturbing, question. The high mountain pass, so tranquil, so sunny, was idyllically peaceful. Far below, on the smooth bay, a heavy trawler glided soundlessly in toward the stone jetty. A small brown rabbit hopped unevenly into view just below our rock perch. It sat up, nose and whiskers twitching nervously. Somewhere, high above the escarpment, in the warm afternoon air, an invisible lark trilled sweetly. A breeze flicked at the gorse and the startled rabbit whisked away. Involuntarily, I met Colum's eyes and we both smiled. My concern evaporated as, wordlessly, we shared the peaceful moment of time suspended, time enchanted.

A sigh escaped me. Time to go, down the last mile through the village of Kilcollery, westward to where Mainstay awaited me.

I must look a sight, I thought, and reached for my bag. At least some lipstick would brighten a face pale from the combined effects of traveling and strain.

"Aha, the lady is feeling better!" Colum teased, stretched full length on the ledge, hands clasped behind his head as he regarded me from one partly open eye, squinting against the sun. "You know, Miss Wentworth, for all your fashionable London suit and that nice French perfume (I appreciated *that* while you were drenching my sweater), you remind me of some kids I photographed recently. Same puzzled, haunted look at the back of the eyes. Now their situation is too much for them, poor beggars. Out of their control. But you, well, I'd be willing to bet you're goin' to sink your teeth in, terrier-style, and not let go till you've got all the answers, old friend Fred notwithstanding. You wouldn't be here otherwise, courage screwed to the sticking point. Am I right?"

"Yes. You are," I said slowly. "That describes it exactly. I hate scenes and fights, but I can't simply let things drift, can I?"

"Someone else might. Are you absolutely sure you want to know the answers? No matter what?"

"An odd question, surely." It was my turn to search his face, but he lay back, eyes closed, their expression hidden. "No matter what." Unintentionally, my tone was hard.

"Pity. Well, I tried," Colum said obscurely. "I hoped you might be persuaded to tell Fred Moone to go to blazes or wherever, put the whole thing behind you and come wander on the hills with me instead." He opened one eye and cocked an interrogative eyebrow.

"Nice thought. Maybe later . . ." I began absently, for my attention had been drawn away by the appearance on the road below of another vehicle, a dark green medium-sized van. It had been doing a fair speed as it came over the rise, but it was the jerk with which it arrested its onward progress that made me sit up and take notice. The name on its side fairly jumped out at me. Kilcollery Crafts, Ltd.

Nita Moone! It must be!

The van idled slowly past my parked car but did not stop. The sun was glinting on the van's tinted glass so I couldn't see the driver's face. All I could see was a vague dark shape. Then the van gathered speed again and disappeared down the hill toward Kilcollery, leaving me wondering. Was it Nita? Had she recognized me?

Colum accepted my offer of a lift into the village and we scrambled down the scree to my car. Behind us, a couple of fat little sparrows swooped on the picnic crumbs.

We were halfway down the steep, narrow, corkscrew descent when into my rearview mirror came the dark green van.

From nowhere, it simply settled in behind me, dogging my trail. Unnerved by its sudden appearance, I must have muttered something for Colum turned uncomfortably, hampered by his length in the small car, just as I asked, "Where did that come from?" I nodded toward the mirror.

Colum looked back. "From one of the lanes or tracks, I suppose."

"Whoever is driving the damn thing ought to give me more room," I remarked sharply. The steep banks on both sides of the road were coming at us faster and faster as the incline became more acute. Suddenly the seaward bank dwindled to a mere ditch-and-hump along the edge of the jagged cliff. The sea shimmered and gleamed below, but I was more conscious of the dark green shape that loomed behind.

Was it my imagination, or was it closing up the few yards between us?

No, I hadn't imagined it. The van was pulling closer and closer. God! The driver had better be careful on these turns or we'd both go over the edge!

My knuckles were white. Fear was bubbling up inside me. The van was almost on me, rocking on each twist and turn of the wheel, but always steadying itself. Always returning relentlessly, solidly opaque, to dominate my rear view.

The Ford pulled sharply as I took a turn too fast. That van was getting to me and I couldn't do a damn thing about it!

"What the hell—?" Colum exclaimed. "Joanna, take it easy, for God's sake."

"Tell him that!" I said through my teeth. Gripping the wheel, I deliberately forced my foot to ease off the accelerator and prayed that the van wouldn't come right through the rear window.

I was bracing for the impact when abruptly the van pulled back, as though jerked by a string. Then, just as suddenly, it surged up behind us again. I think I drew my breath in sharply as I waited for the bulldozing jolt that might, if I couldn't wrench the wheel in time, send us bowling forward over the narrow strip of sea grass, and then spinning, tumbling, down, down into the shining water. . . .

At the last second the van pulled out and roared past! It disappeared down the winding slope at a pace that left dust swirling in little puffs along the sedgy verges.

As the silence settled, I heard myself exhale slowly. I concentrated on driving. Very quietly, very carefully.

"You all right, Joanna?" Colum said. "Your face is so white, it's almost green!"

I made a feeble attempt at a laugh. "I've seen impatient drivers before, but that one's bordering on homicidal!"

Although Colum tried to tell me that the van was merely in a hurry and, no doubt, had simply been trying to find a stretch of road wide enough to overtake, I was not so easily reassured.

A warning? But from whom? Fred, or Nita, or someone else? And why? All at once I began to have the tiniest doubt of the wisdom of my impulsive coming.

Then everything, including the van, went out of my head for the memory that had flickered briefly and evaded me earlier came back. With electric clarity this time.

Even as my car slid to a stop in front of the O'Brien

house, I turned to look at my companion with curious, even puzzled eyes. What on earth could have brought *him* to sleepy, dull old Kilcollery? Not some routine assignment, no, not him.

I had just remembered who Colum McCarthy was.

CHAPTER 3

"Of course! The books, the UNICEF exhibition in London! You're *that* Colum McCarthy?" I trailed away into silence as I took in the fact that the large, untidy, brown-haired man who had just shared his sandwiches with me was the gifted man whose photographs of children in war zones around the world had brought him instant fame.

Magazines devoted whole issues to his work. At least one television documentary had wrenched at viewers with portraits of small children with the weary, knowing eyes of combat veterans. To the affluent Western world, long accustomed to slick commercial visions of children as rosy-cheeked little darlings, the McCarthy photographs of hungry, ragged, cynical youngsters surrounded by danger and disease, were as stunning as they were pathetic.

Colum squinted at me and grinned. "Guilty, ma'am."

"I must have been totally engrossed, not to say submerged, in my own concerns, not to have realized earlier . . ." I said. Older than he looks, I was thinking; in his thirties, probably.

His name had been in the news very recently, too. A new book on the children of Northern Ireland. One picture I had not forgotten: an eight-year-old boy, hard defiance on his young face. Armed with only a rock, he was poised to throw it at an armored car lumbering toward him over uneven cobblestones.

The Northern Ireland book had been acclaimed as a silent chronicle of the children who had never known childhood, who were growing up amid violence and hatred that, tragically early, they learned to share.

"What brought you down here, to quiet old Kilcollery? Not your usual kind of subject, or area, is it?" I asked.

"No-o, but a fellow has to eat. I was down here fishing, actually, and I had this idea and I sold it to a historical society. A record of the tinkers who hang out in the hills behind Kilcollery, before they all disappear, that is. Y'see, the government, bless its notion of progress, has this effort on to get them to settle in new housing, learn a trade, fit in with the rest of us, et cetera."

"You disapprove? Surely . . . ?"

"I'm just chary of people settin' up as judges of other people's ways. I don't think people should be homogenized. There's altogether too much standardization in the world already." His mobile face alight, he launched into vivid description of the tinkers' independent, wandering way of life, their dislike of feeling tied down, their quarrelsome, squalid, gypsy camp, and rigid patriarchal structure.

"They're not the colorful Romany lot of the films, you know. These are the descendants of displaced, evicted traders and small craftsmen, put out on the road a long time ago by the Cromwellians and the land laws the cruel English invader inflicted on us poor gentle Irish folk." Colum turned a sorrowful gaze on me but his shoulders shook as he tried in vain to suppress a throaty laugh.

"I teach history," I retorted, "and in a half-Irish, half-English family I've heard all the cracks about the cruel English invader. Anyway, you're getting your own back these days, what with every second politician in England having an Irish surname."

"Sorry. Bad joke." Colum looked sheepish for a moment. Then he changed the subject to speak of the local fishermen whose way of life was also disappearing fast. Young and old, they still went out in the black-tarred canvas currachs at night, just as their ancestors had always done, though their numbers were dwindling now.

"It's a dying town, Joanna, getting smaller every year. Funny thing, as the population falls away and the average age rises, they seem to get closer knit than ever. Even I am a stranger here; they don't take to anyone too easily anymore."

"My family has been here for six generations. I can hardly be counted a stranger."

"I wouldn't be so sure; I'd go carefully, if I were you." His tone, momentarily somber, caught my attention, but he smiled and went on quickly, "Anyway, how about dinner? This evening be too soon? You'll have to eat sometime. There's a nice place I think you'd like. The hotel here isn't open yet; some problem with staff, I heard. I'd like to show you the tinker camp, too, if you're interested. The kids there are a tough bunch; cheeky, seasoned little beggars, God help them. But there's one youngster, a boy called Danny Sheridan. No mother in evidence, about ten or eleven, bright, independent, not like the others, none of the professional whine, probably ought to be in a decent school. I'd like to know what you make of him, as a teacher, I mean."

He was unfolding his length as he spoke, reaching a long arm into the back for his knapsack and cameras. "I am rattlin' on a bit; you should shut me up. About dinner . . . ?"

"I don't mean to be ungracious, Colum, but I'm not exactly here on holiday . . ."

He interrupted awkwardly. "I knew I was talkin' too much. Didn't mean to rush you. Sorry." He extricated himself from the car in one lithe movement and closed the door smartly. "Another time? 'Bye." With a quick nod, he turned away. Shoulders hunched and hands thrust deep into his pockets, he walked up the cracked, weed-filled path to the doctor's old Edwardian house, now strangely shabby. The flower beds, once Mrs. O'Brien's pride, were overgrown and the gate hung at an angle, its metal paint flaking in mute evidence of neglect.

At the door Colum raised a hand but there was an automatic, abstracted look about the gesture, as though he had forgotten me already. My farewell words died unuttered. As I pulled away, I, too, was thoughtful.

Colum McCarthy was a bit of an enigma. For one thing, he knew a lot more than I did about the circumstances at Mainstay. Was that merely curiosity or had he some reason for being interested? True, he hadn't concealed knowing more than I did. Did that mean it was all common knowledge? Then, if Fred was up to something, did everyone here know about it? Could that be why Colum had warned me, so delicately, to tread with care? Did I doubt *him*, too?

"Oh, for heaven's sake, stop it!" I told myself sharply. "Idiot, paranoid, plain tired after the journey . . ." But I

couldn't help wondering whether Colum's interest was in
me or in Mainstay.

I turned left onto the Promenade where great herring
gulls wheeled and screeched above the seaweed-strewn
high-tide line of the deserted strand. I decided against
going left again toward the Moones' hotel. Time enough
for that. My road lay westward, to the right, along the low-
cut stone seawall, pressing on up over the rise of the western headland, Mullaghbeg.

The little yellow Ford skidded to a halt on the broken,
graveled verge where the road ended at the top of Mullaghbeg cliff. I dumped my suitcase on the dusty tufted grass
beside the great wrought-iron gate and stood back to look
at the house I hadn't seen in nearly five years.

Alone in the sun, azure sky arching above, I looked at
Mainstay. Then the memories of angry voices and bitterness faded and the house quietly came into clear focus.

Funny, it seemed smaller than I remembered, despite its
gracious aspect and generous lines. Broad, square, many-
paned windows flanked a large porch with its timeworn
steps and double recessed doors embossed with gleaming
brasses. Neat white arched casements sat squarely in the
tall, brooding, dark-gray slate roof above. Soft pink sand-
stone framed the ground-floor windows and the porch. The
rest of the house was of limestone, rough-hewn blocks now
worn by time, wind, and rain. Still, Mainstay looked
sturdy, immovable, gazing out to sea as if it would without
difficulty withstand another hundred-and-seventy-odd
years of Atlantic storms.

Would *my* great-great-grandchildren see it as I did now,
I wondered, realizing uncomfortably that something of me
was inalienably part of this place. It wasn't simply that I
was the last Wentworth. Or was it? A glimmer of understanding came to me about Grandmother's obsession with
family continuity at Mainstay. The house was now mine;
would I, too, see it as she had if I lived here for fifty years?

I tried to break away from this inopportune train of
thought, to see the place more dispassionately as I walked
up the limestone-flagged path with its border of heavy
white seashells, laid by a Victorian Wentworth nearly a
hundred years ago. In the beds beneath the front windows,

early budding carnations, wallflowers, and anemones stirred in a gentle breeze.

Before I could reach for the brass knocker, the great doors opened.

In her usual primly buttoned cream blouse, black cardigan, and skirt, my grandmother's housekeeper, Peggy, stood in the doorway. She looked thinner and the bright sunlight accentuated the tiny lines at her eyes and mouth. Her expression was grim. Clearly, there was to be no welcome here for me.

"So! 'Tis you, Miss Joanna. You've come back." And not before time, her tone implied. She ignored my outstretched hand.

"I was in Scotland until yesterday, Peggy. I came as soon as I heard." That much of an explanation she was owed; she and her brother, Joe, had been at Mainstay since my grandparents' marriage.

Reluctantly she moved aside as I stepped forward into the hall. The paneled entrance glowed with well-rubbed polish. On either side, the two gracious rooms, dining room and drawing-room-cum-library, looked fresh and inviting, their faded cushions and chair covers a harmonious mixture of colors. How my seafaring ancestors must have loved coming home! I sank into a cushioned chair near the dining-room window. "Mainstay looks wonderful, Peggy, a credit to you."

Peggy stood, hands tightly clasped at her stomach, a vein throbbing visibly in her right temple. She regarded me sourly. Her sharp voice, in contrast to the singsong accent of the region, stabbed at me. "I'll away and prepare your room."

"My old room, please." Disappointment made my tone unintentionally crisp and she colored dully. I followed her to the curving oak staircase with its gleaming brass rail.

"You should have the master bedroom. You are the mistress now." Obdurate, she began to mount the stairs.

"I'd rather have my old room, Peggy," I answered pleasantly but firmly. "That is, unless Miss Moone is using it."

Her head turned sharply and her eyes met mine. "Miss Moone went back to her own house." There was more than a touch of dislike in Peggy's tone, and not a hint of softening toward me. A thrill of dismay sliced through me. I hadn't expected quite so cold a reception. But I was a Wentworth and my chin went up.

"My suitcase is at the gate. Perhaps Joe would fetch it. Right now, I would like some tea. In the library, please, Peggy."

I swung away to sit, stiff and unreasonably angry, on the library window seat. I have no doubt I was meant to hear the loud sniff Peggy gave as she stalked out to the kitchen.

Listlessly I stared out on the sunlit garden. A weight of depression settled on me. Perhaps Fred was right and I shouldn't have come. . . .

Then I saw Joe shamble down the shell-edged path. Impulsively I rushed outdoors, greeting him as he returned, my case dangling easily from one huge hand.

His weatherbeaten face was vacant at first. Then a puzzled frown stole over the heavy features. Like the sun sailing from behind a spring cloud, he smiled. A glorious, happy smile.

"Well, 'tis yourself, Miss Joanna." His voice was slow and warm and pleased.

I shook his big hand heartily. "Joe, I'm so glad to see you. Are you glad to see me?" Dear Joe, he would not fail to welcome me to Mainstay.

"Oh, yes, Miss Joanna." He grinned hugely, the gaps in his teeth making his face look quite crooked. Mournfully he added, "Herself do be gone, ye know. The misthress bain't here no more. She do be gone to heaven, Peg says." He nodded solemnly, an enormous child.

"Yes, Joe, but we mustn't be sad. And I'm here now. Maybe we can go fishing together sometime, just as we used to do."

He brightened and I'd swear he was about to assent joyfully when a queer, shut look descended over his face. He pushed past me toward the house. I caught at his arm but he pulled away obstinately.

With an anxiety I couldn't fathom, I cried, "We are still friends, aren't we, Joe?"

He ducked his head and muttered something about Peg being scared and them shouting at him! Shooting a last frantic look at me, he shuffled hastily into the house, but not before I had seen in his eyes, quite unmistakably, an animal look of fear.

Joe had always been shy, but never surly. And that look of fear was something else. Clearly, both he and Peggy were badly shaken by my unexpected arrival. Joe had appeared to welcome me so happily at first, until he remembered something . . . what? And what had he meant about Peg being scared and them shouting at him? Who were they? Was it only my arrival that had upset the two elderly servants, or something else?

An involuntary shiver ran across my shoulders and a cold finger of apprehension plucked at already strained nerves. But I knew what I was going to do.

I hurried to the kitchen and spoke to Peggy's back.

"You drink the tea, Peggy. I've got to do something in the village. I shan't be long."

On the cliff, outside Mainstay's gate, the yellow Ford scrunched and skidded on the gravel as I turned the car impatiently.

I wouldn't put it off any longer. I was going down to have it out with Fred Moone.

CHAPTER 4

Fred's outer office reeked of musky perfume and nail polish. The "out" tray was conspicuously bare. The "in" tray hadn't much in it either.

"Mr. Moone is in Dublin. D'you want to leave a message?"

Obviously bored, the beehived secretary pursed her too-red mouth and gazed critically at her fingernails.

"When will he be back?" I asked, irritated by this unforeseen delay.

She reached into an untidy plastic handbag. It was monogrammed in large gilt letters, EH. An emery board worked rhythmically. "End of the week, maybe."

And you're taking full advantage, my girl, I thought, angry at the prospect of kicking my heels in Kilcollery waiting for Fred Moone.

"He might be back tomorrow, he said," she added, shrugging.

Crisply I said, "When he returns, please tell him I wish to see him as soon as possible." She made no move to make a note. "My name," I added automatically, "is Joanna Wentworth."

I was unprepared for its effect. The emery board stopped in mid-motion and the girl's head jerked up.

"Of Mainstay?"

There was no doubt I had caught her attention, quite unexpectedly. "Anything wrong?" I inquired silkily.

"Wrong? Why should there be something wrong?" She giggled, nervously, I thought. "I'll give Mr. Moone your message as soon as he gets back. Over on a holiday, are you?"

"No," I replied shortly, and left.

She was scribbling a note when the street door swung to behind me. But as I passed the window, I saw her reach for

34

the phone and tap quickly on its bar. On a sudden inspiration, I crossed the narrow street at a trot and entered the newsagent-cum-post office just in time to hear the postmistress say querulously into her headpiece, "You'll have to wait a few minutes. The exchange says the lines to Dublin are busy. . . . No, Miss Hayes, I can't hurry it up."

The postmistress's dusty-gray head nodded vigorously in my direction. "One moment, miss." Then she bawled, "Da-a-ad! Sho-o-op!" and a little wizened man appeared from behind a drooping curtain at the back of the store.

I bought a newspaper and lingered over some postcards, but I had already got what I came for. The call to Dublin was put through while I accepted my change and assented vaguely that it was indeed lovely weather for the time of year. From my vantage point by the postcard stand, I watched Fred's secretary speak into the telephone. Of course, I couldn't *know* that she was phoning Fred, but the coincidence of last name, the initial on the bag, and a call to Dublin as soon as I left her set my pulse racing.

Now how could I find out whether Fred was on the other end of that line . . . and why my name had instantly riveted her attention?

"English, are you, miss?" The old man inquired, sparrowlike in his neat movements.

His daughter smiled encouragingly. "Staying here in Kilcollery?"

I didn't resist the opportunity. "At Mainstay. I'm Joanna Wentworth. Don't you remember me, Mr. Murphy? I remember you and Miss Murphy very well."

The old man's wrinkled face creased in smiling recognition. "Old Mrs. Wentworth's granddaughter? Sad business, that. Sure, I didn't know you at all. You've grown up." He was settling down to chat.

But Miss Murphy's face had stiffened into a frown. "That's because she hasn't been back to visit in years." Her tone was curt and the emphasis on the word "visit" was directed at me with a displeasure that was almost palpable. "Now, Dad, 'tis time for your tea. Have a pleasant stay, miss." It was unmistakable. I was dismissed.

It struck me that the Kilcollery grapevine had probably learned of the rift between Grandmother and me. It was clear whose "side" they took. Understandable, too, I supposed drearily.

But was it only because of that long-ago quarrel that my unexpected return aroused such hostility, or was there something else . . . ? For the first time in Ireland I felt a stranger, an unwelcome alien, an intruder. Yet Miss Murphy hadn't frowned at the sound of my English accent, but at the mention of my name and Mainstay. . . . Only then was the friendly old man reminded brusquely of his tea. Why?

Exasperated and more uneasy than before, I retraced my steps to the Ford, thinking hard. Had I guessed right about that telephone call? I turned and hurried back to Fred's office.

His secretary was just closing up for the day.

"Miss Hayes?" I hazarded quietly. Her head nodded in automatic acknowledgment. One point for intuition, I thought with a grim little thrill.

"Oh, 'tis you, Miss Wentworth. Isn't that a fortunate coincidence? Mr. Moone just rang, just after you left. He'll be back tomorrow, specially to see you." Her tone was coy. "Can you call in the morning?" The lock clicked on her typewriter case. No mention of a specific time; Fred's law practice obviously was not overburdened.

I nodded. "Thank you. I just came back to ask if my late grandmother's valuables are in the document box here or in the bank." Under the circumstances, the question was a normal one. It was also the perfect excuse for having come back. It didn't matter that she didn't know the answer. I now knew that no sooner had she heard my name than she called Fred. A fortunate coincidence, my foot! But why was my coming so significant . . . ?

"Lucky for me I came back. And that Mr. Moone rang you." I was, deliberately, at my most ingenuous. I rattled on carelessly. "So expensive, now, the phone, I mean."

"Mr. Moone uses it all the time. He never thinks of money at all," was the surprising reply as she gathered up her bag and coat and headed meaningly for the door.

Fred not think of money! I smiled politely but my thoughts were running and racing. . . . Why had she lied? Under instructions? And why was Fred coming "specially to see me"? What would he say tomorrow?

* * *

Before me lay a solitary close redolent of pines and wild thyme. The cottonwool clouds were tinged with pink. High on a hill east of the village, on the Mullaghmore headland road, the lych-gate protested mildly as I pushed it open.

Slowly I walked forward, into the silent graveyard beside the dark gray cut-stone neo-Gothic church. Though the day was still warm there slid through me a chill, a cold feeling of intruding, of disturbing something or someone. I glanced around but there was no one there. I was quite alone.

The long-ago Wentworths lay under worn mossy slabs. Some of the headstones drooped amid wild flowers and weeds. Beside the chiseled granite that bore my parents' names lay a new grave. Sprinkled with tiny shoots of young grass, its humped topsoil was reddish in the evening light.

I knelt down heavily on the grass, my mind a blank. I was conscious only of an enormous weight, a numbing weariness.

A long, thin shadow sliced across the stone before me! I leaped to my feet, every nerve screaming. Then I recognized the newcomer.

"Oh, Doctor!" I was momentarily breathless with relief. "I thought—oh, I don't know what I thought—"

"Why, 'tis Joanna Wentworth! My goodness me! Where did you spring from?" Dr. O'Brien's thin old hand pushed a strand of white hair out of his eyes, and the light blue eyes blinked several times. It flashed through my brain that I had given him as much of a fright as he had given me. "I've just come from seeing the parish priest; he's not well, poor man. The last person I'd have expected to run into, girl, is yourself. What on earth are you doing here? When did you come? Have you been up to the house yet?"

"What a lot of questions! Oh, Doctor, it's so good to see you."

"And I'm always glad to see you, you know that, but what brought you over now? What about your school term? There's nothing you can do here. Not now."

"I only heard yesterday." Despite myself, I flushed.

"No, no, you misunderstand an old man, girl. I don't blame you or intend any criticism, far from it. I'm simply

speaking from long experience, with your own best interests at heart. 'Twould be far better to have stayed in London. Yes, that's what I meant to say. Better to go on with
your own life and let time do its work. Like the time your
parents died—you'll remember your aunt and I agreed
then that it was best for you to go home. Time is a great
healer. Now, I'm only thinking of you, girl, d'you understand? When I lost my Mary—but we won't speak of that
now." He waved off my attempt at condolence. "Wiser to
let the past go, to go on. Time and work—that's the only
way to deal with the shock and the anger—the healing
power of routine—keeping busy . . ."

The light blue eyes stared off into the shining golden
sunset. I had the strangest sensation he was seeing something I couldn't.

"They're not just clichés, not just clichés," he muttered
more to himself than to me, it seemed. "Time and work . . .
something else to do . . . Yes." He turned suddenly to me
and spoke emphatically. "No, you mustn't mope about
here. Back to work is the best way."

"I appreciate your concern, Doc," I began carefully, "but
I can't simply head back to London, not yet. There are
things I must do. Well, there's Grandmother's memorial,
her will, the servants."

He interrupted with uncharacteristic impatience. "Fid-
dle-faddle. You forget, Joanna, I knew your grandmother
better than most. She'd leave none of that to chance, nor
even to you, girl. The servants will be well provided for,
and whatever memorial she fancied she specified in detail,
I'm sure. No need to be upsetting yourself with any of that,
I'll be bound. And sure you could always come over during
your school holidays, in the summer, if anything did come
up, which it won't; I'd stake a large bet on that one. Meanwhile young Moone can take care of everything just as
usual, can't he? I always say, never trouble trouble till it
troubles you, eh, girl?" He attempted a weak chuckle at
his own sally but I was too taken aback to respond, and he
sobered instantly, going on almost crossly, "I don't imagine your school authorities took too kindly to your running
off like this in the middle of term, did they?"

I stared. First Fred, and now the doctor! What on earth!
This was not the kindly, easygoing Dr. Robert O'Brien I re-

membered. Any moment now he would launch into one of
Grandmother's diatribes about duty and responsibility.

But he was old and a friend and he meant well, so I spoke
gently.

"When my parents drowned," I said steadily, "I wit-
nessed the whole thing. I was there. I knew what had happened. There was nothing anyone could say or do to change
that and it took a long time for me to be able to accept what
had happened. This time it is different, worse somehow; I
just can't grasp it. I know so little. I want to know every detail. I need to know before I can accept it, Doc. As much as
can be pieced together, at any rate. Don't you see, I was
Grandmother's only relative and it matters how she died. I
just have to know." The doctor was frowning but I plunged
on regardless. "Why, for instance, was she out on the path?
She liked to walk there on fine evenings, I know; especially on warm spring evenings like this one. But it wasn't
like this then. And Fred didn't say she was going out for
some reason, to meet someone, or anything like that. He
simply said she was out walking. I expect the answer is
quite ordinary and simple, really, but I'd still like to know
what she was doing out there in the storm, if anyone
knows, that is."

"Storm? Who says there was a storm?"

"The Met office at Cork airport. They described it as a
gale. Don't you remember it? You must remember it, Doc."

"You talked to the weather people at the airport? And
what made you do a thing like that? Sure, anyone here
would have told you what the weather that day was like.
Myself, I wasn't here. I spent Easter with my sister, up in
Dublin. I was away for a week or so about that time."

"You were away? Then you weren't the doctor who—"

"No, no, girl. That would be the county man, the pathol-
ogist. A young fellow, not in the job long but very good,
mind you, a very sound man. A country GP like myself
doesn't—besides, these old eyes—sure, I haven't done even
routine surgery in years. But to get back to your grandmother, well, not to speak ill, I mean . . ." Greatly moved,
the doctor blew his nose and cleared his throat noisily.

I looked away, embarrassed by his obvious distress. He
had known my grandmother for such a long time.

The white head nodded slowly. "You know as well as

I do, Joanna . . . well, let's just say that stubborn as a goat would describe her perfectly. You'll agree that after twenty years of bridge with her . . . well, I know what I'm talkin' about, eh? If she took a notion to go out, not the divil himself could stop her. Certainly not the weather. A mere drop of rain prevent her doin' as she pleased? Not her! No, girl—I'm convinced that—I hate to say it, mind, but it was a case of her own obstinacy. A most unfortunate thing to happen. A terrible accident." He sighed gustily and blew his nose again.

He didn't, or didn't want to, remember that my question was why Grandmother "took the notion" in the first place. It would be useless to press him further on the point; he wasn't even in Kilcollery at the time. I sighed in my turn and tried a different tack.

"Something else bothers me, Doc. Why would Fred Moone write to me in London, pressing me to sell Mainstay?"

"He did that! Good God! Why, the young fool!" The angry outburst was startling. Just as quickly, the anger was replaced by an understanding nod. "Hard up for money, are you, child? Mortgages or debts on Mainstay? Death duties? I suppose your grandmother's income was hit hard by taxation. Of course 'tis a bit of a shock for you so soon after . . . I take it young Moone is worried about the cost of keeping the place; upkeep of a big place is a real problem these days, eh?" His kindly face wore a shrewd, knowing look.

"I don't honestly know. Of course, the will can't be through probate yet," I said vaguely, somehow suddenly feeling the need to go cautiously, to hedge. I could hardly go around accusing Fred to his old acquaintances on the flimsy basis of suspicion alone. I felt my color rise warmly.

The doctor's eyes narrowed against the clear evening light. He patted my shoulder with the gentleness of old.

"I think you can depend on it bein' something like that. But you shouldn't worry your pretty head. Take my advice and leave the dreary stuff to young Fred. He'll take care of everything. I'm surprised you came over at all; you know he's taken care of everything for your grandmother for years. You can safely leave it all to him. Now, seeing that you are here, come along with me. I'll take you down to my house. At least we can see to it that you're not all alone up in that big old house. You'll give an old man the pleasure of your company over a real old-fashioned high tea?" He smiled invitingly. "All you youngsters seem to want to look like bedposts. Not like in my day. I have a grand housekeeper who'd love to feed you up."

"I know." I smiled at the doctor's surprised face. "I met Colum McCarthy earlier today."

"Ah, that explains it. Yes. Nice fellow. In college with Kevin. Kevin's out in Africa still, with the World Health people, you know. Getting on very well, too."

"That's great. Colum's a friend of his, then?"

"A college crony. I gather they were on the rugby team together. Mind you, I hadn't heard of McCarthy before he landed on the doorstep looking for Kevin and I'd no idea he was a—what did Miss Murphy say?" The doctor scratched his head in playful solemnity. "Ah, yes—a celebrity. We got talkin' anyway and the upshot was that I offered him a bed while he was workin' here. Good to have some company in the evenings again. Plays a decent game of chess. . . . There's a thought now! McCarthy'd be more your style than an ould fellow like me. Keep you from mopin' about at Mainstay for the evenin'. I wonder if he is free . . ."

"You wouldn't! Don't you dare, Doc. Anyway, this is my car," I said hastily as we reached the Ford.

"Oh! You have a car! I was going to offer to take you as far as Cork. I'd enjoy an outing and the car's much more comfortable than any bus. We could have a grand chat. I'm free enough tomorrow."

"Everybody wants me to go away." I was beginning to be very irritated.

"Oh, no!" The doctor sounded shocked. "I'm only thinkin' of you, girl. Right now, believe me, home's the best place for you. There's no sense in broodin' here, sittin' about with nothin' to do, mopin' at Mainstay, when you've work waitin' for you. Of course, 'tis up to you, but if you take my advice . . ."

I interrupted smoothly. "Yes, it's up to me. About tea, Doc, I don't think I can come this evening, but thank you for the invitation. Peggy is expecting me back and I haven't unpacked yet."

The doctor looked nonplussed. "Oh dear. Pity about this evenin'. I'd have liked it. You're set on staying, then? Myself, I think you're making a mistake, but young people these days never want to take advice from their elders, do they?" He smiled in a belated attempt to rob the remark of peevishness.

I took hasty leave of him before he could say any more. I drove back along the Promenade toward Mainstay, feeling more confused than ever. Only one thing seemed clear: the unmistakable, startling, and none too comfortable impression that in Kilcollery I was an unwelcome intruder.

Everybody wanted me to go home.

Well, not quite everybody, perhaps. But even Colum had as much as warned me to tread warily. To leave things alone.

To leave what alone?

In my growing uneasiness, I spoke the puzzling question aloud, but the tranquil golden evening returned no reply.

CHAPTER 5

After a strangely disturbed night, the starched sanity of the breakfast table was soothing.

Such dreams! I was wandering in a clinging mist. Faces loomed and changed. Nothing was as it seemed at first. Then I was on the cliff path. It was raining. I was sliding, slipping on the muddy incline, falling, falling, scrabbling at the grassy edge, while over me a dim blurred figure towered, laughing. . . . A low, chilling laugh that froze my blood! . . . I couldn't hold on! I was sliding, falling to certain death! My clutching fingers found only air. . . . The jagged rocks were rising to meet me . . . I was helpless. . . . Then I hit the floor with a thud and woke up in a tangle of bedclothes, my skin clammy with perspiration though the night was cool.

I lay in bed, shivering, for a long time, falling asleep only in the red light of a fiery sunrise. Red sky at morning, shepherd's warning, or was it sailor's warning? The nursery jingle echoed fitfully in my brain. Red sky at morning. There would be rain later in the day. . . .

At the dining-room door Peggy coughed. "That breakfast won't eat itself," she remarked sourly.

I reached for some toast and poured some strong black tea into my cup.

"About the misthress's clothes . . ." Peggy folded her hands tightly at her stomach. "I should sort them. The thing is, then what's to be done with them? The misthress gave some things to a tinker of a beggarwoman who came by a few weeks ago, but what's there is much too good to go to them tinkers."

"I don't know, Peggy. Can't we leave that for the moment?"

"The moths will get at them," she warned stonily. "The misthress was very fussy about moths."

43

I could not deny that. "Very well, Peggy. You'd better go through them and I'll think about what's best to do."

Hastily I finished my eggs and bacon and, tossing my suede jacket over one shoulder, escaped out of the house, away from Peggy's disapproving, brooding presence.

The cliff path was dry and dusty between the limestone ridges that formed natural steps for part of the way down to the cove. Out here in the chill, clean, salty sunshine, I shook away the dream-dread and descended with care. The cleated soles of my walking shoes gripped the rock safely and the sea wind blew gently in my face.

The tide was low and the dark brown rocks were cold. I folded my jacket into a cushion and sat down. High above, Mainstay stared blindly, straight out to sea. What had the old house seen? What secrets was it holding? I shrugged mirthlessly at my own fancy. The cove lay still and calm, its blue water plashing rhythmically along the rocks and swirling lazily up over the silvery sand at the base of the towering cliff.

Suddenly, I knew that I was not alone! I turned swiftly, raking the rocks, the cliff, the sedges high beyond Mainstay . . . I thought I saw a movement. The breeze in the gorse, perhaps, or a small animal. I exhaled. A long, slow, steadying breath. I scolded myself for being jumpy and settled back to my contemplation of the peaceful cove.

Then, a clatter of rocks behind me, and I was on my feet again, breathing hard. A long sigh escaped me as I sighted the small boy making his way slowly toward me across the rocky ledge. He stopped a few feet away and leaned against a high rock, a wary but curious young wild thing.

Tousled reddish-brown hair topped a freckled face and clear blue eyes. His clothes were torn and dirty but the Wellington boots, now poised as though to pivot for swift flight if need be, were surprisingly shiny and new.

"Hello!" I said, and smiled.

He ducked his head as though about to butt something. "Who're you?" The tone was ungracious, even resentful. "Nobody come here before, only the old lady and she's dead now." Pique gave way to childish awe and preoccupation with sensational detail as he added, "Fell off of the path. Up there. Where I'm pointin'. Down onto them rocks."

I swallowed. "I know," I said.

In quick succession the freckled face registered disappointment and curiosity.

Did this child know something, anything, about my grandmother's fall, or was he only reporting a hearsay piece of news? I realized that if I wanted to ask questions I must be very careful not to frighten him away.

I said, "I'm the old lady's granddaughter, Joanna."

"She never said nothin' about you." He was still wary.

"We weren't—well—we had a sort of fight."

The young face cleared. "I get you." He nodded sagely. "Like when the Big Fella takes after me an' beats me with his belt an' says he wished he never laid eyes on me."

"Not exactly like that, but never mind. Who's the Big Fellow?"

Blue eyes widened incredulously. "You never hear of him! He's only the chief of the tinkers. He's huge. Nobody can beat him." Envy and pride strove with painful memory. A grubby hand strayed to the seat of his pants and he rubbed remembered injury.

"Why does he beat you?" I heard myself ask.

"No reason sometimes. He gets blind drunk, an' he's my stepfather." The boy shrugged as if this was adequate explanation. He kicked at the rock and suddenly sat down, folding himself into a comfortable cross-legged position with the lithe grace of healthy youth. It dawned on me that the preliminaries, from the boy's point of view, must have been satisfactory. I had been accepted.

"What's your name?" I ventured and sat down too.

"Danny Sheridan."

Of course! I might have surmised as much if I hadn't been so preoccupied with my own troublesome problems.

"So you are Danny Sheridan." He looked startled, so I added hastily, "Colum McCarthy mentioned you."

"I didn't do nothin'!"

"He didn't say you had. He simply said he knew you."

"Yeah, well, I help him sometimes when he's takin' pictures." He wriggled and squirmed his way to the nearby edge of the rocks and stared down into the green depths that lapped and swayed along the rim. "You goin' to live here now?"

"I don't know. Maybe for part of the year."

He squinted up at the house. "She was okay, the old lady. How come she was your gran? You're English."

"My father was her son. We lived in England. I teach there now."

"In a school?" Danny's tone was wary again and I remembered Colum on the subject of the government's efforts to settle the tinkers in houses, to send their children to school.

"Yes, but it's a girls' school," I said quickly.

"D'you teach readin'?" The surprising question was asked in an offhand tone, but the foot that had been kicking at the rocks was arrested in mid-motion.

"Sometimes," I temporized, wary in my turn.

"I used t'go to school! When me mam was alive. She was a housekeeper. In a big house, in the town. An' I was learnin' readin' an' writin'. I used to read her what I learned."

"She must have been very proud of you."

" 'Course, I don't go no more." The shrug was too elaborate and belied the offhand tone. "I got too much to do. I got a book, though, of me own. She give it to me." Boastfully, defiantly, the strange child jerked his head in the direction of Mainstay! "She used to read me stories out of it, all about Finn an' the Fianna an' wars an' fightin'! She give me the boots, too! The Big Fella had t'beat a couple of the lads at the camp over them boots. They tried to steal them off of me very feet, the buggers!"

"Don't swear, Danny!" The response was automatic on my part and I bit my lip in chagrin in case he would take offense and run away. But the child only smiled, a sunshine-happy smile.

"She used to say that, too."

"Your mother?"

"The old lady." There was silence for a moment while I digested the extraordinary thought of Grandmother's interest in this ragged, curiously likable youngster.

" 'Course, I *can* read," Danny said. "She was just helpin' me along. Then she give it to me. Put my name in it an' all."

Grandmother had actually been teaching this urchin to read! I was dumbfounded.

A torn, dog-eared, pathetic bundle of pages was thrust under my nose. "See. That's my name there."

And indeed, there, in Grandmother's old-world copper-plate, was a flowing notation, "Danny Sheridan." The date below fairly leaped off the soiled page at me. Holy Thursday!

My thoughts raced. Then I saw the other name, in faded, childishly rounded letters, neatly scored through. John Wentworth.

I spoke without thinking. "Why, that's my father's name above yours. This was one of his books."

Instantly, the tattered book was seized! It vanished, protected inside the grubby shirt.

" 'Tis mine, I tell you! She give it to me for my birthday. You're not takin' it."

"Danny, I don't want—" But I was too late. With a last cry, the strange child fled, back across the rocks and up the steep path. At the top of the cliff he paused, looked down at me for a moment, and then vanished from my sight. Poor kid! I would have to reassure him that I didn't want to take the book from him. In fact, there were lots of my father's early storybooks at the house, just moldering away unread. . . . Besides, I was going to find that child again. The date on the flyleaf, in Grandmother's own writing, was Holy Thursday, the Thursday before Easter, the very day she died. . . .

A long clinging weed caught at the hand I was trailing in the cold green water. I shuddered and got quickly to my feet. My watch said ten-fifteen. Surely Fred would be in his office by now.

As I retraced my steps up the cliff path, it occurred to me that Colum McCarthy was right about Danny. He was an interesting child, perhaps because of his hunger for a world he'd glimpsed when his mother was alive, perhaps, too, because of my grandmother's interest in him. . . . Would she have said anything to him? Probably not, he was so young . . .

Still, after I'd talked to her erstwhile lawyer, perhaps I would see. . . .

* * *

Fred's outer office smelled even more strongly of the musky perfume. Mercifully, this time there was no odor of nail polish to mingle with it.

"I'm afraid Mr. Moone isn't here. Something came up and he had to go out again. He left you a note, though." Miss Hayes was brightly solicitous.

I slid the single sheet of paper out of the unsealed envelope. The few lines were scribbled as if Fred had been in a hurry.

Elma said you'd been asking about your grandmother's jewelry. It's in the bank, of course. What did you think I would do, hock the stuff? See you later,

> Fred

Not a word about when he would be back. I exhaled sharply in irritation. Then I frowned as I tried to decide about the tenor of Fred's words. Angry? Teasing? Defensive?

"Not bad news, I hope, miss?" Elma Hayes's voice purring at my elbow made me jump. Was she hoping to make me think she had no idea of the contents? In an open envelope? Almost on the same instant, I was ashamed of my thoughts. What was wrong with me that such mean notions came to me so easily here? Did I distrust everyone around me in this tight-mouthed, lace-curtained, closed community?

"No, not bad news. Look, I'll be back later. Did Fre—Mr. Moone—say when he would be here?"

"No." She shook her head and patted her hair, pushing a curl back from her ear. "May I tell him what it's about?"

I glanced at my watch. Almost eleven. "I'll return at twelve," I said firmly, uncommunicatively, and left.

The chipped stone steps up to the bank hadn't changed. Almost everything else had. Cheek by jowl with worn wooden counters were huge, jazzy posters about interest rates. The former air of Dickensian respectability was awkwardly overlaid with a racy commercial image.

I didn't recognize the nattily attired young man who asked brightly if he could help me, nor the two incurious, sky-blue-uniformed young women who clacked at the inevitable gray-enameled machines. Also unfamiliar was the mustached, watch-chained manager who emerged from a carpeted sanctum in response to his assistant's discreet announcement of "Miss Wentworth of Mainstay." For a moment I felt as if I were my grandmother herself come to call.

I blurted something about his predecessor.

"Old Mr. Stanley? Ah, yes. You knew him well? He retired. Some years ago now, that was. Now what can we do for you?"

With the unobtrusive assistance of the natty young man, my financial affairs were dealt with easily. Polite conversation was just as quickly exhausted. I was not in the mood for lengthy, cheerful chitchat about commonplaces. Then, something, perhaps the memory of Fred's note, prompted me to ask about Grandmother's things.

There was dead silence for a long moment. Tactfully, the assistant discovered something he had to do at the other end of the office. The manager harrumphed. I produced Fred's note and waved the headed paper like a talisman, though without letting the manager read the bit about pawning Grandmother's valuables.

Still the manager hesitated, hemmed, hawed, and fidgeted, fingering the watch chain.

The thought ran through me that I really was a stranger in Kilcollery. The shock was unpleasant. And curiously bitter. Embarrassed, I wondered why I had given in to the impulse to ask the question in the first place. Now I was stuck, committed. Then I had an inspiration.

"I don't want to take them out of the bank." I summoned up an air of earnest reassurance. "Merely to see what is there. To do with insurance, you know."

I had guessed right. Honor was satisfied and the official frown cleared at the magic evocation of a serious, if vague, reason.

"Well, in that case—yes, I think we can—of course—er, you won't mind having Miss Thomas, our senior teller, with you while you check? Bank regulations and all that." He smiled to rob the question of any offense.

I smiled graciously back. I might as well go through with it. Besides, Fred would, sooner or later, through the Kilcollery grapevine, hear about my activities. Perhaps if he thought I was checking up on things he might get around to fitting me into his timetable.

I signed innumerable forms—in both Irish and English—acquitting the bank, the police, the world and his wife of responsibility for my actions, giving Solemn Undertakings, etc. I glanced down the list the manager produced from the recesses of a well-worn, carved mahogany desk. The list was cosigned by Fred, the bank manager, and some minion of the Gardai, the Irish police force.

A brisk, fiftyish woman with startling diamanté blue plastic spectacles framing birdlike, bright eyes, escorted me into the manager's room. The same glasses had never failed to fascinate me as a child. But what had the manager called her?

"You don't remember me, do you, Miss Wentworth? Mary Thomas. I was here in Mr. Stanley's time, too. Oh! You do! That's nice. I remember your dad and mam well, too, of course, God rest them. You're very like your dad, aren't you? You always used to come every summer with them, but we haven't seen you in quite a few years, have we?" Playfully, she touched my arm. "My niece now, she lives in New York. Works for the Tourist Board. Getting on very well, too. *She* comes back home every year without fail. All the way from America, every year." She waited.

For what, I wondered. Praise of the dutiful niece? An apology or explanation of my own lengthy absence? I said nothing but opened the long thin green metal box on the table.

Undaunted, she persevered. "England's so near now, what with the car ferries, isn't it? I always felt for your gran, you her only relative away in England all this time and her all alone in that big old house . . ." She paused, the blue spectacles tilted slightly on her thin nose. I remained silent. Dull color rose over her face. She mumbled hurriedly, "Very sad indeed. Yes, well, we'd better get on with the job, hadn't we?"

Studiously ignoring everything but my self-imposed task, I checked the list against the contents of the stark box.

It was a motley and somehow pathetic collection. Heavy Victorian cameos, coral brooches, jets, semiprecious beads side by side with emeralds in worn gold settings, topazes in platinum filigree, a ruby pendant, a sunburst brooch of diamonds and sapphires . . . Mechanically I checked and ticked, until I came to a long shagreen case. A matched set of Claddagh silver. A simple set, not uncommon. A particular favorite among her everyday jewelry. There was the brooch with its companion bracelet and pendant, each with the characteristic heart held by two hands surmounted by a crown. . . .

Suddenly I could not go on. My heart thumped. For one unnerving moment, I saw Grandmother so clearly. . . . My skin was clammy. The world was whirling. . . .

With unexpected strength, Miss Thomas's bony hands pushed me down into the manager's chair. "Are you all right, dear? Why, you look quite pale." Her voice grated as it came and went in my ear. "Just sit a moment. There, there." Briskly but more kindly now, she took charge. " 'Tis too soon for you, that's all. Your poor grandmother's loss is too recent; you're trying to do too much too quickly. Give yourself some time. Here, we'll just put everything back where it was. Lovely things, all of them. Time enough to be worrying yourself. They'll be safe here. Oh, you'd like to go out now? Mr. Malo-ney!" she fluted to the hovering manager.

More forms, presented apologetically. Obediently, unseeingly, I signed. Miss Thomas signed. Mr. Maloney signed.

"A mere formality, you understand, Miss Wentworth. Later, of course"—he bowed significantly—"there'll be no difficulty—mere formality until the court—ah—was there something else, Miss Wentworth?"

Something was wrong. No, something was missing. From the long green box. My mind was dazed, sluggish . . . I must concentrate. . . . Then I got it.

"Grandmother's rings, they're not there. In the safety deposit box, I mean. Neither her wedding band nor her engagement ring."

Miss Thomas coughed. Delicately she tried to draw my attention to the official list of contents.

"I know they're not on the list," I said impatiently.

There was a strained silence. The watch chain heaved gently as Mr. Maloney cleared his throat again.

"It might be that the—er, um, coroner—or the Gardai, perhaps, can—er, shed some light, ahem . . ."

Drearily I assented. He squared the papers with a relieved, decisive tap on the desk. Condoling mechanically with me, he bowed me efficiently out of the bank.

I stood on the slanting steps and breathed slowly, deeply of the clean, cool, salt air. I was tired, bone-tired, and depressed. Nothing was right.

The experience in the bank had shaken me. Grandmother's presence had been so strong, so alive.

But she was dead. And I was a desolate, unwelcome stranger in the place where my family had lived for nearly two hundred years. And I was no nearer finding out why Grandmother had gone out in that storm, or who wanted Mainstay in such a hurry. Or why.

A few large drops of rain spotted the sandy pavement. Overhead, thick dark clouds were massing swiftly.

"Mr. Moone's not back yet." Miss Hayes was brightly cheerful.

Frustrated, I demanded, "Where is he?"

"At the hotel, I think."

"Can you telephone him there and say I've called here twice already?" I was getting distinctly annoyed.

Her reluctant assent only increased my irritation. Can you do anything, I thought furiously, other than polish your nails?

Sourly, she reached for the phone. I watched her dial the numbers. She used a pencil whose eraser tip squeaked faintly as it dragged over the dusty black surface. An ornate dress ring on her right hand flashed. It reminded me of the bank, and the metal box. . . .

"Tell him I'd like to see the post-mortem report. Today," I said pointedly. If that didn't spur him into seeing me . . .

But there was no reply at the hotel. Miss Hayes let the phone ring for several moments before replacing the receiver. She scarcely attempted to suppress a triumphant smile as she swiveled around to me. "Sorry." She shrugged.

"I'll be back," I promised grimly.

"Third time lucky," she trilled airily and not a little spitefully.

I didn't resist the impulse to slam the door.

* * *

The heavy, ridged banks of gray-and-charcoal clouds were sweeping steadily inland as I stood, tired and uncertain, in the cold windy street. I held a brief and rather one-sided debate with myself and finally decided that, sooner or later, facts must be faced, however painful and wherever they were to be found. . . .

A fine drizzle was falling as I pulled up outside the tiny police barracks on Emmet Square. I pushed open the heavy wooden door, wincing as a large, sleek orange cat seized its opportunity, brushing wet fur against my ankles as it slipped noiselessly indoors.

Amid walls covered with yellowing notices about Dog Licenses and Noxious Weeds, Sergeant Burke, a portly fifty, greeted me with an interest that expanded momentarily to warmth at the mention of my name. Stroking the gray stubble that nestled in the deep furrows around his mouth, he ushered me into a sadly splitting leather chair and turned on a bar of the electric radiator between us. He sat down heavily on one of the hard chairs usually reserved for visitors—complainants and defendants alike.

" 'Tis a sad time for you, Miss Wentworth." His County Cork voice lilted up and down the scale. "The wife and meself were terrible upset about your gran. 'Twas a dreadful thing to happen. A fine old lady she was, the Lord have mercy on her soul." He nodded for emphasis. "Ah, but sure now, life has to go on. And what brings you to see me? Is there something I can be doing for you?" Palms spread welcomingly, he awaited my answer.

"I—well, I was wondering about the post-mortem report."

Slowly, the sergeant's face lowered toward his chest. His multiple chins creased against the stiff collar of his regulation blue shirt. He pushed at his tie, tugged at the lapels of his uniform jacket, and hitched the knees of his trousers.

"Oh dear," he said. "Oh dear me. Now what would you be wantin' with that? Upsettin' yourself all over again. You don't want to go into all that medical stuff at all, take my word for it. 'Tis too much, especially for a young woman, too much altogether."

I should have remembered the inveterate tendency of

the Irish male to protect all females, young and old, from
any and all "unpleasantness." I sighed.

"You see, my grandmother's wedding band and her engagement ring weren't with the other things at the bank
and I thought . . ." I saw the sergeant's frown deepen.
I hurried on. "Well, I just wondered whether the coroner . . ." I stopped in some confusion, suddenly unable to
say exactly what my question was. Warm color flooded
over my face.

Quite involuntarily, I had done the right thing. At the
sight of a lady in some distress, the sergeant's inbred Irish
chivalry overcame his puzzlement.

"Of course, miss! Sure, I understand! 'Twould be a matter of sentimental value." In his wish to be helpful, he
supplied what he obviously considered a creditable reason
for my odd inquiry. My spirits rose swiftly, only to be
dampened by his next words.

"I know 'tis important to you, miss, but I wouldn't know
anything about that at all. Young Mr. Moone'd be the one
to find out for you. Let you talk to him."

Silently and in some exasperation, I concurred. But
when would Fred get around to talking to me?

I said, "I'd still like to read the coroner's report."

The sergeant ran a finger around the inside of his collar.
"That'd be in the county records, I'm thinkin'. But I don't
know that you'd be allowed just to go in there, off the
street, like."

I wasn't getting anywhere this morning. "Then I suppose I'd better request it officially, fill out a form or something." Frustration was making me waspish.

The sergeant ducked his head uncooperatively. "Bless
us all, sure, I wouldn't know about that. Young Mr.
Moone, now, he'd know about that. The proper thing to do
would be to talk to him."

I was by now heartily sick of young Mr. Moone, and
more than a little dismayed at the obstacle course that con-
tinually thwarted my simplest inquiry. But the old sergeant looked so pathetically hopeful as he sat on the hard
chair in the middle of his cluttered office that I hadn't the
heart to inflict on his hapless head my annoyance at being
everywhere hampered, obstructed, delayed, or fobbed off

with excuses. After all, it wasn't his fault, really. Or was it? I would not be sidestepped this time.

I said, "Perhaps there is an official form?"

The sergeant ummed and ahhed doubtfully but I said nothing more. Finally, recognizing my silence for the persistence it was meant to convey, he heaved his bulk slowly upright. He crossed the room to a desk cluttered with forms, license applications, and dog-eared official notices and files. He rummaged halfheartedly about, dislodging a notebook and sending a precariously balanced pile of papers sliding. Dourly, he shook his head.

"I can't seem to find anything here pertaining to such an inquiry." The evasive bureaucratic phrase pleased him and he repeated it with growing confidence, adding a nod for emphasis. He moved heavily back to his chair but didn't sit down.

I spoke rather breathlessly. "Then I'd like to write a letter and have you forward it to the county authorities, please."

The spiky gray stubble on his chin stood out and a dull red suffused his face. "Very well, miss. If you insist. But 'tis not at all the usual thing, you know. Your solicitor is the proper person—we don't do things that way at all here—maybe in England, now . . ." His tone had become resentful, even antagonistic, and I was reminded, yet again, that I was now a stranger, an unwelcome foreigner, where five generations of my family had been at home.

There was a distinct chill in the air as, laboriously, he searched for the appropriate address and sealed the buff envelope. Stiffly courteous, he saw me to the station door.

The mist had settled into a soft drenching rain and the wide square was deserted, windswept.

The silence hung awkwardly, with all the constraint of interrupted sequence. All at once I couldn't bear the tension, the distance.

"I hear the hotel will be late opening this year." I uttered the commonplace in a carefully chatty tone. "A problem with staff, I believe?"

The sergeant took the bait. "So Miss Moone told my wife. I daresay 'tis because the work is only seasonal. Mostly student help these days. Sure, I'd say 'tis the same everywhere what with wages goin' up all the time and the

people not comin' to the sea the way they used to. All the
package tours to the Continent, you know." He was warming to this theme and brightening with every word. "Of
course, miss, if you're looking for a place to go of an evenin', there's the Lighthouse. When the light was moved
up the coast a few miles—a year or so ago now—the old
place was converted. 'Tis a restaurant now. Out on
Mullaghmore head, beyond the church, right out on the
point. Grand view of the bay. But sure now, you'd remember the old light, wouldn't you?"

Unable now to get a word in edgewise, I simply nodded.

"A young pair runs the place. Good cooks. Fresh, good
food. Plain but tasty. 'Tis licensed, too, of course. And
there's a lounge as well as the dining room. Comfortable of
an evening, and sure, a wee drop of the hard stuff sometimes helps to keep the damp out, as they say."

I smiled and agreed and we parted cordially.

"Mr. McCarthy called to see you, to ask you out this evening." Peggy's tone couldn't sour that news for me. Yet
she couldn't resist the chance to add a comment or two.
"For all his being famous, he's not a bit stuck up. Chatted
away there like any ordinary fellow. Very interested in the
house, he is. He wants to take pictures of it, he said. Not
like most of the young people these days who wouldn't
know what they were lookin' at. No notion of the history of
a place and no proper regard for anyone but themselves
and their wants." She sniffed loudly.

I wondered whether I was included in her indictment of
young people, but couldn't help feeling glad that she was
at least talking.

"Did he say he'd call back?"

Peggy nodded brusquely. "Well? Will you be goin'? 'Tis
my evenin' out. I always have Tuesdays and Thursdays
and I'd have to know early if I'm to prepare a tray for you.
The misthress always let Joe an' me off by seven. The
bingo starts at half-past." Her lips trembled and then were
compressed tightly. She waited, almost daring me to
change time-honored arrangements.

Hastily, I said I'd look after myself. No need for her to
prepare anything. "Can't we be friends, Peggy, as we used
to be?"

But she merely bobbed her head and left me to my thoughts.

So Colum McCarthy hadn't forgotten me quickly after all. . . . And he was going to come back. . . .

The rain was sheeting down the seaward windows now. Heavy gray clouds ridged inland, lower and lower, settling down on the headlands, blurring outlines in a drifting white haze.

Far below, the mounting waves advanced and receded restlessly. The surge was swirling and breaking in spreading white lace on the dark brown rocks that sliced through the foam in the narrow cove. With every gust, Mainstay heaved and creaked like a sailing ship as the rising wind whispered and whistled in the crevices.

Lunch was a sober affair in stately isolation. I picked at the beautifully prepared food until Peggy's displeased muttering drove me to swallow a few bites before retreating to the library to savor my coffee in peace.

At the window ledge, the sodden climbing rose swayed and scratched, its ghostly fingers rasping eerily along the wet glass in a fitful counterpoint to the rhythmic roar of the tide.

I was very tired, but restless and fidgety. My mind kept running, backwards, forwards. The flight from England, meeting Colum, the green van. Had it been my overworked imagination or had that driver tried to run me off the cliff? I hadn't imagined the new edge in Dr. O'Brien's voice, or had I? And what of the people at the bank, Sergeant Burke, Miss Hayes rushing to tell Fred of my arrival . . . why had she lied? Fred was avoiding me. Why? And Danny. I smiled as I remembered how I jumped when I heard Danny behind me on the rock ledge. . . .

Funny, that. I hadn't seen him come down the cliff path. Yet there he was, on the rocks that could be reached only by the path. How did he get there?

My fireside chair was old and comfortable and the library was warm. On either side of the neatly laid hearth, many old friends looked down from the stacked bookshelves. My eye was caught by a tiny silver-framed photograph of my parents, young and laughing, beside a reluctantly smiling Grandmother, a sleeping baby cradled in her arms. On the mantel nearby sat a portrait I hadn't seen in the house before.

My last thought before I drifted into a fitful, exhausted doze was surprise that Grandmother had placed, facing her favorite chair, a large, well-polished, framed picture of me.

CHAPTER 6

A harsh, ringing noise was echoing through my sluggish brain. Someone was tugging at my shoulder. A warm plaid rug slid to the floor as I struggled upright.

"Mr. McCarthy's here again." Peggy's voice was abrupt as before but her face wore a softer expression. Silently she picked up the rug, automatically folding it over her arm.

I reached out to her, touching the roughened hand. "Thank you for the rug, Peggy. That was thoughtful of you."

She flushed slightly. "More sensible than lightin' the fire. If you're goin' out this evenin', a fire'd be wasted." The words were grudging but she didn't pull away from me.

Colum was down on all fours when I entered the dining room. He seemed to be tapping the base of the wall behind the sideboard. He was listening intently, head on one side, and didn't appear to have heard me come in.

"Looking for secret panels?" I inquired, smiling at my own silly joke. "No priests' holes in this house, I'm afraid."

He started guiltily and looked around, scrambling to his feet quickly, like a small child caught raiding the pantry. "Oh, it's you, Joanna. Glad you weren't Peggy. She'd give me the edge of her tongue, I should think." Fleeting embarrassment gave way quickly to friendliness. "I was just takin' a look at this sideboard. Lovely inlaid satinwood. I was tryin' to find a signature. Is it genuine?"

"Yes, but it's not signed. I gather that reduces the value or something." I didn't really care about the sideboard just now. "I suppose it was the angle, but I thought you were examining the wall itself."

Colum laughed, a little uncertainly. "Don't know what you think of me. I'm always bein' caught out like this, forgettin' my manners, so to speak, but I'm fascinated by

59

old houses and I never can resist takin' a closer look at really old furniture. Gets me into more trouble in museums and things. I even got arrested once. In France. For crossin' one of those braided rope efforts." His reminiscent chuckle was infectious.

He went on more easily. "Some of the stuff in this room alone could grace a museum, Joanna. Your ancestors had taste, bless their hearts. If you get stuck with hefty tax bills, inheritance taxes or such, a couple of pieces from here would find a ready market to help pay the tax man."

His words thudded into my brain. The furniture in the rest of the house was almost all as old and probably as valuable. Was that what the unknown buyer wanted? Was it as simple as that?

"Hey! Joanna!"

"Sorry, Colum, I was thinking."

Dryly, "I noticed." He went on cheerfully. "I thought we might get an early start on the evenin'. It's clearin' up nicely. We could go for a drive along the coast road and then have a leisurely dinner. What say you? I'm still in my working togs, but it won't take me long to change. 'Tis just goin' on six now. . . . How about six-thirtyish?"

"Is it six already?"

"Sorry, I'm doin' it again. Rushin' you."

"Oh, no. It's just that—well—I was—"

"Fast asleep in the library. Yes, I know. I saw you. Nearly blundered in on top of you, but Peggy shunted me in here. Like an efficient sheepdog, bless her. Said she'd see if you were At Home. You could hear the full capitals. She does the best Victorian manner I've ever seen offstage. She can be a bit of a dragon, can't she?" He grimaced comically.

Suddenly I couldn't resist the lure of a brightly lit restaurant and friendly welcoming faces, as compared with the early night I'd thought of, and foraging in the kitchen after Peggy and Joe had gone out.

"I can be ready by six-thirty," I said in a rush.

Colum grinned. "Good. I've made reservations. Not that it was strictly necessary at this time of year. The season hasn't really started yet. It won't be crowded and we'll get a table with a decent view."

"Lovely. It's clearing well out to sea now so we should have a spectacular view of the whole bay."

I was making small talk, babbling a bit. I didn't usually do that. But my own self-consciousness vanished as I saw, with surprise, Colum's color deepen.

He shifted his feet. "I made reservations at Carnmore. The hotel's not open yet. I thought I mentioned that to you."

"Yes, you did, but . . ."

"Then where?"

"When you spoke of the view I thought you meant the Lighthouse." I was thoroughly ill at ease now. Why on earth had I said anything?

"Carnmore would be delightful," I said stiffly, too quickly, just as he said, at the same time, equally awkwardly, "I'll phone from the doc's house."

There was a difficult silence for an interminable moment. Then we both rushed into polite speech again at precisely the same instant. The resulting confused babble sounded so silly that we both laughed ruefully.

I looked up and met his eyes. They were deep and warm, the corners creased in tiny lines. Wordlessly, he stepped toward me and enveloped my hands in his. For a crazy instant my heart flipped, righting itself infinitely slowly under that steady gaze.

At length Colum spoke. "Pick you up in half an hour. Wear something blue." And he was gone.

The hallstand mirror reflected my tousled brown curls as I turned to go upstairs. My eyes were shining and my London pallor had given way to a soft, flushed glow. You're just warm with sleep, I admonished myself sharply and turned away, reminding myself that I was not a schoolgirl to be foolishly, lightly waltzed into a sudden romance. . . .

But despite my best efforts, at the oddest moments a pair of keen gray eyes seemed to gaze into mine with a disturbing warmth. And when the grandfather clock in the hall sonorously announced the half-hour, I was wearing my favorite silky-soft dress.

The rather intimidating saleslady had loftily described its shade as "spring gentian." Less exalted mortals called it blue.

* * *

"Brought you some fresh fish for tomorrow. I'll leave them here where it's cool. They haven't been cleaned yet. Anyway, I think Peggy'd have my life if she found them in her kitchen."

Carefully, Colum put down beside the porch steps a large tin bucket full of fish in water. "Ready? Yes, I can see you are. Nice."

"Colum! Fresh fish! How lovely! Why don't we cook them, now, here at Mainstay, instead of going out? It's been years since I've done that."

For a long moment Colum eyed me doubtfully. "In that frock?" he objected.

"I'll change, of course, or find one of Peggy's aprons."

Colum looked nonplussed. "I thought you might invite me to lunch tomorrow," he said sheepishly.

"We can do that, too," I answered, suddenly happy, and reached for the pail.

"No, no, no. This won't do at all, at all." Colum's long arm took the pail from me and set it down again decisively. He put on an outrageously broad brogue. "Sure, 'tis a night out you need, not more work, ma'am. Oh, yes, I heard about you bein' hard at it in the village. Word gets around." He nodded sagely and tapped his nose comically.

"Besides, my girl, there you are, lookin' gorgeous. Can't be hidin' you away in the kitchen, messin' with smelly fish. Got to impress you with my suave, sophisticated charm. For tonight, that is." He grinned impishly. "You can clean and cook the fish tomorrow!"

I had barely time to close the door behind me before I was swept, laughing, into the blue Triumph sports car that waited on the graveled circle at Mainstay's gate.

All I could utter was "Oh!"

It was a large, almost circular room, with huge windows from polished floor to beamed ceiling. Vivid plants and ferns were massed along the base of the great expanse of glass. Beyond, as though framed, lay the gleaming bay.

Over Mullaghmore head, the clouds were drifting apart. The evening sun was still obscured by a broad gray bank that ridged high into the darkening sky. Near the horizon, the cloud was hemmed by a shining ribbon of gold light.

And the escaping sunrays were lancing down onto a tranquil patch of gilded sea.

"It's wonderful! Oh, Colum, I'm glad we didn't go to Carnmore, even though I love the mountains too. Sometimes I think I could look at the sea forever. I hope Sergeant Burke is right about the food."

"You talked to him today, too?"

"Mmm. Yes, I did." I don't know why I didn't go on to say what I'd gone to see the sergeant about. Perhaps I was simply mesmerized by the play of light out on the golden water and on the age-old rocky cliffs that ringed the bay. We must be very high up here, out on the point of the head, for I could see Mainstay. Just barely. You couldn't see the house at all from anywhere else around the bay. Even from here, the house, high on its own hill beyond Mullaghbeg headland, on the other side of the bay, was an indistinguishable black mass, all in darkness, getting more difficult to discern in the gathering dusk.

"They say you used to be able to see the light from here for many a mile out to sea on a clear night," the young restaurant owner said as he showed us to a window table and produced a small wine list. Colum studied it intently.

Dinner was delicious, far surpassing the sergeant's laconic tribute. Delicate pink lamb, creamy swirls of potato, homegrown vegetables, preceded by shrimp fresh from the sea and followed by a lemon soufflé that was light as thistledown. I laid down my napkin with a sigh of pure pleasure.

"You look like the proverbial cat that got the cream," Colum remarked.

I was watching the approach of steaming coffee. "Mmmm."

"Then I suppose everything's all right. No more questions without answers?"

Instantly, the reason for my presence in Kilcollery flooded my mind again and the dinner was spoiled. My face must have reflected my thoughts, for Colum screwed his napkin into a tight ball. He dropped it impatiently on the table.

"Damn!" he said incisively. "Damn my stupid tongue! I'm sorry. The last thing you need right now is to be reminded . . . but since I have, did I tell you that Mike Fanning is definitely comin' tomorrow? I talked to him on the phone this afternoon. Maybe the three of us could get in a spot of fishin'. Nothing like it for relaxation."

He rattled on vigorously but I heard little else. Instead, willfully, obsessively, my mind went round, and round, and round. Fred Moone, the letters, Grandmother's horrible death . . .

Someone was speaking to me. Something about cream in my coffee. The restaurant owner whom Colum addressed familiarly now as John was standing at my elbow, politely waiting for my answer.

"I'm sorry. I was miles away."

He smiled sympathetically. "That's all right. There's no hurry. We aren't exactly crowded this evening."

I hadn't noticed that the few other people had left already. We had the whole place to ourselves. Outside, stars were twinkling in a great black sky where shadowy, puffy clouds moved swiftly before a lively breeze. It's cold, I thought, and shivered.

"Take it easy, Joanna. It'll keep," Colum said, and a warm hand closed on my cold one.

"You'd be Miss Wentworth, would you?" John interjected, stopping as he cleared our dessert dishes. "Sorry to hear about your grandmother. That was a terrible thing to happen."

I accepted his condolences automatically.

"The name's John, John Fitzgerald." We shook hands. "My wife'll be out in a moment. Her name's Marian." He chatted on in a friendly vein. Somehow I wasn't in the mood for the instant exchanging of life histories he and Colum launched into. But I couldn't help gathering that the Fitzgeralds were returned exiles who hated city life in industrial northern England and had saved to come home to Kilcollery. She had been an assistant chef in an English hotel. They didn't know if they could make a success of the Lighthouse. To help make ends meet, they both taught part-time; carpentry and cooking, at the technical school in Carnmore.

"It means we have to be there for all of Thursday. A bad night for us to lose business here, but it can't be helped," said John, shrugging. "Lucky to get it all in on one day, really."

"John did most of the alterations here himself." Marian's singsong voice, soft and proud, announced her arrival. Introductions over, she went on, "He even made a cozy sitting room out of the light tower. We couldn't use it for the business. Couldn't very well have people falling down the stairs."

"Would ye like to see it?" John put in, his tone quickening with pride.

"I've never been up in a lighthouse before," I said.

"Are you sure you want to, Joanna?" Colum asked. "It's bound to be quite a trek and you're tired after your journey." He turned to John. "Another time, maybe, John. Thanks anyway."

The Fitzgeralds looked disappointed but nodded politely.

"Oh, let's go up now!" I said impulsively.

"There must be hundreds of steps. It's at least sixty or seventy feet, that tower," Colum demurred, but uncoiled his length slowly and stood up, stretching his long arms.

"The exercise will do you good." John Fitzgerald laughed and led the way through the kitchen to the tower door.

"A hundred and ten, a hundred and eleven, a hundred and twelve." Breathless and laughing, we finished the count and emerged triumphantly into the tower room through an ancient stone doorway all of eighteen inches thick.

"Don't put on the lamps yet, John," Marian said. "They must see the view first."

It was spellbinding. We could see for miles. A cold white moon was sailing in a black sky and the waters of Kilcollery Bay heaved gently, rhythmically. The great, craggy cliffs were dim, dark humps crouching over the smooth sea. Now and then, a telltale line of whiteness brushed noiselessly against them and fell again, fading soundlessly back into the shadowy ocean.

Inside, the great light, with its faceted glass reflectors, was still there, dominating the small circular room like a sleeping giant. The moonlight glanced off the cut glass and exploded in tiny dots of color that danced and rippled round the quiet room.

"A condition of sale," John was saying, "is that the coast guard people have access here and can keep the light in full working order. Just as a sort of backup, they said. It's not likely to be needed. Meanwhile, we run the kitchen and all our own electricity with the original generator. That's one reason we managed to start the restaurant here."

I walked slowly around the narrow space encircling the enormous beacon, to gaze inland across the dark expanse of Kilcollery Bay.

"Joanna! Look over here!" Colum said softly. "I just saw a shooting star!"

But something else had caught my eye.

Out there, in the inky black distance, a light was shining where no light ought to be. Someone was in Mainstay!

I strained to see. Yes, I was right. There it was again, and it was moving! My heart thumped and thundered until I thought the others must hear.

"What's up, Joanna? Seen a ghost?" John joked.

I stared hard at the distant house. It was all in darkness now. Was I mistaken? No, there it was again. A light bobbing about, sweeping an arc, dancing quickly from one window to the next. Upstairs? No, downstairs, I thought. Hard to tell from so high up in the lighthouse tower and from clear across the bay.

I rubbed my eyes wearily as the uneasiness, the nameless fear, flooded my mind again.

I became aware of a strange silence behind me.

"Is she all right?" John was asking uncomfortably.

Colum's arm slid around my shoulders and I jumped.

"Come and sit down, Joanna." He led me to the padded window seat. He spoke soothingly. "It's the climb. You're feeling a bit lightheaded. It'll pass in a moment."

I broke through the Fitzgeralds' embarrassed apologies and solicitous inquiries. "No, no! It's not the climb," I said impatiently, wildly. "There's someone in Mainstay. I saw a light."

"So Peggy and Joe are home," Colum said quickly.

"At this hour? It's not yet ten. They went to the church hall to play bingo. It won't be over till eleven, Peggy said."

"Perhaps they went home early for once."

"Not Peggy! Anyway, it isn't that kind of light. It's moving about, like a flashlight!"

"Can't be! Must be a trick of the moonlight." It was clear Colum didn't believe me.

"Look for yourself. Mainstay is over there."

Colum shot a searching look at me. Then he sighed and complied, gazing intently in the direction of my pointing finger. But Mainstay was now in darkness. The light was gone.

"Perhaps it was a reflection of moonlight on all this glass behind us. It could be thrown out onto the windows, couldn't it?" Marian put in anxiously. Nervously she pushed a strand of fair hair back.

"Of course it could. Probably was," her husband answered bracingly.

I said woodenly, "I know what I saw."

Colum spoke gently. "You're tired, Joanna. Perhaps we'd better go."

The Fitzgeralds hastily agreed and we descended the winding stair in strained silence. This time no one counted the steps.

Neither Colum nor I said a word as we got into the Triumph. Then, reluctantly, I said, "Maybe it was only a reflection." Colum grunted assent. He started the car and drove slowly back along the headland toward the quiet town. He turned onto the Promenade and we dawdled along the seawall. He stopped the car and we sat in silence, both gazing out onto the quiet bay where long, low waves rippled and retreated, where an elegant black cormorant fished industriously.

At length Colum spoke. "Come on. Let's walk. It'll calm your nerves. You're as jumpy as a cat."

The sand was smooth and firm and cool and the chilly night was refreshing on my burning cheeks. We walked, neither saying a word, Colum with his hands thrust deep into his pockets and his shoulders hunched.

I pulled my jacket close around me and breathed deeply of the cool air.

"I suppose it may have been a trick of those glass facets in the great light," I said slowly. "Or perhaps I'm becoming obsessed? Seeing things? Oh, I don't know. I just don't know."

Colum said nothing, but his arm closed warmly, comfortingly, around my shoulder. We reached the stone jetty where several little boats and a couple of trawlers bobbed at anchor. Automatically we turned and headed back to the car.

Below Mainstay, the narrow cove was in darkness. The moonlight cut a broad silver path farther out, toward the dim horizon. In the cool, shadowy garden, the scent of wallflowers and early carnations rose, heady and sweet, mingling with tart seaweed and the clean tang of salt air.

Colum touched my face with a gentle finger. I looked up at him.

"Joanna." He stopped. He thrust both hands deep into his pockets and flexed his shoulders quickly. "Better get some sleep. See you tomorrow." He dropped a light kiss on my cheek and was gone. I was sure he hadn't said what he had started to say.

Still, he was right. I was tired. Exhausted. But not from lack of sleep.

I was just about to close the hall door when I remembered the bucket of fish. The metal glowed dully in the moonlight as I picked up the pail and turned to go inside. Then a movement in the shadowy road near Colum's car caught at the edge of my sight. Colum was no longer alone. Stealthily moving closer to him was a huge, hulking man!

Even as I opened my dry mouth to shout an agonized warning, Colum turned, putting the open car door between the two of them. For a moment they stood very still, face to face. They were talking! But something happened, or was said, and the bigger man raised his right arm, fist closed, and shook it several times. Then he pointed in the direction of Mainstay!

Colum didn't move. They talked briefly again and the big man turned on his heel and walked away. He disappeared quickly into the darkness of the steep, tufted cliff. Was he coming this way?

Colum got into the Triumph and quietly slid away down the hill!

On my dark porch, I wasted no time wondering what that exchange had been about. I was alone and that huge man was abroad.

"Come on, let's go inside," I said breathlessly to the fish in their silver prison.

Terror leaped instantly within me as an Irish male voice answered!

"Thank you kindly for the invitation," it drawled. "I didn't think you knew I was here! You're a cool one, ma'am!"

I froze. Rigid with fear, I simply stood, the bucket drooping heavily from nerveless fingers.

A dark shape detached itself from the shadows of the rosebushes and walked up to me.

"How about a welcoming kiss for an old friend?" Fred Moone said impudently.

CHAPTER 7

I was pinioned in an unexpectedly disabling grip. And instead of the peck on the cheek I had idiotically anticipated, I was being expertly and very thoroughly kissed. The world swam unpleasantly. I struggled to free my arms. In the process the fish bucket slopped wildly. Water shot everywhere. It was very cold.

With an ugly oath under his breath, Fred released me and backed off, brushing ineffectively at the spreading stain on his immaculately pressed twill trousers.

But I was not looking at Fred. Instead I was gazing with dismay into a pair of narrowed gray eyes.

"I came back to remind you about the fish, Joanna. I see I needn't have troubled," Colum said into the silence. "Evenin', Moone." With that he swung on his heel and left.

Involuntarily I started down the path after him.

"Hey! Where're you goin'?" Fred's aggrieved question floated after me.

I took no notice. Colum reached his car and tugged the door open. He looked back, saw me, and stopped in midmotion. For a second everything was as if suspended in the scented darkness. Then Colum's gaze slid past me to rest on Fred, still standing on the porch where I had left him unceremoniously.

I called out low. "Colum!"

Then the absurdity of the situation bore in on me and I stopped short, embarrassed, not knowing what to say.

Then the moment was gone. Colum got into his car and once again the blue Triumph slid noiselessly down the hill.

Ruffled and angry, I retraced my steps to the porch.

"What the hell do you think you are up to, Fred Moone?"

"Aha! So the little Wentworth princess is a woman

grown. You're an elegant London lady, Joanna, very elegant indeed. Keen on our friend McCarthy, are we? Let me drop a word of caution in your delicate ear about him, ma'am."

I was too angry to listen to another word. "What were you trying to do just now? Scare the life out of me, sneaking up like that in the dark?" I demanded.

"Ah, Joanna, me darlin', you were so rapt in watching McCarthy—such a tender leavetakin' that was—you wouldn't have heard an army. As for me, I just wanted to see you. I was out for a breath of sea air an' I thought to meself I'll drop up to Mainstay an' apologize for me unavoidable absence from the office this mornin'. It's been a hell of a day."

I snorted.

"Honest! Now listen here, girl, do you think I would deliberately keep you waitin'? It was quite unavoidable, I assure you. But now that I've come all this way at this late hour just to see you, aren't you at least goin' to offer an old friend a drink? A teeny-weeny one? For the road home, so to speak?"

There was an absurdly pleading tone in his voice and his handsome dark face glowed with the confident mischief of a small boy. I was, and I knew it, being subjected to all of his considerable charm and I didn't trust him one inch for all his smiles. Well, at least he wasn't the great, hulking, menacing man I'd seen earlier. I didn't have to be afraid of Fred Moone. I'd known him since we were both children playing on the sand. Despite myself, I relaxed.

Fred saw his advantage and came toward me.

I said hastily, "You haven't really grown up, have you? Always the spoiled little boy who'll try anything to get what he wants. . . . Oh, all right, come on in . . . just one drink. Besides, I have a few questions you might find time now to answer," I added.

Fred twisted the bucket out of my grasp and ushered me indoors with exaggerated courtesy. "Spoiled, yes, bless Nita's soft heart, but scarcely a little boy. Care for a real demonstration, love?"

Emphatically I declined.

Fred shrugged. Without invitation he walked straight through to the kitchen with the fish.

I poured Fred a stiff whiskey and sank into my fireside chair, watching him splash a minute amount of soda into the glass.

He leaned up against the fireplace and thoughtfully eyed the golden-brown liquid. "Seriously, Joanna, a word in your ear. I'd watch it with McCarthy. . . . Can't make out why he's still here. . . . . I'd be wary, if I were you. How long are you stayin', by the way?"

The question was casual enough, but it seemed to me to be loaded with meaning. But I was tired and edgy and probably quite as paranoid as Colum and the Fitzgeralds at the Lighthouse clearly thought me when I thought I saw a light bobbing about in an empty Mainstay.

Had I seen it, I wondered now. Could the light have belonged to the big man who accosted Colum at the gate earlier? What did he want with Colum? Had he been prowling about in here, or had I merely mistaken a reflection?

With a sinking feeling, it occurred to me now to wonder how Fred had come. So quietly. Too quietly. Could it be that he hadn't come across the garden as I'd assumed, but out of the house?

Somebody, or something, had caused the dancing light. If it wasn't a reflection, if it really was in Mainstay, then who? And why? I thought hard, tried to recall accurately. A bobbing light. A light that was looking for something? A furtive, stealthy light that I wasn't supposed to see.

A light I would not have seen if I had been at dinner at Carnmore, miles away. As originally planned.

By Colum McCarthy.

Oh, God . . .

"Are you all right, girl? You look funny or something." Fred's thin dark brows drew together in a frown. "I was askin' if you plan on stayin' long. You won't need to, you know. I take it you want the sale of the place organized. I can do it in no time. Then you and I can go have a few days' fun in Dublin before you go back to that snobby girls' seminary of yours."

So! There was something I definitely hadn't imagined. The pressure, none too subtle, to accept the offer quickly. Why?

"I haven't decided about that yet, Fred," I countered. "By the way, were you in here earlier?"

"Me? How could I? With yourself out, and Peggy at her bingo?"

But he didn't deny it outright.

"About the sale, Joanna?" Fred began.

"Why, I've hardly had time to think!" I lied, with a nonchalance I was far from feeling. "I mightn't sell at all."

His startled expression was ludicrous, but I didn't feel like laughing.

"You can't be serious, Joanna! Not sell? But you don't want this place. You've avoided it for years. And I've got you the best possible offer . . . oh! I see! Tryin' to push the price up, huh? Well, confidentially, I'll tell you something . . . the fellow who wants this place is pretty loaded. He'll pay what he has to . . . if you get my meaning."

Apparently unconscious of the enormity of this betrayal of a client's confidence, he sat down, stretched his legs, and sipped appreciatively at the whiskey.

But I saw that over the rim of the glass he was watching me intently.

I summoned up a light, slightly fretful tone. "I don't know, Fred. It's such a big decision."

"Oh, rubbish, Joanna, you do know. You know that you have nothing but bitter memories of this place. You know you don't like it here; you haven't been back in years. Why don't you leave the worrying to old Fred? Honestly, Joanna, it's a big chance."

"Yes, I know it's a good offer, but the thing is, well, I feel sort of responsible."

"Responsible? What on earth for? You didn't do anything. . . . Oh, you mean Peggy and Joe? Look, they'll be all right. And I happen to know that this fellow will need someone. He's not married. Maybe they'd like to stay . . . I'll try to work something out. . . . Yes, I'm pretty sure he'll agree to keep them on. There, see, old Fred can look after anything. Come on, what do you say?"

Fred's tone, though superficially confident, held undercurrents of edginess. It was apparent he had never considered the possibility I might not want to sell. The thought gave me pause.

I temporized. "Why all the pressure and rush? I only arrived such a short time ago."

"And you packed a lot of rushin' around upsettin' people into that short time, didn't you?" Fred was suddenly acid. Then, apparently remembering his prime objective, he returned to the business of trying to charm me into agreeing there and then to sell. He spoke eloquently of how his client had fallen in love instantly with the house, and had had his eye on it for ages now, etc., etc. I was just being stubborn, said Fred; stubborn and sentimental.

"Perhaps you haven't really thought about having all that cash, right into your hand."

"It's not only a question of money, Fred," I remonstrated. How far would he go? "It's only an idea I have, but I thought I might come and live here."

This was pure invention on my part. I hadn't even thought of that possibility until just now. But Fred had no way of knowing that.

His jaw dropped. "Live here? In Kilcollery? You must be mad!" He fumbled for reasons. "You've never lived here all year. You don't know what a hellhole this town is for young people in the off-season. Oh, sure, it's all right for the old folks with their bridge and their bingo at the church hall, and all that visitin' back and forth endlessly discussin' everybody's business. God, you couldn't stand it! I can't. I live in Dublin mostly. Besides"—he leaned forward and smiled cajolingly—"a pretty girl like you would be wasted, hidden away here. And 'tis such a bleak place in winter, you'd freeze to death. If you weren't bored to death first, that is."

I said nothing.

"A couple more days here and you'll be longing to get out. You'll see," he predicted confidently. He sat back and smiled a satisfied smile.

I let him sit in pleased silence for a moment. Then I said, "Fred?"

He turned an indulgent, expectant smile on me as he sipped at his glass.

I said, "About the post-mortem report . . . ?"

The fiery liquid jerked and spilled. "What about it?" Once again, he was dabbing at the no longer immaculate slacks.

"I'd like to see it, that's all."

"Why, for heaven's sake?"

Equably, I answered, "Why not?"

Fred's eyes narrowed. "All right. I'll see about a copy. Could take some time, though."

It was my turn to ask why.

"Because bureaucrats are bureaucrats," was the reply.

"Then perhaps I gained a little time by sending in a request today," I said sweetly. "Via Sergeant Burke."

"What the—then why ask me as well? Anyway, chances are our good sergeant will either lose it or send it to the wrong place."

"I thought that possible myself. In fact, he was most reluctant to do it at all. Any idea why?"

"He's lazy," Fred replied shortly. "So you want two irons in the fire to make sure. Joanna, what are you driving at?"

I didn't answer directly. Instead, very quietly, I put another question. "Could it be someone is trying to keep something from me?"

It was only a shot in the dark. I didn't really expect the result.

Fred swore and jumped to his feet. He put the glass on the mantel and came to stand over me. He looked right into my eyes.

"You'd better watch your mouth, Joanna Wentworth. You let that vicious little tongue of yours wag too often, spreading nasty insinuations, and you'll be sorry." His eyes were cold and menacing. I scarcely recognized my old playmate. Involuntarily I shivered and shrank back in my chair.

With a mirthless laugh Fred straightened up and went to retrieve his glass.

"All these questions, the post-mortem report, what are you playing at, Joanna? Straight up."

It was a good question. The truthful answer would have been that I didn't really know. The fact was, I was groping, casting about in the dark. But the handsome dark face before me was somber and hostile and, once more, an uneasy chill brushed at the edges of my mind. I decided to hedge.

"Nothing, Fred. I can't think what you mean." Delicately, nervously, I fluttered my hands and tried to look helpless.

He leaned against the fireplace. "You defeat me, girl," he said tiredly. "I get you a great offer for a house you can't possibly want to keep. And all you do is go around asking awkward and nasty questions as if you distrusted me. How the blazes do you think that makes me look, here in my own hometown?"

As an expression of injured innocence it was pretty good. Suddenly I was indeed uncertain and bewildered. Perhaps Colum and the Fitzgeralds and everyone else were right and I was wrong. Wrong to let vague feelings govern my reactions. Wrong to prejudge, to accuse people who only thought to do me a good turn. Seeing things, too, perhaps. My head was aching. I couldn't think anymore.

Fred spoke again, quickly, persuasively. "You'd have to sell the house sooner or later. Why not now? Live here! What would you do, had you thought of that? You couldn't teach, you know. Your degree would be okay but you haven't got the Irish teaching diploma and you couldn't come within an ass's roar of the Irish language requirement, now could you?" His tone softened, became kinder, as though he was now sure I could hold out no longer against his proposal. "No, it doesn't make sense at all, girl. You'd just be hangin' onto the past, against all the odds, and for what? You do see, love? Your best bet is to grab the cash and count yourself lucky. I can have the lot ready for you to sign on the old dotted tomorrow morning and by the afternoon you and I can be in Dublin. A few days' relaxation wouldn't go astray, by the looks of you. A holiday, a shopping spree in the dress shops, what do you say?"

He was right, of course; right in so much of what he said. Yet, somehow, the urgency with which he marshaled the facts for the opposition only made me the more uneasy, even suspicious again. Stubborn as my father, I thought unhappily, despairingly. Why am I convinced I'm right in this?

"Who's behind Heritage Trust, Fred?"

I shot the question at him without preamble and watched with detachment as his mouth tightened.

Then he smiled, deliberately charming. "Actually, it's a bit awkward," he confessed, lowering his tone to a confidential murmur, "but I suppose it can do no harm for you to know. Oh, don't worry, it doesn't involve you in anything wrong or unethical, even as the bloomin' Law Society sees it. It's just that we're sort of partners. He owns half of the dress design company Nita deals with, and it was on his visits down here that he fell for Mainstay. In a big way, too. A word to the wise . . ."

"And he's wealthy?" I pretended to consider the matter.

"Now you're gettin' the idea. Mind you, he won't go too much further . . ."

"Who is he?"

He hesitated only a moment. "One James Gardiner, a Dublin barrister. He doesn't do much at the Bar anymore. Has a lot of interests. We have a venture together with some horses. I'm hopin' to go into it in a big way, very soon." He was trying to impress.

I couldn't go on with this charade much longer. I got to my feet and walked to the window. I stood gazing out into the dark garden, my thoughts in turmoil.

Then I spoke without turning around. The question that had brought me all the way from London to this tight, shuttered village by the great Atlantic.

"What was my grandmother doing out on the cliff path in a Force Eight gale, Fred?"

There was a strange silence. I swung to face him. He was draining the whiskey in a hurry. His brows were pressed together and, as he placed the glass on the mantelpiece, his mouth twisted angrily.

"You really have a nerve, d'you know that? My sister worked herself into ill health over your grandmother, constantly lookin' after her. And all you can do is come over here, after the fact, mark you, and attack the only people who did anything for the poor old woman who was *your* relative. Where the hell were you all these years? That's a much more appropriate question. While we were takin' care of your nearest and dearest!" He ground out the sarcastic tag in a fury, whipping himself up with every word.

I thought quickly. I heard myself apologizing fretfully, speaking emotionally of the shock his letters had been. Doubly so because of my parents . . . I let my voice trail off miserably.

But inside my head, the little bell that his letters had set off was clanging again. Fred hadn't answered my question. Why not?

Why didn't Fred simply say that he didn't know?

He was watching me again.

"I'm just upset, still in a state of shock, Fred. I didn't mean . . ."

Magnanimously, he accepted my words. He made an appointment to see me at his office in the morning to go over my grandmother's will. "After a good night's sleep, maybe you'll see reason about the sale. I'll have the papers ready. Gardiner won't wait forever. Ten o'clock in my office."

As if he hadn't stood me up several times already.

"And enough of this amateur rushin' around askin' stupid questions, my girl. You want answers, you come to me first."

So that he could evade each one with a show of anger that was supposed to intimidate me? Seething inside, I determined to play out the little drama. On the porch steps I asked kindly, earnestly after Nita.

"She's not well at all," was the reply. "So poorly in fact that we can't open the hotel yet. Have to give her time to get on her feet again, the doc says."

"I thought the hotel delay was because of staff shortage."

Fred looked at me sharply but with a great effort I preserved a carefully innocent, solicitous face.

"Yes, yes. Staff are a problem. They always are. But the real reason is Nita's illness. Some bug she couldn't shake. Left her very weak."

Funny that the doctor had made no mention of Nita's illness. But then he, too, had been preoccupied with persuading me to go home to London. Time and work, he'd said. Perhaps he was right. Oh dear, what was the matter with me that I couldn't simply accept what had happened?

"Perhaps I ought to call, cheer her up with some flowers or magazines or something?" I was by now going through the motions, but Fred's rebuttal was surprisingly firm.

"No. The doc was very specific. She needs rest, a lot of it.

And right now, you are not the most restful person to have around."

Fred was enjoying himself, I could see; playing the dominant male giving orders. I had had enough.

"Good night, Fred," I said.

"No hard feelings between us, eh?" It was half-question, half-statement.

Weary and anxious only to end the conversation, I nodded.

"Good girl," he said in an approving tone, and before I could sidestep his reach, I was enfolded in his arms again. "Can't let McCarthy have it all his own way. I've known you a lot longer, after all. Give us a kiss, girl."

Hastily, I ducked my head away. Then I was looking over his shoulder straight into the furious, hostile eyes of Peggy. And on the path behind her was Joe.

Vexed and embarrassed, I pushed Fred away. The hot blush seeped up over my throat and face.

Peggy said nothing. Shaking her scarf out, she proceeded past us to the side door, her heavy tread slow and even. Joe ducked his head and shambled past, following her like an obedient child.

Fred snorted. "That ould biddy! Always where she's not wanted. All right, all right! I'm going. . . . See you tomorrow." Theatrically, he blew me a kiss and walked away. A few moments passed and the night was rent by the sound of a powerful engine, a screech of rubber on gravel and asphalt, and a series of rising gear changes that echoed around the cliffs and died away. I hadn't noticed a car near the house. He must have parked farther down the hill. Odd. Fred had never been keen on walking anywhere.

I stayed on the cool, shadowy porch for a few thoughtful moments. I was dissatisfied. There was something I had forgotten to ask, but I couldn't think what it was.

Slowly I returned to the study. I leaned my head against the mantel. I tried to think but found myself going around in circles. I was just too tired. It would all have to wait till tomorrow.

From the carpet by the window something gleamed and flashed. A tiepin. Gold, shaped like a leaf, with an engraved Celtic motif. It looked expensive. The retaining safety post that held the point was missing.

I was to see Fred at the office in the morning. I would return it to him then. I dropped the pin into the pocket of my jacket and promptly forgot all about it.

CHAPTER 8

Wednesday's dawn was high and clear and silver-cold. I know. I saw it come up.

I had had the same dream. The same terror-stricken stumbling in the clinging mist. Again I was scrabbling for a fingerhold, nails digging into soft, wet earth that was giving way, while below me the jagged rocks of Mainstay's cove waited. . . . Above me, a dim, blurred figure loomed and receded. He was laughing. . . . I screamed, the sound choking to nothing before it could leave my throat. . . . I couldn't die. I mustn't die. Somebody *must* hear. I screamed again. Again and again, I forced the sound up out of my aching lungs. The dim figure was leaning closer! Reaching out, to touch me, to push me . . . !

Then my shoulder was gripped. I was being shaken. Gently, then roughly. . . .

"Wake up! Miss Joanna, wake up!"

My focus contracted, became sharp. And I was staring wildly, uncomprehendingly, into Peggy's eyes.

"You were screaming. Fit to wake the dead."

To wake the dead! I shuddered.

"Are you all right? Why, you're freezing! Well, no wonder. Just look at that flimsy silk thing you're wearin'. You'll catch your death!" Muttering her disapproval, Peggy stalked to the cedar tallboy in the corner. The bottom drawer stuck briefly but she tugged it open.

Then she was tucking a downy quilt over me.

"I'm sorry I disturbed you, Peggy." My tongue was thick. It was an effort to speak. "Did I wake Joe, too?"

"I doubt it. He sleeps like a baby. Don't you worry about him." She turned at the door. "I'll be back in a minute with a hot water bottle."

The long shudders were easing now. I concentrated on trying to forget the deathly cold, the evil presence in the dream, the man who towered, laughing . . . Why was I sure it was a man?

But even as I gathered the warming quilt about me, I knew the nightmare was not over. In that cold dawn, I was finally face to face with the chilling, whispering doubt that had brought me here. Face to face with the terrifying suspicion that I scarcely dared breathe aloud in the silence of my room. . . .

I didn't believe that my grandmother's death was an accident.

I knew now that I didn't believe any of it. It was all too pat, too opportune; Gardiner's offer, Fred's rush, the uneasy feeling that I could count on no one in Kilcollery . . .

For if my grandmother's death was not an accident, there was only one alternative.

Murder.

"There, now. Drink that up," Peggy ordered brusquely, thrusting a cup into my hands.

Obediently I choked down the scalding tea while she pushed a hot water bottle under the sheet.

"Your feet are freezing. And you're pale and thin as a wisp. You need feeding up. An extra egg at breakfast to start with, and plenty of red meat to build up your blood." Peggy frowned awfully as she adjusted the bedcovers.

I laughed weakly at the incongruity of it. Only two weeks ago, outside on the cold, steep cliff, my grandmother fell to her death and Peggy stands here, talking about food and about building up my blood. . . .

"Why did Grandmother go out that evening, Peggy?"

Peggy started. "You mean the evening she . . . ?"

"The evening she was—er, died. Yes."

"I don't know, I wish I did. But it was Thursday. Joe an' me were both out. We'd gone to church because of Holy Thursday, like. Then we went to visit Mary Flaherty. She's a friend of mine from bingo. I wish now we'd been here to take care of the misthress instead. But what with the rain, sure I never thought she'd budge from the study fire till I got back to make her supper as usual. . . . Oh, Miss Joanna, how could I have known what was goin' to happen?" Peggy's voice rose and fell emotionally.

"Peggy! You don't mean she took her own life?"

"God forgive you for even thinkin' such a thing!" In her sudden rage, Peggy was momentarily magnificent. Then she crossed herself and muttered quickly, nervously, a short prayer for the dead.

"I'm sorry if I upset you, Peggy."

She sniffed. "That's as may be, Miss Joanna. 'Tis prayin' for the repose of her soul you should be. Not goin' around makin' trouble! 'Twill only come back on you, you mark my words. An' it won't bring the misthress back, so what good can you do? Wouldn't you go home to London before . . ." She broke off, her face red.

"Not you, too, Peggy. Before what? What do you mean? What do you know? What does everyone but me know? You've got to tell me!"

"Leave me be, Miss Joanna! I don't want no more trouble!"

"What sort of trouble? Peggy, please!"

She interrupted me dourly. "I've said enough. If you're set on causin' trouble, 'tis you'll have to handle it. There's no helpin' people who won't help themselves. I've said my piece, plain as I can. If you don't know where you're not wanted, there's no more I can do."

Her words were like a slap in the face. I shrank into my pillows, shocked and smarting from such a rebuff. I remembered Fred's anger at being questioned, the sergeant's reluctance, the strange silence in the bank at the mention of my grandmother's belongings. And now Peggy . . .

"I won't go!" I said shakily. "I'll keep on and on, until I find out everything!"

Peggy whitened but she held her ground.

"Don't, miss, please! Go home! Leave us alone. I have to look after Joe."

"I can't, Peggy. And what has Joe got to do with anything?"

Peggy's hands tightened on each other till the reddened knuckles showed white. "I'll bring your breakfast up to you. I'll not have it said that I didn't do my duty by you. You'd better get some sleep."

The door closed on these ominous words and I was alone once more. Alone with my dreadful thoughts in the gray dawn.

* * *

"Blast! Blast and damn!"

Raucously, mockingly, a seabird screeched in answer to my ejaculation of disgust.

I was looking down at the front right wheel of my car. It was absolutely, undeniably flat. So was the right rear wheel. And on the ground beside each one lay the tiny rubber valve cap. An unmistakable message. The air had deliberately been let out.

I swept the deserted cliffs with a long look, but there wasn't a soul in sight. Naturally. Someone might be watching, though, from some hiding place among the gorse and sedge. A shiver of distaste and unease ran through me and I almost ran back indoors to hide myself.

"Always remember, child, that you are first and foremost a Wentworth!" Grandmother's arrogant phrase floated up out of the past, an unbidden and unwanted memory. Yet almost automatically, I squared my shoulders and took a deep breath.

"Damn you all, damn you to hell!" I shouted into the sea wind. Immediately I felt a lot better.

Peggy appeared at the hall door. "You called me, Miss Joanna?"

"My car has a flat tire. I'll have to walk down to the village. I'll ask the garage to send up a man with a pump."

"Haven't you got a spare?"

"It's a bit soft. I forgot to check it," I lied.

"Send Joe down with a note. You don't want to be goin' down all that way yourself just for that."

"I have an appointment with Fred Moone."

Peggy sniffed. "Well, in that case . . ." She turned away, back into the house without further speech. The set of her rounded shoulders spoke for her. She had warned me and I was choosing to ignore her words, so she was washing her hands of whatever was to come. . . .

I reached Fred's office at ten-fifteen. It was closed. Locked. Blinds still drawn.

In the newsagent's across the street, Miss Murphy unwillingly told me what anyone could see, that young Mr. Moone hadn't opened the office yet.

"And what about Miss Hayes?"

"Oh, I wouldn't know, miss."

Hastily she excused herself to attend to some customers who had just trooped in, all talking at once. The busy sing-song chatter stopped when they saw me. Then it started again, as a low, secretive murmuring and whispering, with many side glances at me. I resolved to ignore it and picked up a magazine. A glossy, high-fashion production; few words, lots of pictures. Many photographs of the cover girl. Featuring the latest line from a designer even I had heard of.

"Excuse me," a feminine voice said. Someone reached past me to the pile of magazines. It was a surprise to look into the beautiful dark eyes of the cover girl herself!

She was even more beautiful in reality, though the bright daylight disclosed tiny frown lines and a discontented expression.

With a graceful sweep of darkened eyelashes, her gaze dropped to the magazine I held. She picked up a copy. A fragrance as elusive as wild flowers wafted in her wake as she moved away to the cash register. Then she looked back at me with a wide-eyed smile that was no less stunning for being professionally practiced.

I smiled back, wondering what had brought her to Kilcollery.

She bought some other items and paid an openly admiring Miss Murphy. They chatted briefly. Then the model crossed the road to a gleaming silver Jaguar which sat alone in the deserted street. She didn't get in but leaned against the immaculately polished car. Waiting for someone, it seemed.

I put down the magazine and picked up a newspaper. I was dropping the few coins into Miss Murphy's hand when I saw that the blinds were up in Fred's office. I nodded to Miss Murphy, deliberately ignoring her silence, and crossed the street swiftly. But as I approached the office door, the girl by the Jaguar hailed me.

"If you're looking for Fred, he isn't there. It's only James who's in there, James Gardiner, that is, Fred's partner. He'll be out any minute. He said he just had a call to make. Maybe you'd like to talk to him instead? I don't know where the Hayes creature is. Certainly not here."

Her voice was flat and disappointing but she seemed pleasant enough.

"Thanks, but I'll wait for Fred. He should be here any minute. He said ten o'clock."

She shrugged. "Fine. If you don't mind waiting. Personally, I hate it. Fred's a terror for being late, you know." She smiled charmingly again. "We haven't met before. I'm Katrina Sheehan, Fred's fiancée."

"Joanna Wentworth."

"I know. Miss Murphy told me."

I thought fast as we exchanged the mandatory politenesses. So Fred was engaged to this gorgeous creature, a model so successful that I'd known her name before she mentioned it. Fred, who only last night had twice tried to flatter and disarm me with talk of "fun" together in Dublin! How on earth could he afford to run in the same circle, let alone marry the girl? Certainly not on the proceeds of an obviously perfunctory law practice in sleepy Kilcollery. His Dublin interests must be coining! I looked at Katrina with sharpening interest, to find her studying me equally attentively.

"You *are* the girl who inherited Mainstay?"

"Yes." I would say as little as possible for the moment.

But Katrina was glancing quickly, furtively, I thought, in the direction of Fred's office. She moved closer to me. "I'd no idea you were actually in Kilcollery," she remarked with an odd intensity. "Fred didn't tell me. Of course, he was speaking mostly to James. Last night, on the phone, I mean."

"I'm afraid I don't quite understand. Why should he mention me?"

She didn't answer directly. "Listen"—her voice sank to an almost inaudible mutter—"I've got to talk to you. It's important. Could you come and sit in the car? It's freezing in the wind." Delicately she shivered and drew her expensive wool jacket close. "It'll only take a moment and I don't want—anyone—to see us talking if I can help it."

"What about . . . ?" I nodded toward Fred's office.

"James? Oh, he doesn't matter. I can handle him."

But was it my imagination or did she glance around covertly as we slid into the luxuriously upholstered and carpeted Jaguar?

"You must think I'm nuts. A complete stranger and I haul you off into my car like this."

Her car. Not Gardiner's.

I made polite disclaiming noises and had no trouble looking interested in what she had to say.

"I'm going to ask you to do something for me, Miss Wentworth, or rather, not to do something!"

"Joanna." Deliberately, encouragingly, I smiled. What on earth did she mean? "How can I help you?"

Her breath escaped in a little rush. "I just knew you'd be the friendly sort. And when Miss Murphy told me your name, I knew the opportunity to speak to you was simply heaven-sent. I just had to. Look, have you seen Fred yet? I'm not prying. Honestly. I promise I'll explain."

I hedged. "I have an appointment with him this morning."

"He's going to ask you to sell him your house!"

"He is?"

"You didn't know?"

"No." Strictly, if relatively, true. "I've been away. In Scotland." Also true, if not the whole truth.

But Katrina's attention was on her own concerns only. "You've got to promise me you'll refuse!"

"Refuse?"

"To sell Fred the house! Someone else will buy it. Someone is bound to. I know it's a sort of stately home or something with valuable furniture and all that sort of thing. I'll do everything I can to help you; find a buyer, I mean. I know heaps of people with oodles of money. I'll put my lawyer on to it and when he's got you somebody he can do the job for you for a nominal price. He'll do it, don't worry. He makes a packet out of me, and he knows it."

"Fred isn't your lawyer?" In my surprise, the question popped out before I had time to think, but this extraordinary girl didn't take offense.

"Lord, no. I've dealt with the same man for years. No sense in changing. In any case, I always think it's better to keep business and personal matters apart. You never know." The words were obscure, but her meaning wasn't. Then why on earth was she marrying Fred? She answered my unspoken question easily, lightly. "Fred is a charmer. He's good-looking and we get on well. I'd like kids, before

I'm too old. It's just that he gets talked into wanting all sorts of things. . . . Will you promise me you won't let him buy your house? I'll make sure you don't lose. I wouldn't talk to you like this, but there isn't time for beatin' about the bush, he's got all the papers ready. And anyway, you've known him since you were both kids, a lot longer than I have."

My head was reeling at this unaccountable development.

"Why do you want me to refuse?" I asked warily.

Her answer was low, intense, and brimmed with sudden dislike. "Because I don't want to live in bloody Kilcollery, that's why! I'm sorry if the place means a lot to you, but I grew up in a suffocating little town just like this and I couldn't wait to get out of it. I don't want to live here, not even on weekends. I couldn't stand it, the endless rain, the same people all the time, nothing to do but play bingo and visit the same dreary, poky little shops. I'd go out of my mind. D'you see, Joanna?"

I saw all right. More than she knew. It was ironic that her words should have echoed, quite startlingly, the words spoken to me last night to persuade me that Kilcollery was not the place for me.

Words spoken by Fred Moone.

Somebody was playing a very deep game indeed.

I said, "Yes. I do see. But surely Fred wouldn't insist if he knew how you felt about the house?"

"Oh, he knows all right! We had our first quarrel over it." The perfect features contracted. "He just won't listen. Ever since the old lady . . . oh, I'm sorry. She was your grandmother or aunt or something, wasn't she?"

"My grandmother. When did Fred first say he wanted to buy Mainstay?" The question came from nowhere but seemed very important, though I didn't know why.

"About a year ago," was the reply. "She didn't want to sell, I suppose. Though he never mentioned that he'd asked her."

Somehow I wasn't really surprised. Not really. The sinking, lowering uneasiness assailed me again. Resolutely I plowed on.

"And what about James Gardiner?"

"What about him?"

"Didn't he express—ah—interest in Mainstay, too?"

"James! No! Where did you get that idea? He hates the country, even more than I do. Besides, he couldn't afford it!"

Gardiner couldn't afford it? And Fred could? With his own money? Not Katrina's, obviously. And Fred's story of a client in a hurry was just that; a story, invented for the sake of deception. Wearily, I realized I was still asking the same question I'd started with. Why? Why? Why? The word ran around in my overtaxed brain. I shook my head in frustration.

She was looking at me inquisitively.

Hastily I tried to divert her attention. "I must have picked up something wrongly. A misunderstanding, that's all. What did Fred say about me and the house, by the way?"

"Just that it would be up for sale, you never came near the place and you'd need the cash, so it'd be a good thing all round. But it wouldn't. Not for me. You won't sell it to Fred, will you, Joanna, please? Honestly, I'll do everything I can to get you a buyer as quickly as possible. And if it's a matter of needing a loan to tide you over . . ." She paused delicately.

So she didn't know about Grandmother's money. Fred had told her I'd "need the cash." But why did he want Mainstay so badly, so urgently, so much that he lied to me, and to his own fiancée . . . ?

"I've just remembered something," Katrina said unexpectedly. "Something Fred said. About someone else being interested in your house. That was why he said he was in a hurry. That photographer fellow, the famous one. I've forgotten his name. Oh, you must know who I mean. The one with the book on the North. It was in all the papers. Fred said he was sniffing around. His name's on the tip of my tongue."

My heart thudded. "Colum McCarthy."

"That's it! Look, Joanna, I can get my lawyer to get in touch with him and maybe you'd have a buyer sooner than you'd think. And Fred needn't know a thing."

"No need to trouble your lawyer. Colum McCarthy's here, in Kilcollery."

"Oh! Has he been in touch?"

"Not about the house," I answered dully. I was remembering Colum asking Peggy about the house, Colum speaking to me about photographing Mainstay, Colum examining the sideboard in the dining room. . . . Me or Mainstay? A strange sense of desolation invaded my unwilling mind.

I said only, "When Fred asks, I'll refuse to let him have Mainstay."

She grasped both my hands and pumped them enthusiastically. "Thank you, Joanna. I won't forget this. Now, here's my business card. I'll talk to my lawyer about finding you a buyer anyway. And in the meantime, anything you want, even if it's only a place to stay in Dublin, just get in touch, won't you?"

Tired and dispirited, I nodded. It was the easier thing to do.

I opened the car door.

She went on quickly. "I'll be at the hotel for a day or so, I expect, even though Fred doesn't know yet that I'm here. But I'd rather he didn't know I spoke to you. So if we meet, could you pretend we haven't met before? I hate rows and Fred is going to be mad enough that I ignored him and came with James today. But you see, I wanted to try to talk him out of buying your house. Now, thanks to you, I won't have to." She added the last words with a winsome, ingenuous smile, like a little girl used to getting her own way.

I wanted only to get away. I assented quickly and slid out of the car. Her dazzling smile shone briefly. Then she returned to the contemplation of her own picture on the magazine cover, one elegantly manicured hand tracing the silky outline of her smooth hair.

I walked blindly away. Anywhere . . .

Then I bumped into someone. The automatic words of apology died on my lips as Dr. O'Brien hailed me loudly.

"Changed your car already, girl?" he joked. "What did you do with the little yellow peril, pile it up?" He stooped to look into the Jaguar. His face changed abruptly. "What's she doing here? Fred didn't say she was coming down."

Katrina pressed a button. A window slid noiselessly down. The doctor bent down again and spoke to her. It was obvious they didn't need to be introduced.

"Excuse me, Doc," I said quickly. "Have an errand to do."

Purposefully I crossed the street and dived down a narrow alley, making for the Promenade and the quiet sands. I had to think. If Fred showed up at the office now, he would just have to wait for me. That thought made me laugh, a little hysterical laugh that netted me an anxious, suspicious glance from a passerby.

Unseeingly I wandered along the curving shore, my heels sinking into the wet sand, making little glopping noises as I lifted each one.

The sand had been firm and dry when I walked along here with Colum. . . .

I wished he hadn't seen Fred kissing me. . . .

"Miss Wentworth!"

Someone was calling my name. I pushed my hair back from my face and swung around.

A portly man was quick-stepping toward me, tiptoeing fussily across the huge expanse of sand as he tried to avoid getting his suede shoes damp. About fifty, thinning black hair brushed carefully across a pink scalp, a rotund face with pink complexion. A broadcloth coat, buttoned neatly, its Persian lamb collar turned up against the cold salt air.

James Gardiner, surely. Kilcollery couldn't possibly boast his like.

He puffed slightly as he reached me.

"Miss Wentworth, you don't know me. Gardiner's the name, James Gardiner, barrister-at-law. Fred Moone is my junior partner."

Suppressing an edgy giggle, I inclined my head.

"Forgive this unorthodox introduction, Miss Wentworth, but when Dr. O'Brien said you had come down this way . . ." He exclaimed in disgust and flicked a length of clinging weed from his right shoe.

Funny, fussy little pink man. What did he want with me? Katrina having spilled the beans, so to speak, I now knew that Fred himself wanted Mainstay, that he'd used his partner's name merely for his own nefarious purposes.

I said formally, "How do you do?" And I waited.

He pressed my hand earnestly. Despite the chill wind, his palm was warmly damp. "I am so pleased to make your acquaintance, Miss Wentworth. I cannot tell you how much. I was, of course, slightly acquainted with your late grandmother." He smiled. His teeth were small and pointed.

Why "of course"? Fred hadn't said they knew each other, or had he? I couldn't remember.

"My most sincere condolences, Miss Wentworth."

"You're very kind, Mr. Gardiner." An old-fashioned phrase, one of Grandmother's own. Why did the word "sincere" sound so very insincere?

"A most unhappy accident," he went on unctuously.

If it was an accident. I had been so sure in the cold gray dawn this morning . . . but in the daylight, it was different, somehow difficult to be sure. . . .

Then I found myself looking into James Gardiner's eyes.

I remember reflecting quite lucidly that we were of a height, even as I met that curiously flat, expressionless gaze for the first time.

His eyes were black. Without light. A sort of obsidian. They held me frozen, oppressed, hypnotized.

Like a rabbit before a snake.

A mortally dangerous snake . . .

Involuntarily I backed away. My stomach twisted, tighter, tighter . . .

He followed me. That expressionless gaze locked on mine.

Then, in those flat black eyes a tiny curl of malevolence gleamed, swelled, uncoiled. . . .

A strange dizziness was coming over me. My knees began to quiver, then to shake violently. . . .

"Goodness me, my dear girl, are you all right? Here, let me help you. Perhaps you should sit down for a moment." Unexpectedly strong fingers closed on my arm, pinioning it against his side. He guided me, unresisting, to the rocks, only a few steps from the placidly lapping water. There was no one else on the beach. No one on the Promenade. A single car crawled along the Mullaghmore road. Then it turned off and disappeared. Was I alone with the man who drove my grandmother out of the safety of Mainstay, out to her death . . . ?

"I am sorry, I seem to have given you a fright," Gardiner was saying prosaically, pleasantly.

Startled, I looked up. I couldn't believe my eyes. His

shiny pink face was as though new-washed and wore only an expression of kindly, if puzzled, concern.

I shook my head in disbelief. Surely I hadn't imagined . . . ?

He seemed to misunderstand the gesture. "I should have waited and called on you properly at the house, but I couldn't wait!"

"Couldn't wait?" I repeated stupidly.

"To speak to you about Mainstay. Moone tells me he spoke to you last night. I must assure you of one thing; I will be quite prepared to keep the two servants on, if that is all that is holding up your acceptance of my offer to purchase! I realize, of course, that this meeting is quite irregular, but . . ."

I had stopped listening. *His* offer to purchase? If he'd wanted to confuse, to stun, he couldn't have chosen a more effective phrase. Thoroughly bewildered, I sat shaking my head slowly. I tried to recover myself. Too many jolts, too many contradictions. How could I ever hope to find the truth?

Gardiner's pink face was eager as a boy as he stood in front of me, apparently oblivious of the fact that the sandy depressions under his shoes were rapidly filling with seawater.

"But—" I caught myself up just in time. I had been about to exclaim that he hated the country, thus giving Katrina's confidence away. What could he and Fred hope to gain with this game? Or was it that they hadn't got their story straight? Was Katrina wrong?

Perplexed and beginning to feel just a little frightened, I could only listen as Gardiner smoothly expounded his reasons for wanting Mainstay in a hurry. It all sounded too familiar. He had vacated his own house in Dublin and wished to close the sale without delay merely so that he could move in as soon as possible. Where had I heard those words before?

No. Not heard. I had read them. In Fred's second letter. Was that only three days ago?

I frowned in a desperate attempt to focus my sluggish thoughts. Then I met his gaze again. . . .

In that absurdly pink face, the flat black eyes flickered quickly away from mine, but not before I had seen and recognized again that pitiless, malign . . . Dear God! I repressed a shudder. Mustn't show fear. I wanted to run, but my limbs were cold, stiff, heavy. Even my brain felt slow, ponderous. Must go carefully. I was alone with him. . . .

Then, beyond his head, two people swung steadily into view. They were approaching! Two men in worn black reefers and heavy sea trousers. Elderly, grizzled, weatherbeaten, shabby. Two angels couldn't have looked more beautiful. Wooden lobster pots dangled from gnarled hands. They passed right by, nodding a courteous greeting, heading for the small red buoys that bobbed in the deep water off the farther rocks.

Galvanized by their blessed presence, I jumped to my feet, steadying wobbly knees with ice-sharp concentration.

"I'm afraid you have come to Kilcollery for nothing, Mr. Gardiner," I said, carefully enunciating each word with a dry mouth. "You see, I have no intention of selling Mainstay. To anyone."

It gave me a tiny shock to realize that it was the truth.

Then I met that obsidian gaze for the third time and, despite my resolution, I quailed. I drew a sharp breath.

Gardiner just stood. He said nothing. He didn't need to. In some obscure way, we both knew I had just declared war.

What might he have done if the two fishermen hadn't happened along? I didn't know. I didn't want to know.

Averting my eyes from the enmity in his, I bade him a slightly shaky goodbye and escaped up the strand, back up to the houses, the shops, the people, willing my trembling legs to move steadily and straight. . . .

I had no idea where I was going.

CHAPTER 9

The relentless white mist came swirling in from the sea, blanketing everything in clinging dampness. It curled wetly. Sounds echoed eerily in the sudden windless hush. Even the birds were silent.

Still shaken after my encounter with James Gardiner, I stumbled up the steps of the Promenade Hotel. My knees were jelly, but I couldn't stop now.

I stood for a moment under the canopied roof of the seaward terrace. To catch my breath—but I also needed to think. What was I going to say to Fred? If he was here. A slim little red MG sports car and the sleek silver Jaguar sat in front of the hotel. At a guess, the red MG, fast and expensive, was Fred's! So! He probably knew by now, too, that Katrina was here. And Gardiner. I didn't want to run into him again. . . .

A young voice hailed me. "Like to buy some fish? Fresh from the sea. Caught 'em meself."

"Not now," I started to say, automatically rejecting extraneous concerns. Then I saw that the voice belonged to Danny. Scruffier than the first time we'd met, he was wet through, hair plastered down on his freckled forehead. A sad little sight, huddling on the cold wrought-iron bench on the deserted porch.

"You're soaking wet! You'll catch your death!"

"I fell in," was the succinct answer. "If you buy me fish, I can go on home and dry meself off." A shrewd trader, he was quick to size up a customer and take advantage. I looked down into his childish face and felt pity and a curious urge toward protectiveness. Still, I hesitated.

"Go on, they're fresh out of the water. Taste great. An' I need the money. The Big Fella'll kill me if I don't sell 'em." Truculent, pleading, he watched me with bright eyes.

"And Peggy will kill me if I bring her home any more fish to clean," I said ruefully.

"I'll clean 'em! Honest! I know how. I'll carry 'em home for you 'n all."

I couldn't hold out. "How much?"

Swiftly he counted the fish in the pail at his feet. Then, head on one side, tongue bulging his cheek, he appraised me knowingly and named his price. It was, of course, too high, but I was too preoccupied to care.

"You're supposed to bargain," the youngster cried, taken aback. "The tourists all do. You're supposed to say no. Or, too much. Or, somethin'!"

"Not now, Danny. I've got a lot on my mind." I fished in my wallet and handed over some money.

"Here! You're givin' me too much!" Surprise stopped him short for a moment. Then he picked through the money in his palm and resolutely pushed the remainder back into my hands. I had to bend forward slightly to catch the muttered explanation of this extraordinary behavior. Even then, all I caught was a somewhat stumbling, embarrassed reference to an old lady who wouldn't like it, and something about not cheating.

For a moment I was baffled. Then I understood. My grandmother hadn't confined herself to lessons in reading. But had she thought at all of the harsh world in which this boy had to live when he wasn't with her, reading about Finn and the Fianna and that long-ago mythical world of chivalry and honor?

"Just take it, Danny. Get something for yourself with the extra money."

I looked for a doorbell or a knocker.

"If you want the Moones, they live round the back." He pointed to a concrete path that led around the corner of the building. "Hey, what about your fish? Will I take 'em along to your house?"

"Yes. No. It's much too far from here and you're already soaked." My eye fell on Fred's car. "Look, wait for me here, will you? Maybe Mr. Moone can drive us both to Mainstay. I have a feeling I won't be long."

Philosophical acceptance of my eccentricity written on his freckled face, he nodded and settled back into a corner of the iron bench.

I followed the path past the second glassed-in terrace Nita had described—how remote that night seemed now!—and the new-looking wing that towered high and extended back along what had once been a pleasant croquet lawn, toward a long whitewashed bungalow. The high rows of windows, all of them blank and shuttered, were unnerving. I shivered and hurried along. The mist was crystallizing into a thin rain when I reached the Moones' door.

I was just raising my hand toward the illuminated white plastic bell when voices sounded at the side and, around the corner, a scowl contorting his swarthy face, came the huge man I had seen accost Colum the other night! There was time only to take in old, torn clothes, and a rank odor of dirt and stale tobacco. I shrank back as his bloodshot eyes flickered over me, but he merely slouched past.

Then, through the thickening curtain of rain, a voice carried harshly in his wake. "And stay away from here! I have enough trouble to deal with. You'll get your money in due course. Just stay away from here! . . . Oh, good God! . . . What the . . . !" Fred stopped stockstill when he saw me. His dumbfounded face contrasted ludicrously with his smart, man-about-town appearance, but somehow I didn't feel like laughing.

"Hello, Fred, you weren't at the office." I don't think my attempt to sound nonchalant worked very well, but Fred seemed too taken aback to notice.

"No. No. Er, something came up. These damn tinkers! Always pesterin' people. I'd like to run them out of the country. Can't have them botherin' Nita, can I?" He took my arm and turned me about.

"Miss Hayes wasn't at the office either."

"I gave her the day off." He tried to propel me before him.

"Where are we going, Fred? I thought, now that I'm here and you're here, we might get down to business."

"At the office. I left my briefcase there. All the papers are at the office." He was glancing around as he spoke. I followed suit but couldn't make out what he was looking at, or for . . . I turned to ask, but he spoke quickly.

"Can't be disturbin' my sister while she's sick. I thought I asked you not to call for the moment. You know she would insist on gettin' up and servin' tea an' all that. Téll you what, let's you and I have a good long chat over lunch." He headed me back toward the street. "And we'll go through the papers. Everything. The lot." Smoothly, he piloted me down the path and across the wet terrace again.

When Danny saw us he jumped to his feet.

"Dammit!" Fred was furious. "What are you doin', hangin' about here, Danny Sheridan? Be off with you!"

I spoke up hastily. "I bought some fish from him and I asked him to wait for me."

Fred swore quietly. "Then give me the fish, boy, and scat!"

Danny's face, so cheerful earlier, returned Fred's dislike with a mulish glower of its own. "I will not! They're hers, not yours. Anyway, I said I'd clean 'em for her."

Fred was looking at me with a mixture of exasperation and frustration.

"I haven't paid the boy yet," I lied, hoping the youngster wouldn't give me away. He didn't. "Couldn't we drive by Mainstay? I can pay him. He can clean the fish there under Peggy's eye and you and I can go on down to the office."

Reluctantly Fred led the way to the MG, sharply adjuring Danny not to spill the damned fish all over his sheepskin seat covers.

The rain was sheeting down the car windows as Fred drove, too fast, along the windswept Promenade. Gusts shook the tiny car from time to time.

"It's down for the day," Fred remarked gloomily. "Always is when it's preceded by that bloody mist. Is it drivin' you up the wall yet, Joanna?" His tone was faintly tinged with malice.

I didn't answer. Squashed in behind us, Danny was wriggling about, doing something. I couldn't make out what.

Fred snapped, "Sit still, boy! You'll have water all over my car. The bloody salt'll eat into the upholstery." Somewhat mechanically I said, "I'm sorry if you're a bit uncomfortable, Danny, but it's not much farther now and it's better than getting wetter." I had just remembered the question that had eluded me last night. I turned to Fred.

"Perhaps this should wait till we get to the papers, Fred,

but it slipped my mind once already. Is there an inventory of the contents of Mainstay?"

"An inventory! Not that I know of. Why? What would you want one for?"

"A valuer's list, then. Or an insurance list. Anything."

"No. I just said I don't know of any. What the hell are you drivin' at?"

I was silent for a thoughtful moment. What to say. I could hardly say straight out that I thought he was up to something. Not yet. Not till I knew a bit more. Unfortunately, Fred was too quick for me.

"You think Nita or I have been stealin' your bloody belongings, do you?" His face crimsoned and the car rocked as he took a curve too fast.

I let him demonstrate his anger a moment longer. Then I told him about the bobbing, dancing light I'd seen from the Lighthouse. I could have sworn his surprise was genuine.

"Don't you lock your blasted doors when you're out?"

"Of course, Fred. But since when did a lock stop a burglar? I thought an inventory might hold a clue, tell me what a thief might be looking for."

"Didn't you check to see if anything was missing, or moved about, or disturbed?"

"I can't be sure. It's been so long—"

"It's been so long since you last visited your grandmother, you mean, that you can't even remember what's in the bloody house. Not a very long visit either, was it?" Fred needled. "You two never got on very well, did you? Hated each other's guts, I'd have said. True?"

"No. It wasn't like that."

"But you didn't bother to come near the place in years. Not very loving. Hated the whole place. You wouldn't have come even now if—" He broke off abruptly.

"If my seventy-six-year-old grandmother hadn't gone for a last walk in a pouring gale. Was that what you were going to say, Fred?"

There was a long pause. He was breathing deeply. His knuckles showed white on the wheel.

He sighed heavily. "All I'm tryin' to do, love, is make you see what's best all round. For you, especially. Why not hand the place on to someone who'll live there, who'll treasure it, if that's the phrase, and who's willing to pay well?"

I wished now that I hadn't made that promise to Katrina Sheehan to keep her confidence that Fred, not James Gardiner, was the man behind Heritage Trust.

"You'll think about it, Joanna? Reconsider."

"Reconsider?"

"Stop playin' games, girl. James told me you said Mainstay's not for sale."

"That's right." A shiver rippled through me at the memory of those malevolent eyes.

"You're crazy. Plain crazy, girl. D'you have any idea how much it'll cost you to keep the place, and the death duties?"

"No. But it makes no difference."

"Oh, but it does! If you're countin' on your grandmother's estate to do the job, think again. There's not much left."

"What!"

"I hate tellin' you this. I've been puttin' it off. The old lady must have lived high for a long time. Then a couple of years ago she started pullin' most of her stock out of my hands. Must have been dabblin' herself. Even you had no idea of the real state of her finances. What am I sayin'? Sure, even I couldn't do a thing. What's left won't pay the duties. I'm sorry, love." But he wasn't. Not really. I could hear the suppressed triumph in his voice.

Shocked and sickened, I listened.

"You see now why I've been pushin' the sale so hard. You can't possibly keep the house. I wanted to bring you to the idea before I had to tell you the bad news as well, so that you'd not feel it all as much. You'd have the money from the sale into your hands as a sort of compensation for the other. And no debts. And you must admit that that offer is handsome, enough to tempt anyone. Of course, you'll want to see it all for yourself. I'll help in any way I can." He was so earnest, so concerned for me, that I might have believed him.

If I hadn't met Katrina.

Grandmother living "high"? Dabbling in the stock market? "I shall want to see everything," I said. "Every bill. Every step of the way."

"Of course." He paused. "You'll think again, then? James is very anxious."

"How about you, Fred?"

"Me?"

"Aren't you anxious, too?"

"Why would I be anxious, love? About what?" He laughed lightly.

"Enough of this fencing, Fred. You're not simply trying to get me to unload a house I don't want or can't afford. You want more. You want me to turn a blind eye to something. What it is I don't know yet. But I will . . ." I had had enough of caution. It was time for plain talk. I played my hunch. "And, of course, I don't have to be in a hurry, do I? Mainstay won't actually be mine to do anything with until the will . . . and that all takes time, I understand. So why the hurry, Fred?"

Fred swore violently. The car hit a pothole on the headland road and bucked wildly. Gravel chips flew up, noisily clattering under the wheel housings. Fred swore again and lapsed into a brooding silence.

I waited.

"Bloody roads!" he muttered. "Wreckin' my paintwork and the car not even a year old yet!"

"You haven't answered me, Fred," I remarked coldly.

"Bloody right! I haven't and I'm not goin' to. I won't dignify nasty accusations and innuendo with an answer of any kind. As soon as you name another lawyer, I'll turn everything over to him. Be worth it to get rid of you. There's your bloody house. Get that kid and his smelly fish out of my car before I wring his little neck. As for you, Miss Wentworth, you can go to hell. I've given you my advice, my professional advice. If you're too stubborn to take it, if you can't see what's best all round, then on your own head . . ."

His words uncannily echoed Peggy's. Again I was being warned. On the surface, merely to save myself from debts, financial disaster. But below, there swirled ugly undercurrents, threats, an unknown menace. . . . Was I right? Had Katrina told me the truth?

The car skidded to a stop on the wet gravel. I sat in cold silence. Fred, too, sat silent for a moment. Then he flexed his shoulders and slewed in his seat to look at me. With unexpected gentleness, he touched my arm and smiled deprecatingly.

"Look, Joanna, I'm sorry. Honestly. Truce? I'm under a lot of strain just now and I shouldn't take it out on you. I've just had too much work to deal with lately, what with the hotel problems, and your grandmother, and my work in Dublin pilin' up."

Not to mention your fiancée, and James Gardiner, and the sale of Mainstay, and whatever you two are cooking up. . . .

Coolly, I said, "And, of course, Nita's illness?"

"That, too," Fred agreed hastily. "Bear with me, just a little longer, till I get on top of things again, will you?"

I said nothing.

"Not long, honest. A few days," he pleaded, a note of impatience creeping into his tone again. "At most."

I nodded warily. I didn't trust myself to speak. I was wondering why he needed a few days "at most." Why the time limit? Perhaps, after all, his preoccupation had nothing to do with the sale of Mainstay.

The sale of Mainstay. My heart sank as I repeated the phrase and I realized that I wanted desperately to keep the house, that the old place was, at the last, very precious to me.

"In the meantime"—Fred's confidence was returning—"d'you mind if we postpone that lunch? I'm a bit pushed, as I said."

"Not again! I'm getting very tired of being fobbed off."

"All right, all right! I'll be up later this afternoon. With all the papers. That's a promise."

So the lunch date was only an excuse to get rid of me gracefully at the time. To hurry me away from the hotel, from Nita?

He helped me out of the car. Danny climbed out awkwardly. He sneezed suddenly and stumbled. "I'm bein' careful," he protested as Fred reached for the fish pail.

"As soon as I can, Joanna," Fred said.

"As soon as possible, Fred. I'm not going anywhere for the foreseeable future." Deliberately, I stressed the word "anywhere" and saw Fred's eyebrows contract.

"Stubborn as ever. Just like your grandmother. Okay, I'll do my best." Fred nodded an abrupt goodbye and left.

Danny kicked at the ground and spat into a puddle. "I don't like him."

"Don't spit, Danny! Come on. We'd better get inside. The rain's getting heavier."

"I put a fish down the side of the seat," Danny remarked with relish.

"In Fred's car? He'll be furious."

Danny grinned. "He won't find it a while."

"Till it smells to high heaven."

Danny giggled maliciously.

Then I forgot Fred and his car and the fish as the hall door opened and Colum called cheerfully, "Well, well! Two drowned rats! Where have you been, swimming? Oh, more fish. Peggy'll have a fit. I've been making enough mess with the ones I brought last night."

I said, "Better take them to the kitchen, Danny. Through that door."

"I know the way."

"You do? Oh! And tell Peggy I said to give you something to eat. And a towel to dry off with!"

"Better wipe your feet before Peggy kills us all!" Colum called after him. "Well, lady, had you forgotten our lunch date? To eat the fish I brought you last night? You had forgotten, hadn't you? Great for a fellow's self-confidence." He pulled a mournful face but the gray eyes were warm.

I couldn't help myself. Everything else simply slid away. Irrepressibly, gladly, I responded to the invitation in his eyes, to the unexpected respite that offered itself.

I said, "After the morning I've had, I'm just glad to be safely home. Just give me time to change."

Dark eyebrows lifted. "You do look a bit unglued."

"Thanks a lot."

"Saw your car, by the way. Two punctures? What were you doing, drivin' over nails?"

"Someone let the air out."

"Nasty. Someone doesn't like you."

"So it seems. And I forgot after all to go to the garage in the village. Could you give me a lift down there after lunch?"

"No need. I've got an emergency pump in my car. Have to carry it; never know what I'll run into or how far from civilization."

"Thanks." I turned to go upstairs.

Colum put out a detaining hand. "Any idea who? The flat tires, I mean."

"One or two. But whether I'm right . . . ?" I shrugged.

"Tell all over lunch, huh?"

"Mmm." But unexpectedly, I was unsure again. Unsure of how much to say, what to say. To anyone.

But Colum only smiled eagerly. "There's someone here I want you to meet."

CHAPTER 10

By contrast with yesterday, lunch was relaxed and cheerful. Slowly I unwound and felt immeasurably strengthened.

Peggy blushed with pride at Colum's enthusiastic praise of her cooking.

"A far cry from my efforts with a frying pan," he added with a grin.

"Ah, go on with you, sir!" She smiled and dimpled! The warmth hadn't left her face when she turned to me. "You'll want coffee in the library, Miss Joanna? I made a cake this morning; I'll away and cut some for the tray."

Mike Fanning stretched long legs toward the library fireplace. Like Colum, he was dressed for fishing and had courteously seconded Colum's invitation to me to join them if the weather let up enough to take the boat out. Indeed, the rain was easing and, far to the west, out at sea, there was a tiny but widening patch of watery blue sky.

Indoors, however, the chill was damp and penetrating.

I was touching a match to the neatly laid fire when Colum unfolded himself from the chair opposite mine. Without a word, he crossed the room and closed the door with care.

The new flames licked and leaped around the logs. I lit a cigarette and settled back.

Mike stirred his coffee. The spoon clinked loudly in the quiet room. Then he sat forward on the black leather chair that had belonged to my grandfather. It creaked faintly under his weight.

"Well, Colum said you were concerned about things here, Joanna?" he prompted me interrogatively.

I hesitated before replying to this very new ally, Colum's friend. The cavalry, Colum had joked when he introduced Mike earlier.

But now, how much to tell and what to tell? How to put it all, facts, misgivings, vague suspicions? What to say to this blond giant with the assured air, the quiet, measured speech, and the lawyerlike composure? He was remarkably good-looking, with straight, heavy fair hair and blue eyes that seemed to look right into one. Younger than Colum, I surmised. Only fractionally shorter but somehow more compact. Heavier set, probably works out or lifts weights, I reflected. A more self-contained man, too; every movement controlled, every word thought out. I wouldn't like to be on the other side of an argument with him, I thought suddenly. Mike Fanning struck me as a forceful man. . . .

But he is on my side. . . .

Unexpectedly, Colum came to my rescue. "I told Mike as much as I could already," he said.

. I grabbed at the chance Colum, perhaps unwittingly, afforded me. "And what do you make of it, Mike?"

He frowned. There was a pause. "Well, as a preliminary guess only, I'd rule out embezzlement. I won't go into details but in this instance it should be too easy to trace and prove. The antiques notion? I grant you there are plenty of valuable pieces around the part of the house I've seen so far, but . . ." He stopped. He shrugged. "Unlikely, I'd say. Also easy to trace and prove."

"You know a lot about antiques?" I put in.

"Enough," was the answer. "In my business, you pick up a fair deal about a lot of things."

"What exactly is your business, Mike?"

"Colum didn't say?"

"No. Not really."

"Oh." Mike paused thoughtfully for a moment. "Well, I do investigations into all sorts of things, depending on what I'm called on to do, running the gamut from theft to arson. Mostly related to insurance in a way. Of course, it's not the glamorous life you see on television"—he shrugged, tiredly, I thought—"mostly paperwork and grubbing in records, receipts, filling forms, checking accounts, that sort of thing."

I nodded.

He went on, more energetically. "About the antiques angle"—he was checking each item off on strong, broad-tipped fingers—"if you're really concerned about that one?"

"I am, I suppose." Why did he make me feel so doubtful?

"There's the difficulty of secrecy, difficulty of transport, a very specific and limited market, the presence of the servants, assuming for the moment that they are not involved . . ."

I opened my mouth to object, remembered Peggy's odd words only this morning, swallowed hard, and said nothing.

". . . and the fact," Mike continued after the slightest pause, though the blue eyes didn't move from my face, "that Moone's letter offered you the choice of anything you wanted to keep. What makes you think that's not a genuine offer? You think he's trying to cheat you? Out of what?"

Colum shot a sharp look at Mike but said nothing. I was puzzled by the odd turn the conversation seemed to be taking, but I said nothing either. Mike would make himself clear sooner or later, I supposed.

"Might be a blind," Mike mused. "A double take. Drawing attention specifically to the antiques to get your mind away from the house. Either way, it seems every train of thought, especially your concern about your grandmother's accident, brings us back inevitably to the house itself, wouldn't you say, Joanna?" Again, his tone, with its undertone of cross-examination, made me uneasy.

"What do *you* think, Mike?" I challenged.

He uncrossed his legs and crossed them again. "I can't really see that there is a problem at all! A case of overenthusiasm, perhaps. Moone knowing that it's a good offer for the house. After the accident, he assumes you don't want to keep it. Do you want to keep it?"

"Yes."

"I understand you haven't been back here for years. Not even for brief visits? A few days at a time?"

"No. Look, I don't see what that has to do with anything."

"Probably nothing," Mike said, and smiled charmingly. "Sorry, Joanna. I guess I'm getting off the point. It's just the investigator in me. Going after every niggling little thing. Second nature. You—er—came back because of your grandmother's accident, then?"

"If my grandmother's death *was* an accident," I said slowly. Once again, the spider web of puzzlement was choking me. The easy relaxation of lunch had long since slipped away.

Colum and Mike exchanged glances, but didn't speak. Why had Colum thought his friend would be helpful? Mike wasn't helping me at all.

Colum got up, moved to the window, and stood gazing out into the garden. Unhappily, I sensed a withdrawal on his part, a sort of handing on of me and my concerns to Mike, his friend who "knew his way around."

Mike spoke unhurriedly. "All a bit circumstantial, isn't it?" His tone was soothing, implying that I was imagining things, seeing things that weren't there.

Was I? I hesitated, but resolved to go on.

"Something else bothering you?" Mike asked. The implication that things were settled and could now be shelved, that we could all turn our attention to something else, irritated me. But I would not be put off.

"Take your time," Mike said calmly. He waited. I had the feeling he was used to people who wanted to say something but didn't quite know how to put that something into words. His slightly skeptical composure didn't help me. In fact, I was beginning to feel resentful of his very calm.

"People in the village," I began. "I'm not paranoid. It's just that they all seem to behave strangely."

"Strangely?" Mike's blue eyes bored into me.

I flushed under that penetrating gaze. "Perhaps it's only imagination, but they've changed. They used to be so friendly, ready to chatter at the slightest chance. Not now. None of them. Not the bank people, not the Murphys at the newsagent's, not even Sergeant Burke."

"You've been to see Sergeant Burke?" Mike inquired. The blue gaze shifted to the fire. "About your grandmother's accident?"

"About my grandmother's death, yes. I asked him to get me the post-mortem report. He wasn't very cooperative, kept telling me to talk to young Mr. Moone. They've all changed, all of them."

"I told you they'd become wary of strangers," Colum remarked in a reasoning tone.

"But I'm not a stranger. They all know me. And don't tell me it's my English accent."

"Oh, but you are a stranger, you know," Colum said lightly. He sat down on the window seat, the afternoon light behind him. Outside, the light was watery, shifting restlessly over the bleak headland and the wind-wrenched rosebushes. Colum's face was partly in shadow. "You've been absent from Kilcollery for years. You said it yourself. Besides, you're forgetting an important factor. Apart from the people of Kilcollery being an inbred, close-mouthed lot, there's a long tradition in this country of sticking together. As beliefs go, it's ingrained, right or wrong, and it's strongest in the smallest, tightest communities where everyone knows everyone else. You give nothing away." He coughed.

Mike Fanning interrupted.

"Colum means only that they don't want to be the one to inform on anyone. Fred Moone, for instance. If he's up to something, they'll not tell you. If you were up to something, they would talk about it among themselves, but not to anyone in authority, so to speak."

I, up to something? What on earth?

"You're up against that famed Irish streak of bein' agin' the government, Joanna," Colum put in easily. "It goes hand in hand with their fear of bein' tagged as an informer. It's not confined to political matters. Why, there was even an entire country parish, not too long ago, that was placed under church interdict by the bishop because every living soul knew who committed a murder, but not a one would tell. Not under oath in court, not with all that the state could do to promise or threaten."

"True," Mike added coolly.

"But what happened?" I asked.

Colum shrugged. "Nothin'."

"But surely people can't be allowed to—" I began, and stopped quickly.

"That's the English in you again, girl," was Colum's answer. "But I daresay rural England has its moments, too?"

I didn't reply. The implications were startling. But were the easy words simply that? Or a warning? Feeling the need for some distracting action, however slight, I reached for the poker and stirred the sagging logs into new life. A shower of sparks leaped and died. The logs settled with a hiss of escaping gas. Flames sputtered around and in between them. The silence drooped, depressingly, bewilderingly. We seemed to have come to a full stop.

As though reading my thoughts, Mike said smoothly, "I wish we could be of more help, Joanna. Is it possible Mainstay is hiding something?"

"Hiding something!" I started. It was just what I'd thought and dismissed when I looked up at the house from the rocks.

"Something wrong, Joanna?" Mike asked.

"No, no, of course not," I said quickly. I couldn't very well say his manner made me jumpy, uneasy, could I? And that he seemed sometimes to be reading my mind, somewhat uncomfortably?

Colum stood up and stretched. "No priests' holes, or secret caches? Where something valuable might be put?"

"Was that what you were doing when you said you were looking at the sideboard?"

"Sorry, Joanna," Colum said in a conciliatory tone. The silence settled for a strained moment.

"It's clearing well," I remarked. "Let's go fishing."

"Suppose," Mike Fanning said slowly, "just suppose, Joanna, that something is hidden in the house, something pretty valuable, where might it be?"

"I don't know what you mean. I can't imagine," I said crossly. "I've had enough of all this. Let's go out and get some air."

"It's possible somebody else could imagine. And did," Mike said significantly. All at once Colum's remarks about informers assumed a new and horrid relevance.

"You mean my grandmother?" I saw that he did.

Colum crossed the room hastily to me. "Now, don't get steamed up!" he said bracingly. "Mike, don't you think that's a bit much?"

But I was looking at Mike. His face was composed, neutral, a mask. From nowhere, the horror of my dream swept in on me once again. I met Mike Fanning's blue eyes, and I knew that, like me, he was sure that something was badly wrong.

I drew in my breath and I knew I was afraid.

"I know every inch of Mainstay," I said stubbornly.

"You could be overlooking something," Mike insisted politely. Oh, he was courteous, but the steel was there under the smooth manner. "What's that old adage about familiarity breeding contempt?" he asked. "Of course, you're not overfamiliar with things here anymore, are you?"

Colum slumped onto the side of my chair. His arm rested lightly on my shoulders. "You do want to clear this thing up, don't you, Joanna?"

I sighed.

"So we should take a look around," Mike said lightly. "A quick survey." He was on his feet and moving toward the door.

"But what would we be looking for?" I asked, without getting up.

"Anyone would think you didn't want to show off this lovely old place," Colum said with a light laugh. "I've been dying to see it all anyway. Please, Joanna!"

I rose to my feet. I was surprised at how tired I felt but I said resolutely, "Okay. Where do we start?"

As far as I could see, neither the ground floor nor the bedrooms yielded the slightest clue, though Colum and Mike both searched and probed, tapped and listened. Even in Peggy's neatly stacked linen closet.

What on earth were we looking for?

Reluctantly I opened the door of Grandmother's room. Everything was as I remembered it. The velvet curtains, the heavy mahogany furniture, the Victorian bedspread, befringed and bobbled, the handmade lace doilies, the smoky blue cosmetic jars, the mingled fragrances of sandalwood, verbena, and lavender. On the polished dressing table still stood the delicate china figurines I had admired as a child; hands behind my back, at a safe distance; look, don't touch. . . . Colum and Mike were methodically, calmly opening and closing drawers, wardrobes, scrutinizing the very walls. . . . The scent of lavender was filling my nostrils, flooding me with memories. . . .

Then I was backing away, retreating to the landing where I threw open the casement to the damp skies outside

and breathed deeply of the cool salt air. Colum and Mike
joined me moments later. Neither made any comment on
my precipitate withdrawal from Grandmother's room. Perhaps they hadn't noticed. Both seemed thoughtful, preoccupied.

"No Goyas or Turners or Henry Moores," I said.

We descended the stairs to the main hall.

I continued. "The family jewels, such as they are, are in
the bank, and accounted for. But they won't save Mainstay. Fred says there isn't enough to keep the place. And
our search has come up empty, too. We've not been very
successful, have we?"

Mike was silent. Colum just grunted.

"It was a rhetorical question," I added and headed automatically for the library again. But Mike was still examining the wainscoting below the staircase. Colum and I
stopped to wait for him.

"There's nothing under there," I said, slightly irritated.

Mike didn't stop tapping. Without looking up from his
task, he remarked, "You were, I understand, in Scotland
when your grandmother actually died?"

"Yes, I was."

"You didn't return for the inquest here?" The tone was
still neutral but the question was pointed.

"I didn't know about her death until I got back to school
last Sunday," I said, trying not to sound defensive. "We,
that is, a colleague and I, were in the Highlands."

"Somewhere in particular or wandering about all over?"

The cool voice was beginning to annoy me, with its delicate probing, its deliberate pushing. But he was Colum's
friend.

I said only, "We did both. We spent part of the time at a
cottage my friend owns up there. She hurt her ankle,
twisted it during one of our walking tours, so we ended up
staying put for most of the time. Why do you ask?"

"No radio or television?"

"Too many mountains and trouble with her aerial. Reception was dreadful. Besides, we went up to get away for a
while. What with Easter so late this year, the winter term
was very long and we were both exhausted."

"But you must have had to get to the nearest shop, for
perishables, if nothing else."

"Not really. Elspeth—that's my colleague, she teaches French—has an arrangement with a nearby farmer. Works very well. Basic necessities only, of course. Whenever she's there, he collects a standard list of things for her twice a week when he's getting his own supplies or delivering things to market, I suppose. In return for extra grazing for his sheep, I think."

"Sounds ideal," Colum commented easily.

"It was," I answered. Not unlike life at Mainstay, I thought, and was immediately lowered by the nagging knowledge that Mainstay would not be mine much longer. Of their own accord my fingers strayed to the polished oak balustrade with its brass rail. How could I have thought never to return? Deep inside me, the looming threat of losing this, my real home, hurt more and more.

Colum's warm hand arrested the movement of my fingers. "There's always the chance you'll be able to keep the place."

I shook my head. Fred had been so definite.

But he'd lied about Heritage Trust, if Katrina was to be believed. Could he be lying again in order to get me to sign? My heart jumped, but only for a moment. I didn't really think Fred was lying about the money. He knew, as I did, that sooner or later, whether in the probate court or privately, I would learn the state of Grandmother's affairs. There could be no point in lying now. . . .

"I always assumed . . ." I broke off sadly. If there was nothing I could do about it, Mainstay would have to go. But not to the Moones, my heart cried rebelliously. Not to the Moones.

Mike straightened up. "You always assumed there was money. A lot of it." His tone was only faintly interrogative, but one fair eyebrow rose.

I turned away quickly to hide the flush that burned up over my cheeks at the subtle implication I thought I heard in his voice. This afternoon wasn't turning out right at all.

Colum eyed both of us keenly but said nothing. I wished he would say something, anything.

But it was Mike who went on, more kindly now. "I wouldn't jump to conclusions about the estate without expert advice. What you have so far amounts to hearsay, you know."

I whirled, sudden hope rising irrepressibly. He *was* on my side after all. It was just the investigator in him, as he'd said. His rare smile transformed his face for a shining moment and I smiled back, my resentment of his cool manner evaporating.

"Now, about the rest of the house?" he queried.

"But there's nothing to see," I protested. "Just the kitchen, pantry, various storerooms, the servants' rooms . . . Don't tell me, I know. You want to see them all."

"Might as well be thorough," Colum said lightly.

The green baize door at the rear of the hall opened even as I reached it. I narrowly missed colliding with Peggy. She came bustling through in a great hurry. She pulled up short when she saw me.

"Oh, Miss Joanna, I was just comin' to ask if I might have a word with you. It's the boy!" She puffed in great agitation. "Young Danny, miss. He's quite feverish, in my opinion. Like to come down with pneumonia if somethin' isn't done! His poor mam died of it, the Lord have mercy on her." Peggy plunged on determinedly. "I can't have it on me conscience that I let him out of here in that condition, not for the few pence he keeps sayin' that blackguard, the Big Fella, wants off him. 'I have to go,' the child keeps sayin', over and over. 'I have to give him me fish money or he'll throw me out of the camp forever.' The boy is scared, miss. Seems Sheridan beat up an old woman not long ago over some money or some such and threw her out. She never dared come back, at all. So the poor child has reason to be scared. 'He'll beat me,' he says. Enough to tear the heart out of you to listen to him. Oh, if I get me hands on that stepfather of his, good-for-nothin' drunk that he is!"

Peggy's face contracted in anger and righteous indignation. "If the misthress was here she wouldn't allow the boy out in that condition. God love her, she was very good to that child, bringin' him up here for a warm at the fire. Many's the time I heard them in the library, laughin' and chattin' like old friends." Unexpectedly, her voice wavered and tailed off. She sniffed, wiped away a tear surreptitiously with the corner of her stiffly starched apron, and fixed me with a defiant gaze. "We should get the doctor."

I agreed hastily. This was not the time to assure her that I, too, liked the boy. Let her think she had persuaded me.

"I'll go down for the doctor straightaway," Colum offered.

Then everything happened at once. Joe came lumbering through the hall, waving his hands and trying to say something that was quite lost in his agitation. Behind him, from the kitchen, came a racking, wrenching, spluttering noise.

"Merciful heavens! The child's vomiting!" Peggy rushed back to the kitchen. Joe retreated unhappily after her. It struck me that, in his shy, inarticulate way, Joe liked the boy, cared about him.

I jumped as the great brass knocker crashed suddenly against the front door. Mike, who was nearest, opened it. And there, on the doorstep, shaking out his umbrella, stood the doctor himself! The old man stepped over the threshold, doffed his hat, blinked three or four times in the brightly lit hall after the leaden afternoon light, and pushed back his straggling hair.

"Goodness me! A reception committee. I didn't expect . . ."

"Perfect timing, Doc!" Colum remarked to the surprised old man. "Your patient's in the kitchen. This way!"

CHAPTER 11

The doctor lowered himself awkwardly into a fireside chair and accepted a glass of whiskey.

"Thanks, Joanna. No, girl, no water. We don't want to drown a decent drink. I'll say that for your grandmother. A true connoisseur of the palate."

"What's the verdict on Danny, Doctor?" I asked.

"Oh, a chill. Generally undernourished. He'll survive. Gorged himself a bit too fast on Peggy's rich cake, too. Tinker children are hardier than they look. I think they work at that bedraggled, pathetic air in order to bamboozle the rest of us." The doctor's laconic tone became sarcastic. "Always pleadin' that they're misunderstood, that everyone's prejudiced against them. As if they weren't a pack of thievin' rabble for the most part!" Apparently unconscious that his very words attested to the justice of the tinkers' complaint, Dr. O'Brien shifted to a more comfortable position in front of the fire and sipped appreciatively at the golden liquid while the firelight danced in the faceted glass.

"Am I drinkin' alone? Oh dear me. But you were all in the hall when I arrived. Goin' out somewhere?" He raised his glass as if to indicate his willingness to polish off his drink quickly if we were in a hurry to go out.

"No, no. We weren't going out," I replied. "Actually, we were—sort of—looking for something."

"Oh?"

Colum cut in smoothly. "Not looking *for*, Joanna," he corrected me, ignoring my surprise. "Looking *at* this beautiful old place, Doc. Just wandering around, takin' in the beauty of it."

I started to protest, thought better of it, and subsided. It didn't really matter, did it? I said, "I suppose it can wait."

"Of course it can," Colum said heartily. Too heartily.

The doctor glanced from me to Colum and back again.

"Oh, well, now, if there's a grand tour in progress, don't let me stop it. Been a while since I took in the beauty of this place myself." Mischievously, the doctor nodded his acknowledgment of the phrase, drained his glass at a gulp, and eased himself forward on his chair. "Especially with such a pretty guide." He crooked his arm toward me. "I recall the view from the top of the house is spectacular."

"We've already done the top, Doc," I said.

"Oh dear. Then perhaps a word or two about the architecture of the hall, or this fireplace, the dining-room chairs. Your grandmother was always so eloquent about the chairs."

"Another time, Joanna," Colum pleaded. "We ought to be thinkin' about that fishing boat. It's clearing nicely."

"But I thought Mike—" I felt, rather than saw, Colum's face register a silent appeal. Then Mike stood up, stretched lazily, and drawled, "If the lady wants to show us her house, Colum, me boy, the least we can do is cooperate. On your feet, fellow. After you." He ushered me elaborately into the hall and headed toward the dining room.

"We've been that way," I said, and led the way to the green baize door.

"But there's nothing to see in there." It was the doctor who hung back now.

"Agreed," I said, and continued on my way. The three men followed. Through the gleaming kitchen, now deserted. Peggy and Danny must be upstairs somewhere. Joe was digging in the vegetable patch outside the kitchen window, turning each sod slowly, carefully. His face was blank.

With almost equally blank faces, Colum and Mike opened and closed doors, ushering the doctor before them as we proceeded from pantry to larder, from the starched primness of Peggy's room to the curiously impersonal neatness of Joe's. Every few minutes one of them would utter some fatuous, bland politeness about the size of the house, or the days when big houses had large staffs. I was more puzzled and embarrassed with every step.

Back in the kitchen, I stopped at the sink. "After that little lot," I said in pique, "I could do with a drink."

Briskly, I searched the cupboards and found a large jug. "And unlike you, Doc, I like some water in mine."

"Let me," Mike said courteously and took the jug from me.

Then I remembered the one part of the house they hadn't seen.

"The cellar!" I exclaimed. "You haven't seen it yet."

Swiftly and in concert, all three demurred. "No more, please." Colum pretended to massage aching legs. "Another time," Mike said lightly.

"I must agree," urged Dr. O'Brien. "There's nothing to see down there, I'd be willing to wager. Just a lot of vegetables, pots of Peggy's jam, sacks of potatoes, the usual stuff that accumulates in every house. Plus a couple or so of well-stocked wine racks from your grandfather's time, Joanna. Apart from the wine racks, the only difference from one house to the next is the size of the cobwebs!" All three men laughed. The doctor linked arms with me and moved in the direction of the hall, gently but firmly pulling me with him. "You look tired, girl. Let's go and relax in the library. You mentioned a drink?"

But I pulled my arm out of his and crossed the kitchen to a cupboard near the side door.

"Five pounds that none of you can find a single cobweb down there," I cried willfully. "And another five that you'll find nothing more interesting than jams and pickles and wine. But you'll have to go down to find out!" I plunged in among brooms and pans and yanked the cellar key from its accustomed hook.

Colum only barely suppressed a whistle when I pushed the key into an unobtrusive keyhole at the back of the cupboard. Smoothly, noiselessly, the rear panel swung back into the cool dimness.

Mike and Colum stepped past me down the steep curving wooden stairs. Long and narrow, stretching forward under the house, the cellar had literally been dug out of the solid rock of the cliff and smelled faintly, but not unpleasantly, of salt.

The warm draft from the kitchen swirled down, setting the overhead lights swaying and the shadows darting and dancing along the uneven rock wall.

"Vegetables, jams, sacks of potatoes," Colum enumerated cheerfully, calling back toward the stairway. "Just as you said, Doc. You forgot to mention jellied fruits, but no matter. And, ah yes, several very well-stocked wine racks back here."

"About that drink?" Dr. O'Brien remarked hopefully.

"Not a spider in sight," Mike said, emerging from behind the wine racks. "We owe you some money, Joanna," he added with a rueful smile.

"Oh, forget it," I said, slightly ashamed of the impulse that had made me make such a silly bet.

Colum took the stairs two at a time. Mike followed more soberly.

"Find anything else, besides the usual clutter?" the doctor inquired.

"Some very nice wines," Colum rejoined good-humoredly, "and plenty of evidence of Peggy's skill. There's enough pickled and preserved food down there to provision a good-sized shop."

"A dying art," was the doctor's crusty comment, but he was smiling as we returned to the library.

"There ought to be stronger bulbs on those stairs," I observed. "Must see to it before Peggy has a fall."

"Och, she'd know her way around blindfolded." The doctor subsided gratefully into his chair. "These old legs of mine don't care for too many stairs. . . . Only a tiny drop there now. Whoa! I've already had one, and the county matrons are worse than any breathalyzer contraption. I still have a couple of calls to make."

"And we thought you were gasping for another," Colum teased him.

The doctor shrugged. He watched in mock disgust as I added water to my own glass.

"Dilute a fine brew with that stuff. Have you any idea of the things they're adding to the water supply, girl?" he muttered, but almost immediately he brightened again. "Nearly forgot why I called. It's the annual county medical society dinner. They've sent me my usual two tickets. Mary and I always went. . . . But that was then. Now would you honor an old man with your company, girl? I'm sorry it's such short notice, but it had completely slipped my mind until this morning."

"Short notice, Doc?" I temporized.

"Tomorrow night. Now don't tell me you haven't a thing to wear. You could do with an evening out. I could get tickets for you two fellows, too, if you like."

"Tomorrow night!" The dinner, I knew, was in Cork. At least two and a half hours' drive there, not to mention back again in the dead of night. But how could I refuse without hurting the old man's feelings?

A thin hand pushed back a stray white lock. "You've got something else on, have you, girl? Don't worry, if that's the case."

Colum's breezy tones cut in. "Actually, Doc, she has," he lied, quite unabashed. "Dinner with me, and a spot of sightseeing along the coast road. You know, sea air and all that, after London."

There was a decidedly difficult pause. Then the doctor nodded. "Well, you'll enjoy that. Been to Carnmore yet? Food's good. Colum knows the place, don't you? Then I must be getting along. Duty calls. See that she has a good time tomorrow evening, boy, or I'll have a bone to pick with you."

Mike looked up sharply but Colum merely grinned good-humoredly.

In the hall the doctor waved away my conventional expression of regret. "It's a long ould drive. Probably better if I don't go anyway. I just thought to get you out and away from this damned house. You look as though a change of scene wouldn't come amiss. Promise me you'll really relax a bit, get those black smudges out from under those pretty eyes, and we'll say no more about the dinner in Cork. Promise?"

It was blackmail but the old blue eyes twinkled suddenly and, somewhat awkwardly, I said that he had my promise.

"Hope I didn't say the wrong thing, Joanna," Colum said when I returned to the library. "You just looked kind of trapped. . . . Thinkin' of myself as much as you, I must admit," he went on quickly. "Gather ye roses while ye may, or some such. One of these days you'll be headin' back to your eager pupils, I suppose." It was an observation, not a question.

From nowhere, a dull weight of depression crushed me. "I suppose so," I assented almost inaudibly.

Abruptly, Mike stood up, clapped his hands vigorously and stamped his feet. "Let's go fishing, get some air, a breath of sea wind in our nostrils. Do us all good," he said unusually energetically.

Colum's face brightened. "Coming, Joanna?"

"Yes. Oh! What about Fred? It's only half-past three. I ought to give him a little longer, even if his record on keeping appointments is rather lamentable lately. Just in case," I said.

"Leave a message," Colum suggested.

"I've already tried that," I pointed out.

"It'll all keep a while longer," Colum said reasonably, "and you'll be in better shape to deal with business after a good blow out in the boat."

"If the rain will hold off." Mike was looking out the window at the gray afternoon.

"We have two sou'westers in the boat. We'll scrounge up one for Joanna from one of the fishermen."

Mike shrugged his assent.

"Tell you what." Colum turned to me decisively. "Mike and I'll go ahead and haul the boat out. When we've got the tackle organized, we'll come back up for you, Joanna. And if Moone hasn't put in an appearance by then . . . okay? Twenty minutes too soon?"

We compromised on half an hour.

Around me, the old house settled itself peacefully, silently, whispering faintly now and then as the wind caught in the crevices. The fire flickered. A stair creaked. A gust whistled and rumbled in the chimney and outside, the rosebushes bobbed and swayed and were still again.

I sat in the gathering dusk of the leaden afternoon and watched the shadows grow in the corners of the old house. With every moment of reacquaintance, Mainstay became dearer. . . .

A quarter to four. Fred wasn't coming. Damn him!

I jumped to my feet. I needed action. To blazes with Fred. I would go on down to the jetty and borrow a sou'wester for myself. Purposefully I headed to change my clothes and almost screamed with shock.

There, in the gloom of the darkened hall, advancing oh

so slowly upon me, was the hulking, ragged, black-browed man I'd seen with Colum and again at the hotel!

Gigantic arms hung loosely from brawny shoulders as he moved one step forward. Then he stood still, wary and poised.

The same rank odor of dirt and stale tobacco assailed my nostrils. I moved backward into the library. He came on. I retreated in panic until my legs jarred up against a small table. It fell over. I bent down and set it upright very slowly, very carefully, as though the outward calm of my movements would somehow avert the looming horror.

But he stepped forward again. Then he smiled, baring yellowing teeth in a wolfish leer!

A sob rose in my throat. Quickly I suppressed it. Mustn't show fear. How did he get in? Why had no one heard him, or stopped him? *What did he want?* If I screamed, would he attack before anyone had time to answer my call for help?

Mainstay was silent. Not a sound. On edge earlier, I was plain terrified now. No match for the brute strength that faced me. I would have to outwit him. The bellpull by the fireplace would be too slow and would summon only elderly, defenseless Peggy. It would have to be the door. A flickering glance measured the distance to the hall door. Could I maneuver unobtrusively? Could I make it? Was I trapped?

I swallowed back the unwanted memory of my dream, the huge figure looming over me in the darkness as I scrabbled frantically for a fingerhold in the loosening sea grass of the cliff edge.

I didn't believe in premonitions.

Then the man spoke. A harsh, deep voice that snarled something, the guttural sounds growling in his throat. Like a dog. And another step brought him closer!

I stood tensely, at bay. I hadn't understood a word, but the rapacious expression was unmistakable. My breath escaped in little gasps. One of my knees started to shake uncontrollably. I reached down and gripped the table edge tightly. The bloodshot eyes followed the slight movement and came back up to meet mine.

Then he spoke again, this time mumbling more quickly. To my amazement, he removed his filthy cap and, twisting it between grimy, horny hands, he spoke once more, this time slowly and with emphasis.

Miraculously, my brain cleared and I understood. He was speaking, as did so many of the people in Kilcollery, in Irish. The words he had uttered were, providentially, one of the few Gaelic phrases I had learned on those long-ago summers here.

A simple greeting. A centuries-old salutation. God and Mary be with you.

Stupid with relief, I dredged the answer out of the silt of long-buried memory.

"*Dia is Muire agat is Padraig.*" God and Mary and Patrick be with you.

Inwardly sagging with the aftereffects of shock, I tried to look resolute. Slowly and clearly I said, "What do you want?"

Did he understand me? Gaining confidence, and feigning a peremptoriness I was far from feeling, I repeated the question.

Head on one side, he was listening carefully to my voice, clearly not an Irish one. A flash of cunning was quickly replaced by a servile bobbing of the head.

"You do be a sthranger here, miss?" His English was halting and thick. "I am come to have speech wid de other misthress, Miss Moone."

"Miss Moone is no longer here," I said as authoritatively as I could manage, though I couldn't control the wobble in my voice. At least my knee wasn't shaking anymore.

But why had he spoken in Irish? To scare me? Why?

There was a pause as he ground and twisted his cap tightly. But he made no move to go. "She would be in de town, wid Mr. Moone?"

"I expect so."

Still he stood, barring my way out.

"She's not here," I said with emphasis.

He leered knowingly at me. "Dan Sheridan, now, he be here." It wasn't a question.

For a split second, I didn't connect "Dan Sheridan" with the youngster I'd brought home. Then I did.

"Thass right, miss. I do be his father. What d'you want wid him? What are ye doin' to him? I do have a right." The slow, hesitant speech was truculent.

What to say? What did I want with young Danny? To help him, that was all. As my grandmother had. But not with reading lessons. Then how? Confused and puzzled and not knowing how to answer Sheridan's question, I retreated behind the fireside chair I had left only minutes before.

The Big Fellow—he was well named—followed. He stopped only inches from me and spoke again, but the tone was no longer truculent. Instead it was pleading, yet with a nasty undercurrent.

"The boy shouldn't be here, wastin' his time. He didn't bring me no money yet neither. He have to earn his way, miss. He can't be doin' nothin', sittin' around here wid books. What good are they to him? He have to earn his keep, see? Unless you would be wantin' to pay somethin' for his time, like? That'd be all right wid me, an' I'm his father, so what I say goes. Just you slip somethin' into me hand, miss, an' we'll say no more about Dan comin' here. He can come then all right." One bloodshot eye closed in a slow wink.

His meaning was horribly clear. I shuddered, as much in disgust as in rising horror. My flesh crawled as the filthy smell of him reached me again.

Inwardly recoiling, I drew myself up very straight. "I think you should go. At once."

"What about me money? Here, you can't keep him here for nothin'."

"Nobody's keeping Danny here. He needed some food and to dry off his clothes, that's all. Now will you please go?"

"Just a few pence, miss. A rich lady like you can spare a little to help a poor ould fella."

He was coming at me again. Frantically I grabbed my bag, scrabbled in my wallet, and surrendered most of the loose change I had into his filthy palm.

The red-rimmed eyes darted swiftly over the coins. "God bless you, miss." The pious farewell was belied by the greedy face as he leered again, baring those horrible teeth. But he was backing off, going away.

He bypassed the main door, headed for the kitchen. Of course! He must have slipped in that way. Perhaps while Joe was working in the garden.

The Big Fellow's hand was raised to push the green baize door when he halted, turned, looked at me. Oh, God, he was coming back! Then he pulled off his cap again and crushed it between those powerful, frightening hands.

Slowly, and with great difficulty, he spoke once more, this time in a furtive, sibilant whisper. Each word was shockingly, terrifyingly clear.

"You will be the new young misthress, I'm thinkin'." It was as though he was searching for words. Or trying to make up his mind. "*Eist liom,* listen a while. This place do be evil, wicked. Go away, now. Away wid you across the water where you came from. You'll be safe over the water."

Another pause. I held my breath.

Then, into the listening, prickling silence, he growled horrifyingly in a hoarse, guttural croaking, "Where there's been one murther done, there could be another. Get away wid ye while there's still time!"

Dirt-rimmed, bloodshot eyes glared into mine for a long moment.

"You mean my grandmother?" I whispered in horror. My dream! It wasn't my imagination! Had I sensed something, or stumbled into dreadful comprehension in some shadowy, intangible way? My groping hands found the balustrade. I hung on for dear life. "Was my grandmother murdered?" I whispered.

The tinker retreated. He shifted from one foot to the other. Then he tapped his nose with one finger. There was something frighteningly furtive about the soundless gesture. As if he, too, was afraid.

"I daren't say no more," he muttered stealthily, glancing about as though he might be overheard, "but you done the Big Fella a good turn—" He patted the torn pocket where the coins I'd given him jingled faintly. "Get on away, miss. Now." A conspiratorial nod and the door sighed into its cushioned frame behind him.

I was alone in the polished hall.

I didn't hear Peggy come down the carpeted stairs. I started and cried out when she spoke.

"Merciful heavens, Miss Joanna! 'Tis all right. I didn't mean to give you such a turn."

"The tinker! The Big Fellow! Peggy, he was here! He told me to go away. He warned me . . ."

Peggy interrupted me in vexation. "Sheridan? I hope you didn't let him over the threshold. The thievin', drunken, dirty—"

"I didn't let him in. I found him here, in the hall. He told me—"

But Peggy wasn't listening. "That Joe!" she exclaimed in annoyance. "Must have left the side door open again. I'll give him the back of me tongue." She turned to leave, but I held her back.

"Peggy!"

She seemed to see me for the first time. "Why, Miss Joanna! You're shakin' like a leaf, an' your face is all white. Like you'd seen a ghost." She laughed, but there was little humor in it. "Mind you, Miss Joanna, that fella's enough to give anyone a fright, with the size of him. But you've no call to be upset now. And he's not half as fierce as he looks. You just come along back to the fire and Peggy'll get you a nice hot cup of tea. Settle your nerves in no time."

Talking all the way, she half led, half pushed me to a chair by the library fire and bustled away to the kitchen. Moments later, sharply watchful, she stood over me while I gulped down a scalding hot cup of tea I didn't want at all.

Once more, I tried to tell her what the tinker had said, but I gave up when she obstinately persisted in her notion that the whole terrifying incident was best forgotten.

"Sheridan do have bees in his bonnet, but he wouldn't harm you," she agitatedly assured me. "Him and his like do just be out for what they can beg or steal. Never an honest day's work, ho no, not for the likes of them. You didn't give him money?"

"I did, but that was before—"

"You shouldn't give them nothin'. 'Tis only encouragin' laziness."

"It was only some loose change, Peggy, and anyway, it was after that that he warned me to go. Peggy, he spoke of murder!"

She paled and reached out to grip the arm of the nearest chair, almost as I had done earlier.

"Did he mean my grandmother, Peggy? Did he?"

She swallowed and her eyes widened in fear. "No!"

"But you know something, Peggy! Tell me!"

She took a deep breath.

I waited.

It seemed to me that all around us Mainstay waited, too.

Then Peggy's breath came in a little rush. "I don't know what you mean, Miss Joanna! Leave me be."

"But Peggy . . . !"

"Imaginin' things, you are. Believin' a tinker? Nonsense, wicked, lyin' nonsense to get money out of you. You just drink your tea an' put that fella out of your mind." She chattered on, nervously at first, then more determinedly. I pressed her but she regained a mulish composure and I could get nothing out of her. Reluctantly I decided to wait. At least she was talking to me now. Later, perhaps, she might be persuaded . . .

She reached down and took the empty cup from me. "Mind you, Miss Joanna," she said from the door, "you'd want to be careful who you let into the house."

"I told you, Peggy, I didn't let him in. He was already in the hall."

"Not him!" she snorted. "I mean the fellow with Mr. Colum!"

"Mike! What has he to do with anything?"

"Pokin' about." Her voice was sharp, resentful. "Who does he think he is? You'd do well not to get involved with him."

"You didn't mind Colum's interest in the house."

"He only wants to take pictures of the old furniture and the plasterwork and such. There's no harm in that."

"What are you getting at, Peggy? What do you think Mike wants?"

"I'll say no more," was the exasperating answer. "A word to the wise." She compressed her lips. "I'll away now. I could do with a cup of tea meself. That child has me worn out with his chatter."

Danny! I'd forgotten about Danny.

"He's still here?"

Her face softened. "Wrapped up in a blanket, in front of the heater in my room. Tellin' Joe a story he was, if you don't mind." Peggy's tone was gruff. Anyone else might have thought she was annoyed. I knew better.

"Waste of electricity," she grumbled, "but there's not

room for him in front of the kitchen fire, what with all his clothes hung on the wooden clothes dryer. Such holes! Glory be! And the boy is all arms and legs, comin' out through the seams everywhere. There do be no way I can mend some of them things, and his poor mam always so neat in herself and careful of the boy, the Lord have mercy on her."

"How did she ever take up with Sheridan, then?"

"Oh, he was a fine, handsome, well-set-up fella when he took the trouble. But since she went, he hasn't bothered. And what with the drink, you see . . ."

I saw. All too vividly. Poor Danny!

Quickly I fished in my wallet and pressed some notes into Peggy's hands.

"Do the best you can, Peggy. And get him some clothes in the village when you have time. Warm things. Tell me if you need more money. I must go and change. Colum and Mike should be back for me any minute. It's after four already." I raced up the stairs. "And if Fred Moone calls, tell him I've gone fishing!"

Peggy's voice, warmly and unexpectedly approving, floated up after me. "Your poor grandmother would be pleased. The Lord bless you both. I'll take the boy down to the draper's just as soon as he has a dry stitch to wear!"

I pulled on my thickest, warmest Shetland wool sweater over my shirt and jeans, and thrust my feet into two pairs of socks and rubber-soled canvas shoes. It would be cold out on the water.

My watch said four twenty-two! Where were they? Probably on their way back up from the boat slip. Unless they'd run into some sort of snag. I might as well go on down. Perhaps we would meet on the way.

I shrugged into my old serge jacket. It had stood up to much over the years and wouldn't mind a touch of sea-spray.

On my way through the hall I shivered but resolutely pushed away the remembered shock of Sheridan's appearance. But his final words echoed in my head.

Murder, he'd said.

I hurried down the path. Suddenly I wanted above all else to see Colum's welcoming smile, to be with him, safely with him. He would listen when I told of the Big Fellow's frightening words. Then, cheered and strengthened, perhaps I would know what to do. . . .

Overhead, the thick clouds swirled and billowed, closing on the lone patch of blue, piling up in gray and white masses, moving swiftly inland before an unseen wind.

Down here, the air was still and heavy with moisture. Mainstay's shrubs drooped under the weight of glistening droplets and the gate dripped water as I swung it open.

Still no sign of Colum and Mike.

Ever drawn by the sea, I walked across the graveled sweep and stood drinking in the wild beauty before me. The silver and black expanse of the gently heaving Atlantic, the rugged cliffs, the dark headlands rimmed with grass, that reached out intrepid, narrow fingers of deep brown slanting rock. And closer, the deadly little cove where green water foamed through the narrow entrance, rising and falling along the ledges even in a calm sea. The quietly rocking surface gave no hint to the unwary of the powerful, sucking undertow that lurked, a monster, below the innocent waves. The tide was coming in, the surge washing the rocks lazily, rhythmically. . . .

Then, on the deserted cliff behind me, I heard a footfall!

It was only the faintest whisper on the soft, cushioning grass, almost lost in the soughing of the waves. Almost, but not quite. No friend would come up so quietly. . . .

I whirled, heart thumping, hands raised, clenching themselves into fists even as the newcomer met my unnerved gaze. Once more, I was looking into the flat, black, reptilian eyes of James Gardiner!

CHAPTER 12

The shiny pink face was bland, void of expression. It was those eyes that frightened me.

"All alone, Miss Wentworth? Out here on the cliff, hmm?" His appearance was as sleek as before, but his voice held a new sharpness. "I was just coming to call on you."

"You were?" I was acutely conscious that only a few feet away waited the edge . . . and the deadly drop to the rocks. . . .

"Ye-es. I thought I might speak to you again about the house," he asserted, but his attention was not on me. He was looking past me, down into the cove, and the opaque eyes were narrowing in a manner I didn't like.

As though to permit him a better view, I stepped aside. Away from the edge.

But he moved, too, contracting the space between us again. Slowly he wet his lips, the pink tongue sliding, darting, disappearing. "Er—might one ask what you were watching so intently down there?" He smiled, but the smile didn't reach those terrible eyes. "I can't seem to spot anything of interest myself."

A ruse to catch me off guard? Or simply ingratiating conversation? Warily I slid away another step.

Again, though glancing around him with apparent interest in the landscape, he closed the space I'd thought to open.

"Oh, nothing much," I said, making a desperate attempt to sound nonchalant. "Just rocks and sea and gulls and gannets and things. I like birds. Do you?"

I had to get past him, back to the road at least. Even if I had to push past him.

"Come, Miss Wentworth, must we talk about birds?" The snakelike eyes were fixed on me now.

It was time to speak up. And to get going.

"Look, Mr. Gardiner, I don't want to talk about the house and I've already made that quite clear." I nodded an abrupt farewell and made to step past him.

He blocked my way again. This time there was no mistaking the hostility I had felt from the start.

He said, "I would be prepared to—ah—increase my offer."

I said the first thing that came into my head. "I know."

He stiffened.

"I mean, I thought you might, but it doesn't change a thing."

Wisely or not, I was getting under his skin. He was making a visible effort to control himself.

"Let us stop fencing, Miss Wentworth. We both know what the situation is."

"Do we?" After almost three days here, I still seemed no nearer to knowing what was going on, or why the lies and evasions.

In a desperate outward attempt at calm, I shrugged elaborately and suddenly strode past him, quickening my pace as I reached the graveled sweep. But he recovered, came after me and an expensively gloved hand shot out, painfully closing on my arm and jerking me to a twisting stop.

"Katrina Sheehan's not to be trusted, you know," he hissed venomously. "I saw you together this morning. What did she tell you?"

"Nothing. I mean—we simply met over a magazine rack in the shop. Now I must go. I'm expected," I added despairingly. Where were Colum and Mike? They should have been back at least half an hour ago!

"You don't stand in the wind talking about magazines," Gardiner rasped unpleasantly.

"People have been known to," I answered coldly. Fear and anger were combining to make me less cautious. "As a matter of fact, she also kindly condoled with me on the death of my grandmother."

Then an odd thing happened. A shiver ran through him. I felt it, quite clearly.

Sharply, I said, "Afraid of something, Mr. Gardiner? What do you think Katrina Sheehan and I talked about?"

He didn't answer. Instead his gaze dropped to his own

hand, still clenched on my arm. It was almost as if it didn't belong to him. Slowly, he released the pressure, patted my sleeve, and straightened his gloves. There was something final about the gesture, something oddly remote, as though he had already left me.

"Afraid? Nonsense. You're imagining things. Two young women? You talk about anything, and nothing." He steepled his fingers, sank his chin onto his chest. "She's a flighty girl, interested only in her own face. Not at all reliable. She didn't speak—ah—of my interest in your house?"

"No. Why should she? We'd never even met before." Neatly put, I told myself, and quite true. And I was moving now, toward the road.

He came after me. "You're going down into the village? I thought you were heading down the cliff path. I'll walk with you."

I quickened my step. "I'm late as it is."

For a plump man, he moved surprisingly fast. "I won't slow you down at all. A pleasure to see you safely to your destination." Coming from anyone else, the words might have sounded reassuring.

"This is quite a dangerous area, isn't it?" he added conversationally. "Slippery in wet weather, and it's so often wet. You'd do well to stay away from that path altogether. Very slippery. And the sea grass at the edges of these cliffs can be treacherous too, even at the best of times. Don't you agree, Miss Wentworth? Miss Wentworth!"

But I'd broken away. I ran back up the road. I couldn't take any more of his veiled warnings, that unctuous tone. Not another moment of him.

"Just remembered!" I called back breathlessly. "I forgot my cap. I'll need it out in the boat."

Gardiner stood in the middle of the road. He was smiling. The damn man was smiling! "Shall I wait for you, my dear?"

I shouted back fiercely. "No, don't. Don't wait!"

The smile widened. It was not a pleasant smile. Then he turned and went on, vanishing from sight around a bend in the road.

I slammed Mainstay's gate behind me and, heedless of drips, leaned against its wet surface, panting with relief. From my pocket I pulled the shabby navy cap I always kept there, and stared at it while my breathing returned slowly to normal.

Belatedly I hoped it didn't matter that, in my effort to establish convincingly the unimportance of my encounter with Katrina, I had inadvertently revealed that she knew who I was.

She had airily said she could cope with James Gardiner. I wasn't so sure.

Would he have passed the boat slip by now? Perhaps I'd stay put for another moment or two. Just in case.

And surely Colum and Mike had launched the boat by now? Where were they? In a moment I would go on down and find out. When Gardiner was well gone.

Keeping a sharp eye out this time, I slipped across the sweep again and along the cliff to where the limestone ledges we always called steps began their sloping descent. My gaze idled along the rocks, over the patch of white sand, the creeping green water, the shifting, scraping pebbles that rolled noisily with each wave, forward, backward, surging, subsiding. . . . One foot almost went from under me on the third step. A slimy wet ooze spread across the worn stone. Gardiner was right, the path was treacherous.

Come to think of it, that wasn't all he'd said. I tried to recall his words. He had warned me, threatened me. Then he'd told me to stay away from the cliffs. Away from the cove . . . With a sense of rising interest, I realized now something I should have seen earlier. Gardiner had been almost as taken aback when he met me, as I was to see him. Why?

"Staring intently," he had said. His exact words.

I caught my breath. Was that why I was suddenly sure there was more to his warning than mere dislike? Was he really trying to scare me, just because he'd come upon me gazing down into the cove?

Was I paranoid? Ready to start reading tea leaves, or seeing omens in the fall of every leaf?

Nevertheless, slowly, and with infinite caution, I descended the steps, scrambled down the steep slope and across the rock ledges and boulders to the rapidly diminishing patch of white sand.

I didn't spot it until I was almost on top of it.

A boat.

A small, narrow, sharp-keeled rowboat, badly painted in a streaky blackish-brown. Inside and out. Both of the oars and the metal oarlocks, too.

Then I looked again.

No! Not badly painted. Deliberately camouflaged.

By day, out on the gleaming water, it would look no more noteworthy than a currach, the fishermen's black-tarred canvas shells that lay drying in a row near the jetty. Even by night, out on the open sea, it would be a dull patch on a moonlit ocean, invisible on any night lit only by the stars.

Beached like this and pushed in as far as it would go under the rocky overhang, the black-brown streaky paint was enough to blend with the rocks, to conceal it completely.

Unless someone came down into the cove. As I had.

From no more than a few feet away I noticed the tiny dried trails. Water had been dashed on the scuff marks where the boat had been dragged up from the water. The smooth little runnel marks, invisible if you weren't almost standing on top of them as I was, were quite dry. And on such a damp day.

Someone, some little time ago, had gone to extra trouble to ensure that the boat's presence was not advertised.

Gardiner? Somehow I couldn't see him messing about with boats, or streaky paint, or negotiating the tricky currents and undertows of the cove.

But had he known about it, and that it was here now? And tried to scare me off because of it?

Sand clung in lumps to the bottom. The oars were still damp. No sun to dry them, even if they hadn't been tucked away under the shade of the rock. The boat wasn't secured by any rope or chain. The boatman, or woman, must be coming back soon.

Experimentally I laid hold of the gunwale and tugged. Heavy, though empty. Still, it shifted slightly. A strong man would have little difficulty. I let go and the boat settled back a fraction of an inch. The oars slid sideways with a clatter that echoed around the cove. Quickly I looked up, but no one came in answer to the noise. As far as I could tell, I was entirely alone. No one on the rocks, no one on the path or up on the cliff. No one out on the hump of Mullaghbeg headland.

Why would anyone who wanted to walk or climb come in by sea anyway? No, there had to be some other reason.

The sand squelched under my shoes. If someone was going to reclaim the boat it would have to be any moment now before the water rose over the rocks and cut off access to the little strand. Most of these rocks, except for the ridge along the base of the cliff directly below Mainstay, would be six to eight feet below water at high tide, and that ridge sat under a steep, curving overhang that couldn't be climbed and was only a few inches wide at its highest point.

The tide! It was coming in! I must go.

Damn! I'd already delayed too long to get back across the strand without a soaking. Even as I watched it, a long, heaving, curling wave splashed on the shore and rolled lazily in, spreading wetly over the sand. It looked quite normal, except that because of the very narrow entrance and the reef formations there, this cove had a dangerous peculiarity. The tide, held up longer by the reefs, once over them didn't retreat but came on and on, swelling, deepening, swirling fast.

Pools of water were already forming in the depressions my shoes were sinking into as the strand became waterlogged. I stepped back hastily, dismayed and just a little anxious. How could I have forgotten just how fast the tide was here? Or how long it would take to climb across the rock ledges? Even if I moved quickly, could I outrun the tide? There was one way.

My eyes on the familiar, if tricky, route, I returned at a run to the boulders that littered the shore at the base of the massive cliff, and began the return climb. This was no time for leisure. Heedless of knees and elbows, I scrambled up, up toward the ledge that ran almost all the way over to the safety of high ground on Mullaghbeg, muttering in annoyance at my lack of vigilance. Damn the boat, and Gardiner, and whatever was going on! Because of my preoccupation, the easier way back was already cut off.

Ahead of me lay one deep inlet I would have to jump, a fissure that ran some way back into the cliff. Thank God I was wearing shoes that should grip.

My attention now on safe footing on the damp lichen and weed, I stepped and reached, stretched, crawled, or jumped until finally I made it to the flat rock by the fissure where the sea was already swirling and heaving, rising higher even as I looked. . . .

Must catch my breath. Only a moment. I daren't delay. Just long enough to ease the painful stitch in my side.

Out there, where the water was tossing and breaking whitely, my parents had disappeared forever. . . .

The sky was lowering again, the wind getting up, even down here. My shoes were unpleasantly, coldly damp. They must grip! Surely the ledge on the other side had been bigger, wider?

The creeping green water surged and subsided. But the level was higher. I must jump now.

The ledge was so narrow, so far below the rock I was on. And the overhang stuck out so far . . . I would have to take a run at it.

Then something caught my eye.

A cigarette butt. On the rock at my feet. A rock that was six or more feet under water at high tide, twice each day.

A dry cigarette end that was still warm to the touch.

I jumped away from it, stifling a cry. But even as I backed off, mesmerized by the dirty scrap of rice paper and the partly squashed yellow tobacco, I knew I was no longer alone!

No sound, no glimpse, just animal instinct.

And fear.

Warning bells clanged in my brain. I wheeled sharply. The heel of my shoe caught in a crevice. I pitched forward. A needle of agony shot through my twisted ankle. I was falling . . .

Then something hit me. Just over my left ear. Something cold and hard.

Pain exploded through me. I crashed to the rock, hands outstretched in a vain attempt to protect myself from further blows. I think I tried to call out, but my throat only croaked a low moan. And there was no one to hear, except the one who had hit me.

Consciousness was slipping from me. But I mustn't black out. . . . Feverishly I peered upward, trying to clear the cloudy blur in my eyes, to see that looming dark bulk. . . .

Then the fireworks exploded again, roaring in my ears with a deafening rushing noise that kept getting louder. . . . And I slipped away, down, down, into the deep velvety darkness where, at a great distance, tiny lights swayed, danced, flickered, and were snuffed out. . . .

CHAPTER 13

I was swimming frantically. But I wasn't getting away.
Something was holding me back, dragging at tired arms
and legs. I was flagging. Something was heavy, soggy. It
was pulling on me . . . then a wave splashed in my face and
I woke up.

Woke up to see the water all around me. Creeping up the
rock where I sprawled, one arm pinned beneath me. I
couldn't feel my arm. The water was icy cold. I couldn't
feel my arm! I raised myself on the other arm, gingerly,
slowly, and looked around in disbelief. Seconds later, the
circulation began to return to the numbed arm in agoniz-
ing needles. Not broken after all, thank God. But how did I
come to be here?

Then I remembered . . .

And the pain came raging back. Piercing, knifing . . .
Cautiously I touched the side of my head, behind my left
ear, where it hurt the most. Tears started to my eyes and
spilled over. I dashed them away. Something warm and
sticky was running down my neck. My hand came away
red and wet.

Must stop the bleeding. A handkerchief. Dabbing at it
wouldn't do any good. Must press firmly. It hurt to press.

A wave broke over my legs. I scrambled to my feet in
panic, crying out like a kitten as my right ankle collapsed
sideways under me and I fell to my knees.

And the pain rocketed about in my head.

The handkerchief was floating away. I grabbed at it,
missed, grabbed again, and caught it. I wrung it out,
pressed it against the cut on my head and crouched awkwardly, unmoving. For a blazing second the salt stung. Im-
mobility helped. The cool wet cloth was calming. The pain
subsided to a dull roar.

Then I saw it. A few feet away. A rock about the size of a fist.

With blood on it.

My blood.

Oh, God, that looming presence behind me hadn't been another nightmare. Nor a figment of an overburdened imagination.

Someone wanted me dead.

Or unconscious. To drown in the rising water. A moment or two of struggle in the gurgling, suffocating waves. Then, oblivion.

Perhaps he was watching even now. Watching me labor to my feet and collapse again, terror-stricken by the cold green water that heaved and surged all about me.

I must take hold, clear my head. Cold water in my face to rouse me from the paralyzing grip of nightmare. Someone laughed hysterically. Then my laugh died as I came to realize fully my position.

My ankle stabbed again. Was it broken? I tried it cautiously but it gave way each time. Heedless of the pain, conscious only of my danger, I pressed and probed. I didn't think it was broken. How could I make it take my weight?

Perhaps, if I anesthetized it . . .

I crawled to the edge of the rock and lowered the whole foot into the icy depths. A desperate gamble. Only a few seconds and I couldn't feel the pain anymore. Much.

Then I remembered the boat. Pressing the dripping handkerchief to my head, I scanned the cove, but the boat was gone, its rocky hiding place long since underwater. The sucking, slapping water that was creeping closer.

I didn't want to die. I wouldn't die. I would *not.* "Do you hear me?" I whispered despairingly into the wind.

But the uncaring wind simply tossed the waves and swooped and eddied in the fluttering sea foam.

Slowly, agonizingly slowly, I inched and dragged myself back and up against the rock face, all my weight on my good leg. With an enormous effort I half lurched, half hopped toward the fissure. Even though I knew I couldn't jump it now.

Not on that ankle.

The ledge on the far side was under water, too. And I was sliding on the slippery weeds that clung and waved in an inch of water. I backed up against the rock face again, looking around wildly for inspiration. Anything. Please.

Then, out of the corner of my eye I saw a clump of purple anemones and pink sea thrift in a crevice higher up under the curving overhang. A narrow ledge stretched along and away from the flowers. They could only grow where the tide didn't reach! But could I get up there?

Handholds, footholds, cracks, fingerholds. Desperately my eyes leaped about, searching, as I clung like a fly to the underside of the crag. I hadn't even thought how I would hang on till the tide receded. I just knew that those tiny blessed spots of color represented safety, a place where the creeping water would not come.

I had never gone so far into the cleft before, even as a child. The cove was too dangerous for swimming. My father and I had come here only to fish, from the farther rocks by the deep water, at low tide.

My hands were cold. My grip kept slipping. Fingers closed on minute cracks. I inched and clung. The feeling was returning to my ankle. And it was beginning to rain.

Choking back fear, I pressed up against the broken, scarred rock, working my painful way in across the face in a sort of crazy diagonal, hampered by the blinding headache that was now settling in behind my eyes. I blinked away the raindrops and clung and slid and clung again among the long, black-shadowed rocks and angled ledges.

Then I saw something. Something that made my heart race and thump with sudden hope. Something in the cliff that I'd never seen before.

An opening! What I'd taken for a dark shadow was a gash, an elongated mouth, naturally hidden by a protruding, slanting outcrop, and well in under the concealing overhang. A cave, a blessed, wonderful cave.

But it was below me, and only a few simple feet above the inner end of the flat rock. The rock that was now awash. Would the cave be high enough inside?

Recklessly I slid down, landing in a crumpled heap. The rockets in my head exploded again. But the water was cold and shocked me into swift movement regardless of pain. I struggled to my feet and splashed toward the dark hole as the rain thickened and leaped high off the rocks all around me. Dizzy with hope, I scrambled the last few steps with scant regard for bleeding fingers and icy feet.

Then I was inside, blindly pressing forward into the dim interior, stumbling over the jagged rocky floor. My eyes strained to adjust. And I scarcely believed what I saw. . . .

More like a narrow passage than a cave. It went back some yards, and my feet were telling me that the floor sloped upward!

Galvanized, I lurched forward recklessly, hands groping joyfully for support, feet pacing unevenly but faster in wild hope. Then I hit my head on the rock ceiling and fell with a cry. I crawled forward, inch by painful, leaden, despairing inch until I met the wall. There I crouched in the dreadful gloom, cold, wet through, finished. The cave was too small. My safe haven, by a cruel trick, was no more than a trap. And I was exhausted, spent.

No reserves of energy for the second try at climbing the cliff toward the friendly flowers. Even if I got there, I knew now I hadn't the strength to hang on long enough, till the dreadful water retreated to the cold gray sea.

I was going to die. Disheveled, wet, shivering and burning with fever, I laid my tired body on the sandy floor to wait for the end.

Perhaps I should leave a message in the sand, I thought sluggishly. A last message. The last will and testament . . . Sand! But there shouldn't be sand. Not if the cave was under water at high tide. Not if the water I could hear lapping in the darkness was going to cover everything in here. . . .

Feverishly, alight with sudden hope once more, I groped about me. Except for the rock face at my back, my questing fingers found only air. I rose cautiously to my knees, feeling all about me, reaching above my head. Still nothing. I stretched my arms, high as they would go. Still nothing! I lurched once more to my feet, expecting every second to crash against the lowering ceiling. But still there was only air. Then how had I hit my head!

A ledge? A single low ledge? Was the cave big enough after all?

Light! That was what I needed. My jacket pockets yielded only two bars of chocolate. I always got hungry out fishing. But I had put my cigarettes in my shirt pocket, and where my cigarettes went . . . yes! There they were, and mercifully, miraculously, still dry. There were only three matches in the box. I had taken the wrong one, but I didn't care about that now.

I lit one and, shielding it against vagrant drafts, looked around with a fearful excitement.

And knew I was not going to die.

The cave had only seemed to end. In fact, with a sharp twist, it continued at an angle upward into the blackness.

And were those rough steps? Hacked out of the very heart of the cliff?

Then the flame stung my fingers and I dropped the match. It sputtered briefly on the rocky floor, setting shadows dancing, reeling grotesquely. A last flare and the gloom closed about me again, darker and more dazzling than before.

But I had seen what I most needed to see. The high tide mark of seaweed and unmistakably darker rock was behind me. A few precious, life-saving, wonderful inches.

I used the second match to light my blundering way up the rock staircase. Despite the pain that was coming in waves now, I stumbled and limped, up, up, till I fell at the top, collapsing in an exhausted heap against the rock wall of a dimly glimpsed wide chamber. There I huddled, while the roar of the rising sea in the cave below thundered, rolled, reverberated, and the fireworks in my head crashed and exploded before burning eyes.

Sleep. The irresistible urge flooded over and through me. I lay down, folding my hands under my head. Consciousness was too much just now. I would sleep. Just until the tide water went down. Just for a while, a little while . . .

No! No! I mustn't sleep! Somewhere—in another life, an uneventful tranquil life—I had read or been told that head injuries were perilous things. Something about concussion. Or was it fractures?

I mustn't sleep! I might not wake up. Ever.

Needles of finest torture to sit up again, to draw chilled legs up, to rub my ankle. The gloom was rocking all about me. It steadied, dipped briefly, then was still.

Song. Yes, sing a song. That would keep me awake.

I would sing every song I knew. But under my breath, so as not to wake the lurking hammerer in my brain.

How many songs to freedom? How many miles to Babylon? Or was it Bethlehem? Mustn't let my mind wander. That way lay the frightening dark, the sleep without end. Sing!

But quietly. In a whisper.

Until the tide went down . . .

I think it was the silence that woke me.

Woke me from a fitful doze, a sleepy detachedness dominated by high, thin, cracked, half-uttered melodies. I had run quickly out of songs, been through every nursery rhyme, every fragment of poetry, every advertising jingle, got hopelessly lost in muttered childish prayers, muddled my way through symphonies, stumbled through Bach preludes and finger exercises and sonatas learned on our old upright piano . . . jerking painfully to rouse myself whenever I drifted toward the deadly insensibility I feared. I thought of Colum. . . . Had his gray eyes glowed with a special warmth for me? Did his breath catch when he looked at me, as mine did when the deep yearning stirred, budded, flowered in my heart? He was here! Here with me, now! I reached out my arms with a glad cry and the hammerer in my head lashed out and told me I was a fool, seeing things. . . . Hopelessly I nodded, just an infinitesimal movement, and the hammerer subsided into an uneasy sleep. . . .

Until the stillness woke me.

The cave below wasn't thundering.

No rush of stones rolling and receding, no deep echoing. While I sang and mumbled, the tide had paused, eddied, then turned, swayed, drifted, and finally flowed back out to lose itself in the great ocean. I was safe! Free! I was alive!

I would save my last match until I absolutely must strike it. I would wriggle and squirm my way to the top of the rock steps. I would bump my way down; I couldn't trust my wobbling legs.

With a great glad exhalation of relief and confidence, I cast about me for the steps, eyes straining through the dimness. Surely they couldn't be far. Had I gone in the wrong direction?

Then my questing hands found something. A hard, heavy obstacle. Made of wood. Wood? In a cave deep under the cliff below Mainstay? Rough wood. Not sanded, splinters catching at my fingers. A box of some sort. No, boxes. More than one. Piled on top of one another. Three, four piles, maybe more.

I had only one match.

I couldn't find the steps without that tiny light, so I would have to use it. I would look for the stairway first, I promised myself. Then, if the match lasted long enough, I would take a look at the boxes.

The match flared, settled. I shaded it with my hand. Found the steps straightaway in the dancing half-light. I had indeed been going not toward but away from them, toward dark recesses at the rear of the chamber. Then I turned. Looked. And didn't believe what I saw.

Crates. Long, oblong, unmistakable.

And just as the match guttered and flickered out, I saw the symbols stenciled along the rough sides in patchy black paint.

Even I could recognize the Cyrillic alphabet.

As used in the Russian language.

I stumbled out into a golden-orange, high, blue evening. Smoky traces of cloud above, stranded cottonwool pulled into long tinted streaks by stratospheric winds. The gilded sea mirrored the soft, late, falling sunlight.

I don't know how I made it up the path. I don't remember much.

Except that, at Mainstay's open gate, I saw Colum.

Then he saw me.

I faltered. He came with a rush, great headlong strides closing the distance between us. He called my name in relief.

"Thank God! I've been searching everywhere! Where—?" Then he really saw me, took in my condition. "Oh, my God! My poor love! What happened?"

"Someone tried to kill me," I whispered, and the strength drained out of my legs, my arms, my leaden body, and I began to topple slowly forward.

But this time, powerful arms scooped me up like a feather as the darkness swirled and swallowed me again. . . .

A cool cloth was stroking my temples. I struggled to rise but a firm hand pressed me gently back against the worn leather. My grandfather's chair. In the library at Mainstay.

"It's all right, now. You're safe," Colum's voice murmured soothingly. "We've sent for the doctor. It's all right now."

His face swam into view for a moment. Just behind him loomed a stern-faced Mike Fanning. Then I let go and slid down into the soft darkness again.

"No, the ankle's not broken, just twisted. And the cut on her head will heal well enough. Her hair will hide any scar. Still, she'll need X-rays, to be sure. Bruises, exhaustion. What happened?" Dr. O'Brien folded his stethoscope back into his bag. "Ah, you're awake. Nice mess you've made of yourself. No, no talking. Sleep, that's what you need. How many fingers am I holding up?" He shot the question at me. I croaked the answer.

"And now, how many?" He whipped out a silver pencil light. Obediently I followed it. Left, right, up, down, one eye, the other eye . . . At length he straightened up, slipped the tiny light into his bag and pronounced me conditionally unimpaired in essential respects, "Such as your eyesight, young woman. Though, mind, you're lucky, I'd say. What were you doing to get in such a state? By the condition of your hands I'd guess mountaineering, with no experience and no rope!" he finished sarcastically.

I managed a weak laugh. "Near enough, Doc."

"Where, for God's sake, child? And why?"

"The cliff below Mainstay. The tide was coming so quickly . . ."

He started. Then he roared, "Is it a death wish you have, girl, that you'd not stay away from the place that killed your mother and father, and you watchin' it happen?" His tone softened, pleaded. "Promise me you'll not be so foolish again?"

The clammy darkness was gathering about me again in

rushing, all-enveloping waves. "I—I didn't mean to this time, Doc." I was blacking out. I made a tremendous effort. "I was almost safe, but someone—hit me . . ." I knew the words were sluggish and slurred now as consciousness swayed and receded. Must tell them about the cave, and the steps, and the boxes . . . the wooden boxes deep under the cliff. . . . "A few steps from the door," I heard myself say quite clearly.

"Exhausted," the doctor snapped loudly. "She needs sleep. Lots of it. I'm going to sedate her to make sure. Better get her upstairs to her bed, Colum."

Then I was being lifted, supported. A needle pricked my arm and I knew nothing more.

I was on the cliff path again. It was raining. I was sliding, slipping on the mud . . . now I was on the rocks. The water was lapping higher. No escape. I was going to die. Unless I could climb the sheer overhang that loomed above me. . . . But someone was coming, someone who would stop me, strike me down, someone who wanted me dead! It was all blurred. My arms were stuck. Someone was holding my arms! I couldn't get away. He had caught me. . . . Then he was shaking me, rocking me, cradling me, kissing my hair! I sighed, nestled close. I was safe after all, safe and warm. . . .

"There. That's better." Colum's voice was low and calm. "Now for the pills the doctor left for you . . . good girl . . . and another sip. That's my girl. Now lie back, love. Rest. No more songs, just sleep . . . sleep . . ."

With the soothing murmuring in my ear, I drifted away. . . .

I lay and watched the Virginia creeper outside my window make shifting, shadowy patterns on my bedroom wall. Dancing early sunlight gleamed palely on the brass rail of my rumpled bed. The first sunlight of the day that touched with a gentle finger the dark stubble on Colum's chin and the deep, exhausted crescents under his closed eyes. I lay, floating, detached from everything, content to let my gaze slide over his features.

As if in answer to an unspoken call, he stirred. The gray eyes opened. For a timeless moment, the sleepy, lazy con-

tentment in them matched my own. Then the flowered
wing chair in the corner creaked and groaned and he stood
up, stretching. He looked at his watch. "Mornin'. How
d'you feel?"

"As if I'd been run over by a train." My voice sounded
strangely faraway, not mine at all.

"Be back in a jiffy."

I had never had thin soup with croutons of Peggy's
brown bread so early in the morning before. It was delicious, but halfway through I laid the spoon down in sudden
weariness.

"It's too heavy," I said in surprise.

"Effect of the pills. Let me." Colum took the spoon. Com-
petently, easily, he fed me the rest of the soup.

I watched him set the empty bowl on the tray. "Thank
you," I said indistinctly, inadequately to his back.

"My pleasure."

Then I took in the quilt and pillows piled on the wing
chair. "You've been here all night?" Around us, the house
slept.

He nodded. "You needed someone. To help with the
nightmares." He subsided into the chair and wriggled his
shoulders.

I looked down at my rumpled bedclothes. "Bad?"

"Bad enough. Peggy wanted to sit up, but she was worn
out." He grinned suddenly and the weariness momentarily left his face. "At least you knew I was here."

"I did?" I was remembering the kisses on my hair. A
dream?

"In some ways," he remarked idly, impishly, "it was the
best night I've ever spent."

The words hung in the air between us.

Then I blushed. I busied myself with the bedclothes and
for the first time noticed that I was wearing a voluminous
flannelette nightgown, a blue paisley print, with long, ruffled sleeves and prim collar.

Colum's eyes followed mine in some amusement.

"I got as far as your jacket. Then Peggy shooed me out."
But by this time I had recovered my composure.

"I wouldn't have minded," I whispered, with a ghost of a
smile.

Colum grinned again. Then a comical expression of dismay crossed his face. "Nearly forgot. Doc left some more pills for you. No arguments, doctor's orders. Sleep's the best medicine, and all that."

Through already hazy eyes I watched him replace the glass of water on the night table. A butterfly kiss touched my forehead as I drifted away on a golden cloud. I was smiling. This time I knew I hadn't dreamed it. . . .

CHAPTER 14

The tranquil afternoon sunlight was sliding past my window when I woke again. Leaves rustled gently against the sill and a warm whispering breeze fluttered the half-open curtains.

I eased cautiously upright. The world didn't whirl, but I ached all over. The hammerer in my head slept fitfully. I sat very still.

The door opened noiselessly and Colum's untidy brown head leaned into view. For a moment he wasn't quite in focus. Then my eyes cleared.

He saw that I was awake.

He lounged easily against the jamb. His clothes were, if anything, a whit more rumpled than usual, but his chin was freshly shaven and the purple crescents were gone from under his eyes. He belonged comfortably within the polished dark enclosing wood. It crossed my mind that the first Captain Wentworth was probably as tall; the generous lines of Mainstay suited large-framed people.

"Hello, sleeping beauty."

"Hello yourself, prince."

"Better?"

"I think so," I said cautiously. "No more pills. Please!"

He spread his hands wide and waggled them about. "You've had the lot. See?"

I nodded toward the window, careful not to make any sharp moves. "Lovely day."

His eyes didn't budge from my face. Slowly he nodded.

"Pity to waste it all," I hazarded.

The only reply was a noncommittal monosyllable.

"I'm getting up," I announced, a little too vigorously, and my head swam again.

"Sure you're up to it?"

"No-oo, but I'm getting up anyway."

149

"In that case, I'll go and run you a warm bath. I insist. Besides," he added disarmingly, "doctor's orders. He left a herbal rub for you, too."

Then full consciousness thudded back. And memory.

"Colum," I said urgently, "I must talk to you."

"Later. Bath first." He smiled as he answered me. "Then we'll talk all you want."

Incautiously I nodded and promptly paid for the sudden movement.

Colum frowned but said nothing.

Like the Cheshire cat, the brown head was the last part to vanish. It returned abruptly. "The bath'll probably hurt a bit. I wouldn't advise washin' your hair yet either."

"I'll try not to come unstuck."

It did hurt. And not just a bit.

But it felt marvelous just to be alive.

I managed to limp toward the stairs, my swollen ankle newly strapped up in clean gauze and encased in a soft slipper. And, despite exquisitely aching muscles, I had even succeeded in brushing my hair, well, most of it.

I was doing nicely until I began to think.

I thought I knew who had tried to kill me.

And why.

I groaned as I realized that almost twenty-four hours had elapsed since the attempt on my life. Enough time to return with a larger boat and spirit away the contents of the cave, in darkness, probably, at low tide, hours ago. . . .

And by now, the fist-sized rock, the only vestige of the attack, would be new-washed and innocent. I should have carried it with me. But, as evidence went, the rock wouldn't have been very convincing, proving only that it had been in violent contact with my head. In any case, I didn't have the "evidence." It was down in the cove and the tide had been in and out several times since.

I hadn't much to take to the police. I knew that.

And I couldn't be sure of Sergeant Burke.

So it would have to be someone higher up. In Cork?

But would they believe me there? Or politely, compassionately, put it all down to hysterics or delayed reaction to Grandmother's horrible death?

Then I had an idea. A crate. Just one crate would furnish

all the evidence I needed. If they were still there, if they hadn't been moved yet . . .

I couldn't do it on my own. I had tried to shift the top one and couldn't budge it at all. But Colum could. Easily. And, together, we would figure out what to do.

Then I realized something else. Something that chilled me to the bone.

Once what had happened was known, once it was common knowledge that I was still alive, that I hadn't died down there on the rocks, it wouldn't take a genius to surmise, no, to *know*, just how I had escaped. And a version of what had happened, including the fact that I was very much alive, albeit somewhat dented, would be known all over Kilcollery in due course. Probably was already. The village grapevine could be relied on. Then what would he do?

The silent house almost screamed the answer.

Come after me, of course. And, this time, make sure.

Peggy met me at the foot of the stairs.

"Are you sure you should be out of your bed, Miss Joanna?"

This time I didn't mind the slightly truculent tone. I was glad that she cared, and thankful for the very ordinariness, the reassuring safety of her presence. She hovered uncertainly.

"I'll get you some tea." But she made no move to go.

"No, thanks, Peggy. No tea."

"But you've eaten nothing."

"I had some soup. Honestly, I'm not hungry. It's probably the pills. Where's Colum?"

"Mr. Colum had to go. That Mr. Fanning came for him. Something important, I heard him say." It was more than clear from her tone that Peggy still held Mike in aversion. She sniffed. "Mr. Colum said to tell you he would be back as soon as he could and not to stir till he came." She recited the message like an obedient child. "Those were his very words."

"Oh?"

"Yes. Are you sure you don't want some tea? How about a nice glass of milk. You should take something. That's a nasty cut. You'd want to be more careful, Miss Joanna."

"I'm all right, Peggy, really. Just headachy and sore, but it'll pass." And I would be careful. Very careful.

She followed me into the library.

"The boy was here. Askin' about you, he was."

"Danny? That was nice of him."

"He deserves better than that ould rip of a stepfather." Then she dismissed the subject of Danny. "Miss Joanna," she began, hesitantly, but with an underlying determination, "I don't like to bother you just now, what with your accident and you not feeling at your best, but, well, I've got to talk to you, tell you somethin'." I could hardly catch the words, uttered as they were in a tone that dropped lower and lower.

But I came out of my brooding, preoccupied state in a hurry when Peggy closed the door. Secretively, as though she didn't want to be overheard. . . . She turned, fixed anguished eyes on me. " 'Tis about the house, Miss Joanna, this house . . ."

Then the great brass knocker thundered imperatively on the front door.

Peggy started and squeaked in fright.

I started myself. "Ignore it, Peggy," I said urgently. She was just about to confide in me. She mustn't be interrupted. Not now.

But I was too late. She had already collected herself. The eyes were veiling themselves, her face was once again set in its customary impersonality. Smoothing an already immaculate apron, she said obstinately, "I have to answer the door."

I wasn't really surprised to hear Dr. O'Brien's authoritative tones.

"Aft'noon, Peggy. Your mistress awake yet? Ah, Joanna! Up and about, I see. A good sign. Healthy young woman that you are, with any luck you'll suffer no long-term damage, eh? But best be sure. I arranged for X-rays in Carnmore at the County Hospital, so you may as well get your coat. I'll take you there right away. No time like the present, seeing that you're on your feet."

"Is it really necessary, Doc? I'm all right. Better every minute."

"White as a sheet, and with an intermittent headache by the looks of you. Come along, girl. Better be sure than sorry with a head injury. And I'll give you something later to make sure you get another good sleep tonight."

I nodded cautiously, so as not to start up the throbbing. Stay put, Colum's message had said. He believed what I'd said about being struck. But of course he hadn't meant the doctor. And I should have the X-rays. The doctor was right. "We'll talk when I get back, Peggy."

"Talk, girl? What about? Nothing else wrong, I hope?" the doctor inquired lightly.

"Oh, no, sir," Peggy replied stolidly. "Just bills and household matters. Like the menus. That sort of thing, sir." But her eyes dropped and there again was that quick, tight, nervous clasping movement of her hands that I had noticed before. And she avoided my gaze.

I said nothing in reply to what I knew must be a lie. She hadn't closed the library door so circumspectly merely to speak of household matters. And I couldn't recall ever having known Peggy to lie before. No, she had been going to talk . . . I couldn't go now.

But Peggy now met and held my eyes as she said, " 'Twill keep till you get back." It was her best toneless-servant manner, usually reserved for pushy tradespeople. "We have enough in to be goin' on with."

I nodded temporary assent and limped out of the house with the doctor.

His battered old Austin made heavy weather of the steep mountain road. With every twist the car creaked, and its springs were decidedly unsound. In automotive terms, the Austin looked the equivalent in age and fatigue of the doctor himself. And it had over ninety thousand miles on the clock.

"You do a lot of traveling, Doc?"

"A fair bit. To Dublin, to see my sister. She's bedridden, you know. And, of course, round and round the county. It's a big county. Seems endless sometimes." A wintry smile flitted over the lined face.

Was it only because I hadn't seen him in some years that he seemed disproportionately aged? Not just older and more worn, but somehow fragile, vulnerable, strained. Overworked, I thought.

"There are other doctors. Surely you don't have to—"

Testily he interrupted. "You know, there's a lot of the

old lady in you, girl. I may be old, but I'm not incapable. I'll retire when I'm good and ready."

I opened my mouth to object to what I considered a willful misunderstanding of my kindly meant inquiry. Then I remembered an encounter in the quiet graveyard on Monday and an old, faraway voice saying stoically that only time and work could heal grief. . . . So I said nothing.

A few moments later, the doctor touched my arm lightly. "Forgive an old man, a touchy, proud ould fellow who doesn't want to be put out to pasture like an old horse that can't work anymore. An obstinate old mule, more like, eh?"

"Never, Doc. Not you. People hereabouts wouldn't know what to do without you."

"They're too scattered, but some of them have been with me since I started. And that's not yesterday. Oh, the youngsters are on the job, more and more of them, easing me out with their machines and their lab tests. But some folk still like to call me. They still need me." He nodded several times and frowned fiercely as though to reinforce the point. "Drat this road! Goes from bad to worse. Divil a penny do they put into fixin' it! Just look at the drainage ditch there. Far too deep and much too close to the road. Be an awful job to get your car out of that thing. Need a towrope at least, I should think. And a damn tractor. Would you believe how long I've had this jalopy? Nearly fifteen years. Old Sam Madigan at the garage does wonders to keep her goin' for me. Of course, she needs a bit of work at the moment." He patted the wheel almost affectionately.

"You've had this car for as long as I can remember," I said. After we left Mainstay, I'd wondered whether to talk to the doctor, to enlist an ally, so to speak, but I knew now I couldn't. I couldn't burden him with the deadly knowledge that pounded in my aching head. I couldn't worry a tired old man. After all, what could he do, except become alarmed, angry, urge me to be careful, to go to the police. The former two I'd achieved on my own. The latter two I was going to deal with in my own time. With Colum's strong arm for aid . . . if the boxes were still there . . .

"You know," mused the doctor suddenly in an annoyed tone as we hit another pothole, " 'tis only six or seven miles to Carnmore as the crow flies. The damn mountain range adds three at least."

"Pity we're not crows."

The doctor grunted and lapsed into silence. Even an inquiry about one of his favorite sports, sea angling from his own boat, elicited no more than the terse comment that "it wasn't what it used to be in the old days, and damned expensive now, too."

He roused only once after that, when we came upon a stretch of roadwork that hadn't been there when I came this way on Monday morning. But there they were now, the familiar yellow-striped barriers and beacons closing half the road, the hunched gap-toothed workers swinging worn picks and pitch-stained shovels, the asphalt lorry, the giant greenish diggers, and the dusty steamrollers. One man was pouring something, probably tea, into battered tin mugs. Over all lay the unhurried calm of endless time.

We joined a line of miscellaneous vehicles. We sat and waited.

The doctor snorted. "I knew it! Stuck behind a horse and cart, I'll bet."

"Well, at least they're fixing the road."

The doctor harrumphed and muttered impatiently.

A lethargic flagman gave an indeterminate signal with a grubby flag, and everybody surged forward eagerly. There was indeed a lumbering farm-cart in the line but it was pulled by a very new-looking tractor, not a horse, and the driver obligingly and, to my mind, quite dangerously, hugged the edge of the drainage ditch, sending faster traffic onward with a cheerful wave.

Dr. O'Brien reluctantly acknowledged his action with a glowering nod, wrenched the gears, and sent the Austin forward with a lurch.

The X-rays in the small but well-equipped County Hospital didn't take long.

"No fractures," the white-coated young doctor told me. "But you'll have what I might call a hangover for a while. Nothing to worry about, though."

I thanked him without comment. After all, he didn't know how I had come by my injury.

"I'd stay off the booze." He grinned. "It won't help."

I laughed politely and escaped quickly from the ether-and-antiseptic air.

Glimpses of the sea, shimmering under the acutely angled sunrays of evening, soon were flashing and gleaming through the high crags as the road twisted and squirmed through the jutting mountains. The roadwork was deserted now, the heavy machinery parked and padlocked between the barriers. A few rusty night lamps sat forlornly on the paving, glowing faintly pink in the warm air as they awaited the fall of night.

Everything seemed to be waiting. Even the birds were still.

"Glad Carnmore hadn't bad news for you, girl," the doctor remarked gruffly as the Austin labored up the hill toward Mainstay. "Feeling better? You've got some color in your cheeks. Not so bad now?"

"Not so bad." I told myself that the statement was relatively true if a certain amount of redefinition was introduced.

"No lasting ill effects anyway." The doctor's tone was one of relieved finality. "Then I recommend relaxation. Good as a tonic. I happen to know young Colum's made a booking at that place at Carnmore I suggested. He'll be glad to hear the X-rays cleared you, eh? Then an early night after a good dinner, girl. I'll give you some pills to take. Make you sleep well. Best thing. The state you were in last night, I'd not have been surprised if you came down with pneumonia. Hardy constitution. Runs in the family. Still, take care for a day or two, promise?"

I almost nodded, remembered the lurking hammerer in my head and assented verbally instead. "Thanks for everything, Doc."

"I just wish you'd taken my advice and gone back to England. But I daresay you'll be heading back any day, eh?"

"I daresay." I wasn't going to get into all that again.

We had reached home. Funny how quickly, how easily, I had slid into thinking of Mainstay as "home." I struggled out of the Austin, suppressing a wince or two.

"Thanks again, Doc."

"No more mountain climbing now! How did you come to be climbin' about down there anyway?"

"Oh, I just went for a walk." Like my dead grandmother.

"I must have hit a slippery patch. Well, as you said, Doc, no long-term harm done."

He fumbled for the gear lever. Then a sunray, escaping from the massing clouds, bathed his face with sudden pitiless light, robbing me of all speech as I took in the deeply etched furrows from nose to chin, the blurred, thickened contours of his cheeks, the papery folds under sunken eyes. But his glasses were no thicker than before and the clear blue eyes were sharp and penetrating as ever. Clear blue eyes that now took grave leave of me.

"I'll look in again, Joanna. In the meantime, nothing to worry about. Rest and relaxation, now, mind. Goodbye, girl." The Austin jerked twice and moved away.

I summoned up a farewell smile. A smile that quickly died as I reflected on the recurrent assurance that I had "nothing to worry about."

I hadn't imagined that attempt on my life. Nor the bloody rock. And the crates in the cave were no dream.

From the hundreds of caves, large and small, that riddled the broken coastline of the southwest, I knew why that cave had been chosen. It wasn't only because its entrance was below water at high tide. Nor merely because it was so well hidden by the natural curves of the cliff that even I, a constant visitor for years, hadn't known about it. That wasn't all, as I'd realized down there . . .

And I knew why my grandmother had died on Holy Thursday.

Holy Thursday. I remembered a pathetic, torn, dogeared storybook with a copperplate inscription.

Then I remembered something else and drew in my breath in a soundless whistle of horror.

Peggy and everyone else would have to wait. I must find Danny Sheridan. And quickly. For he could be in as much danger as I was!

High above Mainstay, I paused to catch my breath, to rest for a precious moment. The goat track up the steep slope had proved more difficult than I'd thought, the angle of ascent more awkward than I remembered from carefree childish forays. My ankle hurt and I was aching and hot from the exertion, but I daren't delay.

Before me lay the moor, starred with gorse and flowering thornbushes. Scattered, limpid, mirror-still bog pools reflected the leaning wild flowers and the billowing silver clouds that were gathering in the indigo sky. No breeze stirred the bullrushes, nor the clumpy heather, nor even the soft grasses.

It was still and warm and close. And oppressive.

I wasn't sure exactly where the tinker camp would be, but beyond the moor, beyond the raised path that wound between the pools, lay a hollow in the mountains. A likely place. It was sheltered and rimmed on one side by a clear, clean, rippling stream. Ignoring my protesting ankle, I pressed forward urgently. And found the camp just where I'd guessed it to be.

It was small, squalid, and haphazard. But at least Sheridan Senior was nowhere to be seen.

Six caravans in all, their colorful circular tops marred by peeling paint and shabby, torn canvas flaps at the half-doors. I had an impression of unwashed milk bottles, littered scraps of paper, orange peels, yellow canisters of bottled gas. A few shaggy piebalds grazed nearby, their liquid eyes following my approach toward a group of sharp-faced women whose quick chatter faded into silence when they saw me.

"Good evening." My polite greeting sounded constrained even to me. "I'm looking for Danny Sheridan."

No one answered, but wary glances passed between them. A young woman sidled around behind me and slid away in the direction of the farthest caravan. She disappeared inside.

"He ain't here. What d'ye want wid him?" It was an older woman who spoke, her speech hesitant, reluctant, suspicious.

What on earth to say? I looked around wildly for inspiration. None came. Belatedly I realized that I should have thought this out.

The older woman said something to the others. I couldn't understand her; had she spoken in Irish? They shifted about, gradually enclosing me in a loose circle. I started as a skinny hand grabbed my left hand, turning it palm-upward. A young woman with tangled black hair and bright eyes.

"Tell yer future, lady? For silver, mind."

They were all around me now, pointing at my clothes, my shoes. Decidedly ill at ease, I scrabbled in my wallet and produced a couple of coins. The black-haired young woman released my hand to take the money. I seized the chance to back away. The women behind her jostled each other out of the way, murmuring, now begging. The young woman tried to grab my hand but I refused. She shrugged. The chorus strengthened. I handed out some more coins and backed away. Danny wasn't here. And I shouldn't have come.

"You're from de big house, aren't ye?" The older woman gestured vaguely in the direction of the sea, toward Mainstay.

"Yes. Can you tell me where Danny is?"

She shook her head. But as I retraced my steps toward the moor, the low secretive chattering that followed me swelled to an urgent noise.

After the mingled smells of cooking, damp earth, and wood fires, the scent of the bog was thin and clean. I plodded painfully homeward, heavy with doubt and confusion. Had I been unwise to go in search of Danny, to point him out? My shoe struck a pebble and a needle of pain shot through my ankle. I pulled up short with a stifled, exasperated exclamation. I bent down, rubbed at my leg.

Somewhere behind me, a bird flew up out of the bracken, winging skyward with little thrusting, fluttering movements. I watched the tiny thing wheel and soar, glide, and then dip quickly down into the thornbushes. And the silence settled once more.

I limped on toward the fiery west, now lit by a slanting sun that glowed between the rising mass of rain cloud.

The gorse rustled, a soft swishing sound. Some small animal, probably. But despite myself, I quickened my pace as much as my ankle would allow.

Then, somewhere behind me, in that echoing, oppressive stillness, I heard a crunching noise. And a twig snapped.

I whirled around, but the path only stretched empty, quite bare. For a second my whole being was in my eyes and ears.

I saw no one. Heard no one.

Yet I felt a lurking presence, an indrawn soundless breathing.

Perhaps he was even now circling, creeping . . .

Then I unfroze and ran. Stumbling, crashing, blundering between the spiky gorse and the leafy, prickly thornbushes.

I didn't look back once. And I didn't slow my headlong pace until, chest heaving and with a painful stitch in my side, I came to the top of the goat path once more.

And felt safe within sight of Mainstay. . . .

CHAPTER 15

He was on his feet, deep in thought, staring out the library window. The set of his hunched shoulders suggested concentration, tension. I thought I detected impatience, too, in the way he shifted restlessly from one foot to the other.

"Hello, Colum," I said quietly.

He started violently and whipped around. Then my hands were crushed between his.

"Joanna! Thank God! Where the blazes have you been? The doctor came home ages ago, said he dropped you off here. But when I came up, Peggy said you hadn't come back yet from the hospital. I thought—oh, I don't know what—where were you?"

"Looking for Danny Sheridan. Colum, I want to talk to you."

"Sure. But you'd better sit down. The doc said the X-rays were clear, thank God. But how are you feelin'? You look a bit ragged around the edges. Have you eaten at all? Peggy said you wouldn't touch a thing earlier. Not good enough, but we'll see about that shortly, if you're up to it, that is. Are you? The doc seemed to think it'd be the best thing all round; said somethin' about relaxation. Must say I agree with him."

"Colum!"

"Rattlin' on again, am I? Sorry. It's just relief that you're not out there again in some other sort of trouble."

"Some other—what other sort of trouble?"

"Oh, I don't know. You seem to get about so much." He shrugged. "Stuck somewhere with four flat tires or somethin'."

The example sounded lame even to me. "Colum, my car's at the gate."

He mumbled something about worrying anyway. I had to smile.

He hadn't sat down, but continued to pace about.

I bent forward to rub at my ankle. A soothing circular motion. And became aware of a throbbing, a rushing in my ears.

Colum had stopped pacing and was looking at me. He was speaking. It was an effort to concentrate, to understand his concerned inquiry.

"I—I'm all right," I said, but my voice sounded thin and faraway somehow. . . .

When I came to, Colum was rubbing my hands. The plaid rug was tucked around my legs. I lay still against the soft upholstery. The faintness passed slowly, leaving a slightly sick taste at the back of my throat. Joe lumbered in, a moony curiosity fixing his features, a glass of water clutched tightly between huge hands. Colum took it from him and held it to my lips. Obediently I sipped.

Joe ducked his head. "Peg do say she be makin' the tea, sir." He recited the message glibly, bobbed his head again, and shambled out of the library.

"And you'll eat it, girl, if I have to spoonfeed you," Colum added with mock severity. "Enough of alarms and excursions. . . . Food first, then we'll see . . ." He glanced at his watch. "Good God, it's after seven already."

"Doesn't matter, does it?"

"Yes, it does."

"Why?" I struggled upright.

"Why? Well, because you haven't had anything to eat all day, of course." He went to the library door and set it half open. He stood, apparently listening. Then he swung away to the window where he gazed out into the gathering gloom. He flexed his shoulders, went to the door again, and out into the hall, every movement quick, impatient. I heard him pace across the tiled floor toward the kitchen. Then the steps stopped. A pause, and he was back in the library again, pacing up and down at the window.

"You're like a yo-yo. Sit down, Colum. Please!"

"How long does it take to make a simple pot of tea and set out some bread and butter?" The words were ground out between his teeth.

"I'll last." I eased myself fully upright. "Come and sit down, Colum, please. It's important."

He demurred briefly, smiled, slumped into the chair opposite mine and folded his arms. "All right. Shoot!"

I wasted no time getting to the point. "In the cliff below this house," I began quietly, "there is a cave."

Colum stiffened. There was no doubt I had his full attention now.

"A large cave," I went on. "At high tide its entrance is concealed. Oh, it's well hidden even in the ordinary way by the way the cliff juts in and out. And in that cave there are crates, wooden crates, piles of them, worth a fortune to those who share . . ." My hands were grabbed in a bruising grip. I think I cried out. Colum's gray eyes were boring into mine.

"Go on!" he urged. His tone was harsh.

"Those crates"—I flinched at the intensity of his face—"Colum, those crates . . ." But I never finished the sentence. Instead, from the kitchen came a cry, then a tremendous crash of china, breaking glass, and a heavy thud.

Colum leaped for the door. Heart thumping, I limped after him. The door to the kitchen was ajar, wedged by the brass weight that usually sat on the hallstand. Wedged so that it wouldn't swing back as Peggy carried the teatray through.

The teatray was now upside down on the floor in the middle of a splintered, spreading mess of tea leaves, butter, jam, sugar lumps, shards of glass, and gilt-edged fragments of china, all sliding about in a pool of milky-brown liquid. Faint curls of steam hissed and evaporated.

Just in front of the open cellar door, Peggy lay crumpled on the floor, a freshly broached jar of her own jam still in her hand. Her legs were splayed, arms flung out awkwardly. Like a rag doll. Or a discarded puppet.

Her face was drained of color, her breathing loud and uneven. A bubble of saliva slid slowly down her chin. Her mouth was dragged down to one side, twisting her heavy features into a rigid grimace.

Beside her, on his knees, Joe was sobbing. Tentative fingers touched hers and fled again as he folded his arms and hugged himself close, rocking back and forth calling her name piteously, like a lost child.

Colum exhaled slowly. He pushed the cellar door back. The lock clicked and held.

I dropped on my knees beside Peggy and lifted her head onto my lap.

"Heart or stroke, I'd say," Colum breathed in my ear. "Did she have a heart condition?"

"I don't know, Colum. Oh, God, I don't know."

Joe gave a great cry. "She's goin' to die!" He began to thrash about, knocking a heavy kitchen chair. "Don't ye touch her! She be dyin'!" He pulled at the fallen chair, righting it and thrusting it behind him, away from Peggy.

"The doctor, Colum!" I said rapidly.

"Yes, I know. I'll go right away. The thing is, should we move her or not?"

"We must keep her warm, I think. A blanket. Joe, get a blanket or an eiderdown. Now!" He only moaned in fear. "Now, Joe!"

His great, pain-filled eyes swung to me, cleared, focused. He nodded, mumbled something, shambled off in the direction of his room.

Her hand under mine was very cold. And getting colder. I spoke fearfully. "I think a blanket won't be enough. She's freezing. I think we have to risk it and move her to her bed. Oh, God, I wish I knew what to do!"

Colum scooped her inert body and cradled her to his chest. "She's surprisingly heavy," he gasped as he struggled to his feet.

She lay on her bed, unconscious but still breathing in that ragged, noisy way that was so frightening. I loosened her skirt, opened the top buttons of the familiar cream blouse, smoothed back the gray lock that straggled across her pale forehead. I pulled up the eiderdown, tucking it around the still figure. How many times had those work-roughened hands done the same for me?

"Oh, Peggy, hang on. Please hang on!" I whispered, sinking to my knees beside her bed. A speechless, quiet Joe joined me there, holding out to me a faded patchwork quilt. The one from his own room. The one Peggy had made for him years ago. He stood, in mute misery, looking helpless and already bereft.

"I'll just get you a chair, Joanna," Colum said. "You'll have to stay with her while I go for the doc."

I nodded, my eyes never leaving the bed. With all my

soul, with every fiber of my being, I was willing Peggy to hold on . . . till the doctor came. . . . Her hand was so limp!

Colum slid a chair under me. I sagged into it without letting go of Peggy's hand.

"I'll be back as fast as I can, girl. Don't let anyone in till I come myself, unless it's the doc. Oh, God, why did this have to happen now?" He left the room precipitately.

Then I remembered something and stumbled after him. He was already loping down the path when he heard my call. He skidded to a halt and swung about, his face registering fright.

"Danny! Colum, you must find him! After you get the doc."

"What the—?" The dark brows contracted.

"Please! Don't ask questions now. There isn't time. Just find him and bring him back here. He'll be safe here. Please, Colum! I'll explain later."

He nodded and raced off down the path.

I retreated into Mainstay, clicking the great lock home with care. Apprehensive, I hurried through the kitchen, sidestepping the shattered mess on the floor, noting that the heavy chair Joe had knocked over now stood in front of the cellar door. I shivered as I turned the side door key in the lock.

Joe had pulled Peggy's rocking chair close to the bed and was sitting in it, rocking gently, stroking her hand and singing a queer, off-key song almost under his breath. Singing to her a lullaby she couldn't hear. He didn't look up when I entered the room. Nor even when I slid wearily, fearfully, into the chair Colum had brought for me to keep vigil. And, together, Joe and I waited for the doctor.

And waited.

Seven forty-two already. Where was the doctor? He couldn't be out. Not now.

Seven forty-three. Had Peggy's breathing changed? Was that a car? I strained to listen. Seven forty-four. Hadn't I read somewhere that the first half-hour after a stroke or heart attack could mean life or death?

Then there was a short series of sharp taps on the distant side door and Colum's voice called my name. Thankfully, I flew to the kitchen and tugged the lock open.

Two men in navy uniforms, carrying a folding stretcher,

followed Colum into the house. I stumbled after them to Peggy's room.

"Can't find the doc. Out on a call, I think. His house-keeper's trying to locate him by callin' everyone she can. He didn't leave word," Colum said rapidly. "So I phoned the county people at Carnmore, told them it was an emergency and these fellows came tearin' here."

A young man in a white coat strode in past us.

"Dr. Roberts," he said briskly, indicating the tag pinned to his breast pocket. "Clear the room, please."

"Resident. House doctor at Carnmore," Colum said to me.

Joe was resisting all attempts to get him to leave the room. He flailed at the ambulance men.

"He's her brother," I cried.

The young doctor nodded. "Let him stay," he ordered. "We don't have time to fool around."

A few minutes later, swiftly, efficiently, they took Peggy out of the house, the doctor holding aloft a plastic bag whose long tube ran down into a needle taped to Peggy's arm. Joe went with them, still clinging tightly to Peggy's other hand. He let go only to climb into the ambulance. He settled himself beside her. Nobody objected. It wouldn't have done any good. The men secured the stretcher straps.

"I'll need a few particulars," Dr. Roberts said.

"I'll get my jacket and be right behind you in my own car," I answered hurriedly. My eyes couldn't seem to tear themselves away from that dreadful pulled-down mouth.

"Fine. Meantime, her name. The one she usually answers to."

"Peggy."

"Surname?"

Then I went blank. I gaped at him. But from the depths of memory swam up jumbled pictures of many years' Christmas gifts, carefully hand-knitted things, each bearing a small card inscribed in Peggy's laborious, upright handwriting: From your affec. friend, Peggy Curran.

The doctor looked at me curiously. "Age?" Another pause. "Sixtyish, perhaps?" he prompted.

"Mid-sixties, I think."

He made no comment but my color rose anyway.

"Allergies? Is she taking any medicines? You don't know. Next of kin?"

I indicated the silent Joe.

The doctor assessed him for a split second. "I'd better put you down as well. If you reach Dr. O'Brien before we do, tell him to get in touch right away. Urgently." He climbed into the ambulance and sat on the bunk opposite Peggy. "Right, fellows, let's step on it."

"Hold on a sec, Doc." This from Colum. "Joanna can't follow along for a while. Can't drive herself for the moment. Just recovering from a fall. Head injury."

I interrupted impatiently, frantically. "Then you'll have to drive. Peggy's all that matters for now. I must go."

"Joanna, calm down. Have you forgotten about Danny?"

I had. Completely.

"We'll come as soon as we can, Doc," Colum said.

The doctor nodded. The men latched the rear doors and, seconds later, the silent white vehicle was rolling away down the hill, gathering speed smoothly. We stood, watching, somehow rooted, until the mesmerizing flashing light vanished into the dark depths of the stifling dusk.

I tripped once on the path back to the house. Colum steadied me. "Watch your step. The light's tricky." He released my arm, thrust his hands deep into his pockets. "Must be a storm brewin'." His brows were knitted again. He moved quickly, tensely.

Automatically I headed up the steps, reaching for the brass door handles. Locked, of course.

"We came out by the side door, remember?" Colum reminded me brusquely. "You look all in. Better rest, at least for a while. I'll hunt up young Danny."

He stopped at the side door. "Care to tell me why you're so concerned about the boy?"

"He knows, Colum! About the cave, and its contents, I think," I replied hurriedly. "Find him, Colum! It's important!"

"As fast as I can. Another thing, did you see who hit you last night? No?" I shook my head. Frowning, he raced off.

He didn't need to remind me to lock the door.

Alone again. In an isolated house. With no telephone. Resolutely I foraged, made some tea, a sandwich, tried to

ignore the smashed mess on the floor, found I couldn't stay
in the kitchen and not clean it up, bent down to do so, and
nearly fainted again. . . . Concentrated solemnly on knotting myself into a bundle that had some chance of staying
together till this thing was over . . .

Left the kitchen light on so that no one would inadvertently step into the jammy, squelchy jumble that disfigured
Peggy's spotless domain.

It was cold in the library. Surprising, that. It was so
warm and close outside.

I slipped out to the dark hall and found my fleece-lined
suede jacket. The keys to my rented Ford jingled faintly
against the company's large metal nameplate and settled
back down into the depths of my pocket as I slid the com-
forting downy warmth about my shoulders.

I sat on the library window seat. In the dark. That way, I
told myself, I could see out better, out into the garden, over
the cliff, up into the scudding clouds that were accumulat-
ing and rearing high in the strange, still gloom. It wasn't, I
told myself, because that way no one out there could see
me.

I paced restlessly. Turned and paced back the other way.

Sat down again, huddling into the velvet cushions.
Thought I heard a car. Thought I saw a heart-stopping
movement in the shadowy garden. A furtive, flitting,
dodging shadow. Then the climbing rose scratched at the
glass beside me and I jumped, every nerve screaming.

My face was hot, my fingers ice cold and clammy.
Pressed them to my temples. Cool water, yes, that would
be much better. I would go upstairs quietly and splash
cool, refreshing water on my burning cheeks. I reminded
myself that the doors and windows were locked, the house
was secure, no one could get at me here.

I was halfway up the curving, carpeted stairs when a
key scraped in the front door lock!

Only Peggy and I had keys to Mainstay, and Peggy was
unconscious, ten miles away, in Carnmore County Hospital!

Heart thudding, hand over mouth, I backed soundlessly
up the stairway as the great door swung noiselessly in-
ward. A compact dark shape moved slowly into the dark

hall. Then a second. Larger, taller. Two men. Not Gardiner. Not Fred. Then who? Oh, God, who!

They stood by the open door. They were talking in low voices. Waiting for someone else? There were three of them?

Cautiously, fearfully, I inched toward the balustrade, leaned infinitesimally, strained to listen. Had they come after me? Did they know I was in the house?

I couldn't hear what they were saying. Silently I slid down a few steps to the curve of the stairway. I daren't go farther. Then two whole phrases floated up, phrases that transfixed me with horror.

". . . dead before she hit the ground . . . one easy thrust and that was the end of her chatter . . ." It was the shorter man who spoke.

The taller man said nothing.

The shorter man went on. I caught something about a knife.

A murder? To be committed, or already over? My head reeled, but I strained still farther to hear all I could.

"A model, wasn't she? Engaged to Moone?" the first man was asking dispassionately.

Oh, dear God, they were talking about Katrina! She was dead. Oh, God, why? The chilling answer came all too fast.

". . . necessary, I suppose, if she knew . . . couldn't take the chance . . ." The shorter man's tone fell back into too low a murmur for my straining ears. But I had heard enough.

If she knew, he'd said, in that nightmarishly ordinary tone. If. They had murdered Katrina without even being sure that she knew? I had to clap my hands tightly over my mouth to suppress the sob that rose in my throat.

They mustn't hear me. It seemed they didn't know I was here. Perhaps I still had a chance, a slim chance . . .

Then, into the prickling silence, the grandfather clock in the hall heaved and began to chime the hour. The luminous hands of my watch glowed against my wrist. Ten to nine. The hall clock was fast. Incredibly, I made a mental note to set the hands back ten minutes tomorrow.

The taller man exclaimed something that was lost to me in the noise the clock was making. Then he groped about, feeling along the wall, coming toward me with every step!

I shrank back. Had he heard me, sensed my scarcely breathing presence above him? Then he snapped on a wall switch, raised his left arm, and shook back the sleeve of his well-worn dark suit. Instantly the other man barked an instruction, and the taller man swept his hand swiftly across the switch again, plunging the house into darkness once more.

But not before I had seen and recognized the taller man. And seen and recognized the gleaming cuff link in the white shirt beside the expanding watch bracelet. The gleaming shape of a leaf, a damning scrap of gold engraved with a Celtic motif.

The link that matched the tiepin I'd found the night of the strange, furtive light in an empty Mainstay. The pin I had thought was Fred's. The pin that my groping fingers now found and clutched in my pocket.

But was it possible? Surely I was wrong. Wrong about the two men in the hall, about their involvement in Katrina's death, in the unholy business it had taken me only four days to stumble into in my rash, obstinate zeal to know the truth about my grandmother's death. But could I afford to go down there and find out whether I was wrong? Even as I asked myself the desperate question, the shorter man was speaking again, and his words slammed into my hot brain, ending all hope.

"We can trust John to keep the kids who found her under wraps. At all costs this thing mustn't leak out. Tinker kids, aren't they? Nobody'll worry if they don't come home early. Or if they don't come home at all." And he laughed, a low chuckle that made my hair stand on end.

The man I'd recognized uttered a sort of grunt, by way of assent. Then I froze.

"And the other girl?" the older man was asking, very quietly. I didn't need to wonder who the "other girl" was, didn't need to have him add, "the one who owns this place now."

But I had to strain to hear the low-voiced answer.

"She'll be taken care of . . . not to worry," said Mike Fanning. Casual words, cold, commonplace phrases that conveyed the ease of disposing of me. . . .

They moved out onto the threshold and stood there in the suddenly deafening silence. They were no longer talking. Everything was arranged. The time for talk was over, it seemed. Now they waited for something. Or someone.

I scarcely dared breathe. Katrina was dead, and I was next. I had been all too right. They would try again. This time they would make sure I didn't escape.

I shrank, shivering, against the brocaded wall, crouching in the darkness. Mike Fanning, a murderer. Or at least a willing accomplice. Mike Fanning to whom I'd "told my story," who had pretended to look for answers and plausible explanations, all the time to draw out what I knew, to determine with that cool precise mind of his whether I was a threat to their plans. Mike Fanning, whom Colum trusted.

Colum! Oh, God, probably even now on his way back here with Danny. Who also knew. Else, how had the boy appeared behind me on the rocks that first day? He had not come down the path. He must have come from the cave.

Yes! Danny knew. About the cave. About the crates, too, probably. And their contents? Had he, as I had, recognized the shape of the boxes and guessed what *must* be inside?

Guns. Russian guns.

Smuggled guns that could lie for weeks, months maybe, in a safe, dry, well-hidden cave, until it was time to bring them up the remaining sloping passageway at the back of the cave, through the slickly oiled doorway I'd found there, into the false cellar that must lie behind the wine racks, and on up through the house. The isolated, lonely house with no telephone, where an old lady and her two terrified servants would offer no resistance that could not be swiftly, ruthlessly overcome. . . .

The cellar that was always faintly salty, that was about twenty-five feet below where I crouched in shock and horror. . . .

I must get away. To the police.

But how? The front door was blocked. And those two couldn't fail to hear if I tried to slip down and past, through the baize door to the kitchen and the side door.

My head was aching again with strain and fatigue. I pressed my fingertips to my burning temples, but that did no good at all. My hands were sticky, hot, perspiring. Yet I was shivering. A moist dampness was breaking out all over me. Rocking back and forth soundlessly, wild-eyed and terrified in the dark, I fought back the grim throbbing and the sick taste in my mouth. What a time, I thought in silent hysteria, what a time to come down with a fever. . . .

Then a car roared to a halt at Mainstay's gate and hurrying steps raced up the path. The third man? The one they had been waiting for?

"Ah, good, you got our message," the shorter man greeted the newcomer rapidly. "No time to lose. Katrina Sheehan's dead and all hell's likely to break loose."

There was a muffled exclamation.

Mike Fanning's voice, now urgent, floated clearly up to me. ". . . very little time to get everything set. The landing's on, tonight. We just got word from the Libyan end. Been some trouble there, our man was late on the air. . . . Have to be ready about midnight or so . . . just got to keep everything quiet till then."

"Moone and Gardiner?" The newcomer was panting, gasping for breath.

"Making their preparations right now."

"They've been ready since before Easter." The shorter man's tone was edged with sarcasm and contempt.

Since before Easter. Since the Thursday before Easter, to be precise. When my grandmother fell to her death. I was roused from my bitter, despairing thoughts by the sound of my own name.

"Joanna? Where's Joanna?" the third man was asking.

"We haven't seen her at all," Mike Fanning replied.

"At all? There's a light on at the back. She must be in the kitchen. Unless—"

Thrusting past the other two, he dived across the hall and through the green baize door. The first two looked at each other, then rushed to follow, hard on his heels, while, unseen on the shadowy stairway, I shook and shivered in a sudden despair that had nothing to do with fear. Nor even with the fever I was undoubtedly running now.

For the third man, the man they had been waiting for, was Colum McCarthy.

CHAPTER 16

It was all too horribly, hopelessly clear. The reason for
Colum's presence in Kilcollery, his knowing so much on
that first sunlit day on the hill high over the tranquil bay,
his vehement denial that there had been a light in the
house on Tuesday evening. That first nonchalant mention
of his friend Fanning, who would be coming to Kilcollery
"for a spot of fishing," who was used to "looking into
things."

Which of them had organized it all? I didn't know. I
didn't really care. Colum was the one with the contacts
among the men of blood who would pay well for the contents of the cave and for the additional cargo that was to be
landed this very night, in the teeth of imminent danger of
discovery. Katrina was dead, and I . . .

Oh, God, when I had sent Colum in search of Danny, I'd
said the boy knew about the cave and its contents. And
Colum McCarthy hadn't stopped to ask what contents.
Because he already knew. And I had betrayed Danny to
him . . .

I would see them all hanged if I could.

Swiftly, noiselessly, I slipped down the carpeted stairs
and shot across the hall out into the night. My shoes made
no sound on the grass. Even the gate stood open. No telltale squeaks from damp hinges.

The night air was heavier than before, more sultry. In
the distance, thunder growled. No lightning here yet,
thank God. One flash and I would be seen.

The yellow Ford sat prosaically at the gate. Beyond it, a
maroon Mercedes and the blue Triumph, the latter at an
angle. Dark skid marks sliced along the asphalt behind
the blue car. A warm wind was soughing in the grasses.
Long Atlantic rollers splashed as they broke on the rocky
reefs.

173

I slid my key into the passenger door lock, the door away from the house, and then froze as my eye caught a movement in the Mercedes. There was somebody else, a fourth! Shaking with fright, I dropped to my knees on the wet verge. Nothing happened. He hadn't seen me!

Gathering all my courage, eyes glued to that still, dark figure, I inched the door open. I wriggled into the passenger seat. Bumped painfully across the handbrake to the driver's seat, keeping my head down and ignoring the wrench in my ankle when I had to twist my foot sideways.

Infinite care, now. Not a sound till takeoff.

I inserted the key in the ignition and eased the passenger door in without closing it.

Clutch depressed, key ready.

First gear made a soft click.

I poised my feet on accelerator and clutch, adjusting the position until the clutch was almost released.

Lights went on upstairs in Mainstay. They were looking for me. . . .

If the engine would fire the first time . . .

The car was facing almost in the right direction. One quick wrench would send her bucketing straight down the hill.

Mentally apologizing to the rental company for what I was about to do to their gearbox, I turned the key. The engine fired into noisy life and the car leaped forward. The Mercedes door opened. A man jumped out. He was right in front of me. I was going to hit him! Grimly, I realized that the road was too narrow to avoid him unless I wanted to drive straight across the sea grass and over the cliff. To die where my grandmother had . . .

I steered straight for him. I saw only a white face. Then, at the last second, he leaped for the ditch. Rubber squealing, I roared past down the hill, accelerating all the way.

Pursuit wouldn't be long getting organized. They couldn't let me get away.

Away to where? Telephone? No good. Besides, all that talk about informers. Who could be trusted? I thought briefly of the Fitzgeralds. They had a phone. But it was Thursday. They would be in Carnmore, teaching. The doctor's house? Too near. I'd be caught before I could get the stupid Kilcollery switchboard to wake up and answer. There was nothing for it. It had to be Cork. Unless on my headlong way through Carnmore I spotted the police barracks. It would have to be easily visible. I couldn't afford to reconnoiter in a strange Irish town in the dead of night.

Thunder growled as I raced through Kilcollery, heading for the Cork road. I wished I knew the road better. I might have risked dousing the headlights, to vanish into the stormy night. But I dared not. In any case there was only one main road out of the village. They must guess where I was going. I would just have to go hell for leather. I settled myself for a difficult night drive over unfamiliar, twisting, narrow mountain roads. At high speed.

Light flashed somewhere behind me. Involuntarily I slowed for a tense moment on the dark highway. A vivid fork of lightning stabbed into the hills on my left. Thunder crashed, rolled, reverberated. I breathed hard and pressed the accelerator to the floor. Then, on the road far behind me, two tiny pinpricks sparkled and were gone. Not lightning this time. Headlights.

The small car was responsive, well tuned for a rented car. I thanked heaven for the chance that had caused Aunt Christine to ask one of her friends to teach me to drive. A man whose business was cars. Whose weekend relaxation consisted of test driving and cross-country rallying. I, too, had conceived a liking for the latter sport. He and I had for some years been a team. In treasure hunts, time trials, mud races, whatever the club could dream up for a Saturday filled with slippery, twisting, arduous trekking. Thankful for all I'd learned on those fast and furious trips, I whirled now around sharp corners, ruthlessly changing gears, up and down, trying to get every turn of speed out of my small car. It was balking slightly at the steepness of the climb and I tore the gears in fear as I forced the pace.

Lights flashed again in my mirror. Still at some distance, but gaining.

I hit a short straight and roared along it, headlights dancing wildly on the drainage ditch as potholes jarred the car's springs. Then it was hairpin twists and turns again. It was taking every ounce of strength I possessed to whip around them at such speed without sending the car rocketing into the deep, wet dikes that lurked in the dark all along the mountain road.

Another sheet of lightning lit the landscape in an unearthly purple glow, almost blinding me for a second. Thunder cracked and rolled. The car lurched and my heart with it. I fought for control, battling the swaying mass for a mouth-drying moment. Miraculously the car steadied and roared onward through the night.

Then it started to rain.

Huge, sheeting, spreading splashes that bounced and rattled deafeningly on the roof. I thrust at the wiper lever and opened the window. I couldn't risk having the windows steam up. Ventilator switch? I knew the Ford had one. Couldn't find it. Had to slow a fraction to reach over and jab at the other window winder, to let the glass down even a crack. I was getting soaked now anyway, but at least I could see where I was going at this breakneck pace. Just about.

Damn the rain. On an unfamiliar mountain road, hurtling along at night, the last thing I needed was a skiddy surface. The light Ford had taken the twists of this murderous road very well so far. But in rain, how much would her steadiness and gripping power be reduced?

The rain, I knew, gave my pursuer the advantage; he was bound to know the road better than I did and didn't need to worry about what was around the next of these horrible corners with wet crags rearing high and gloomy on either side and dim stretches of lonely moorland falling away in the misty air.

The lightning forked jaggedly across the turbulent sky. And the timpani among the heaving, racing clouds was answered by the piledriver in my aching head.

There. They shone, twin beams. Headlights. Gleaming behind me as the relentless pursuer rapidly closed up the distance between us. Electric brilliance lit the countryside, flashed along the car behind, glancing over chrome and glass. A blue Triumph.

Colum's car.

A cry escaped me as I took in that fact. Convulsively, I jerked in the seat, cramming the accelerator to the floor, my misery too deep for words.

It was Colum who was behind me. Colum who was

in fast, efficient, ruthless pursuit. Colum whom I had thought to love, whom I did love, desperately.

He had played me expertly and was now intent on landing me, exhausted and helpless, so that he and his cohorts could complete their profitable business of supplying arms and explosives to the insatiable guerrillas of Northern Ireland. Which side? I didn't know, but it didn't seem to matter.

Which of them had silenced Katrina? Which of them had tried to kill me? I didn't know that either, but they were all equally guilty in my eyes. All of them.

Biting my lips with determination, a cold, hard fear knotting my throat, I drove like a demon through the desolate landscape while, all around, the thunder rolled and the lightning stabbed across the massed, fleeing clouds. The peals were coming less frequently now. The storm was faster even than I as it swept inland, chased by the cooling air from the sea.

Despair was a real thing, I thought incredulously as I glanced in the rearview mirror where the twin beams cruised in tandem with my car. The pursuit—I would not think of him as Colum lest I break—was steady and pitiless. Yet it seemed to have slackened mysteriously. The Triumph was staying at an even distance from me. Why?

His horn sounded once, twice. A raucous, mocking noise that tore along my nerves and only stiffened my resolve. My thumb reached for the plastic disc on the wheel in front of me and I answered with a defiant racket of my own.

Then I spotted the small pink light, low on the roadway. Dead ahead. Glanced in the mirror and noted with trepidation that the Triumph had crept closer. Suddenly I knew why. He, who knew this road better than I did, knew about the roadwork just around the sharp corner, a few short yards away. Did he think I'd have to slow, maybe stop, to get around the barriers? What was he going to do, cut in front of me? Or come up alongside and run me into the ditch as the barrier loomed up at me out of the darkness?

Well, we would see about that. . . .

Lips set and teeth clenched, I slackened for a second, only a second, and then jammed the accelerator to the floor, sending the car leaping forward crazily, my left wheel gunning straight for the warning light. There was just a chance he hadn't seen it, a slim hope that he had forgotten the roadwork or wasn't certain of the barriers' location. It was worth a try . . .

If I could hit and smash the tiny pink light . . .

I cried out in hysterical exhilaration as I hit the first one cleanly. I heard it crunch beneath the wheel. The light was gone when I shot a glance back. I gunned hard for the next one, hit it sideways. Enough to send it spinning into the ditch. I missed the third. It didn't matter, though, for we were on top of the barrier.

The Triumph was only feet behind as I swept around the curve and gasped as the yellow strip loomed up, taking even me by surprise.

I hit a switch and the headlights went out.

Accelerating with everything the Ford could give me, I noted with grim satisfaction that the Triumph was keeping pace. Almost on top of me now.

Ten yards from the barrier.

With a wordless prayer, I slammed on the brakes.

The Triumph's brakes squealed and shrieked in frantic response.

From underneath the Ford came an ear-piercing screech, shattering the night, as the wheels locked and the suspension heaved convulsively. The Ford began to skid, the front slowly turning to the left. The acrid, sickening stench of burning rubber filled my nostrils.

Behind me, the Triumph was helpless. Locked and skidding blindly, heading straight for the deep drainage ditch. There was a crunch of metal collapsing as the blue car grazed along mine. Then it toppled slowly over the side of the road into the waiting drain, coming to a jarring stop at a steep angle, nose pointing down into the mud and rear wheels spinning uselessly in the air.

I caught a glimpse of Colum's furious, white face as I released the brakes on my car and steered to the right, exerting every aching muscle to pull the car around. For a hopeless second it seemed I'd made my move too late. I gritted my teeth and pulled. Arms straining against the weight and impetus of the sliding car. Then, miraculously, she shuddered around, clearing the treacherous edge by no more than a whisper. The wheels came unlocked abruptly and she spurted forward. Instinctively I ducked as I hit the barrier straight on and pieces of wood flew up. One caught in the bumper, dragging noisily along for a few feet. Then it cracked loudly, broke, and fell away. I had done it. I was through, and safe. I had beaten them.

With an exultant cry, I punched the headlight switch and raced through the gears in a crescendo of noise.

The Triumph's engine revved and its reversing lights glowed briefly, uselessly, then flickered out.

Shaking all over, I sped away into the dark night. I had gained a brief respite and some precious time. Unless, I thought, breath catching in horror, unless there was more than one car after me?

Nothing appeared in my rearview mirror. No more relentless headlights gleamed on the road behind. Nothing for miles back. And the blue Triumph was well and truly stuck in the drainage ditch.

They must have been confident of Colum's ability to catch me. I was, after all, only a girl.

I smiled bitterly and blessed those long-ago rallies where I had learned to throw a car into a blind, headlights-out, screaming skid and get safely out again. Part of the trick was instant memorizing of the road's contours. I hadn't really believed Bob when he'd said, in all seriousness, that that particular skill might someday save my life. Breathlessly, I conceded the point to the absent Bob.

Even though he didn't, and couldn't, know that it wasn't a car with defective, failing lights that had menaced my life, but the man I had thought I might someday . . .

Instead, he had pursued me tonight to stop me. At any cost. No . . . no! . . . I was shouting, but no sound emerged.

The silent scream of anguish died away in my aching head. For all his involvement with illicit arms trafficking, my fevered brain told me, I couldn't and wouldn't accept that Colum's hunt after me tonight, if successful, would have ended in murder. . . . Surely they would just have held me, along with the tinker children they'd spoken of, and Danny, if they could find him, until it was all over?

My heart turned over within me as I realized drearily that in a last, hopeless attempt to exonerate Colum McCarthy I had, incredibly, forgotten about Katrina.

No, they couldn't, and wouldn't, let anyone go.

I swallowed a sob. Which of them had killed her? Struck me? Did it really matter which of them?

Oh, yes, yes, it mattered. I cried out into the rain, now falling softly in that drenching, misty Irish way. Oh, yes, it mattered dreadfully.

Mind racing miserably, I retraced my every step since I had sat on that sunny ledge, reluctant to travel the last mile or so down into Kilcollery. What premonition of disaster, of this despairing sense of loss that was now gripping me, had delayed me on that sunlit, high perch? That warm gray rock where I wrestled with the uneasy suspicions that had catapulted me out of my peaceful life in England into this maelstrom of violence and murder, to race dangerously, miserably through the night to bring back the police to arrest the man I'd thought to love, the man I did love. . . .

How could I have been so wrong? So trusting? How could I have been so wrong about Colum?

Then everything came back. Everything we had shared, the moments like precious shafts of sunshine on a gray day, his easy camaraderie with Danny, his laughter, the teasing banter, the simultaneous gentleness and strength I thought I'd observed in him from the first, the insight his photographs revealed. A reassuring presence in a fright-filled night, warm arms holding me close, telling me I was safe . . . kisses on my hair . . . everything flooded back in soul-shattering, painful detail. A cry of anguish broke from me as the moon sailed out into the clearing sky and gleamed along the running ditches. A black and silver sky like the night we went out to dinner . . .

Abruptly I spoke aloud. "No," I said, and repeated the word in wonder, then with gathering certainty. "Not Colum. *Not Colum.*"

I stamped on the brake. The car skidded to a shrieking halt. The echoes died away in the looming hills.

"No," I repeated with rising feeling. "No! No! No!"

Unless every scrap of sense, of judgment, of sensitivity I'd ever had had deserted me, unless the very universe had been turned topsy-turvy in the last few hours, things could not ring so true and be so false. I wasn't wrong. I couldn't be.

I sat very still in the silent car.

If, I reasoned slowly, if I was ever again to know a moment's happiness, the smallest, tiniest glow of contentment, I must not let it end like this. Colum was no murderer, of that I was sure. And I could not believe he was a money-crazed, vicious panderer to violence, a cowardly, profiteering middleman. No, not he. There was an explanation. There had to be, and I wanted to hear it from Colum himself.

The reversing gear clicked softly into place. Slowly I made a quiet three-point turn on the deserted road, there in the high gorge, among the starlit Irish mountains.

I loved him. And I was going back.

CHAPTER 17

The rain was drizzling lightly again when I got there. He was sitting, morose and uncomfortable, inside the steeply angled car, gloomily watching the raindrops slide down the glass when my headlights came to rest on him.

A few yards off, near the wrecked barrier, I pulled over. Slowly, deliberately, I switched off the ignition. Ignoring the rain—I was already well and truly wet all over anyway—I climbed stiffly out of the car, rubbing my aching arms. I limped toward him.

He sat there, unmoving, just looking at me. Then he pushed open the door and clambered down into the road.

We stood, about three yards yawning coldly between us, the only sound the soft murmur of the rain in the grasses. Beside us, its twin exhausts hanging loose, lay the once sleek blue car, muddied all over and with a collapsed front right side.

It was all too clear that Colum was in a towering rage.

"Well, well," he drawled dangerously quietly. "Came back to see if you killed or only maimed me? Hell, you shouldn't have bothered. The next passing farmer would have done nicely, thank you very much."

He turned back to the ruined Triumph. His hand went out, followed the contours of a rear light. Almost like a caress.

"I'm sorry about the car," I began.

"I'll bet." He thrust his hands deep into his pockets. "The insurance'll take care of the damage and then I'll sell her to the first buyer who comes along. I won't drive her again."

The rasp in his voice took my breath away for a moment.

"But you love that car!"

"Not anymore. Anyway, her rear axle's probably a write-off. Even rebuilt, she'll never be the same."

All around us the soft rain dripped and trickled.

"I'm really sorry about your car," I whispered.

Abruptly he swung around to face me.

"Now that you're satisfied you haven't killed me, why don't you go? Go on. Get the hell out of here. I won't tell anyone you came back."

"No?"

"No. Go on. I'm in one piece. I won't even try to stop you. If you step on it, and God knows you're capable of that, you'll make the last flight."

"You'd let me go?"

His voice was flat and expressionless. "Why'd you come back, anyway? In a few hours you could be well away, out over the Irish Sea. God knows I never want to see you again."

Then my anger boiled up. "Who the hell do you think you are, Colum McCarthy? *You* don't want to see *me* again. Well, brother, before I go anywhere, I want some answers from you. And then, don't you worry, I'll be off. But not to the bloody airport."

"Why not?" No more flat tones. Now his rage matched my own. "A quick turn at Heathrow and you can be anywhere in the world. And who knows, maybe your pals will manage to make it out, too, and you can look forward to a long, wealthy life in some not-too-fussy South American resort with your old friend and playmate from Kilcollery! Just be sure you boil the water! And I hope you're both miserable! I hope you drive each other bloody mad!" He turned away. He stood gazing at his car. The stiff, straight set of his back spoke volumes.

"Got it all worked out, haven't you?" I retorted furiously. Then my brain suddenly shook off the anger and took in what he'd said. What he'd actually said. Every blessed word.

He stood, hunched now, one finger rubbing the same spot on the poor maimed blue car. Round and round.

While the joy bubbled up inside me.

In carefully, deliberately neutral tones, I spoke to his back. "When you looked for me in Mainstay earlier, did you happen to notice my handbag in the library?"

"No."

"Well, you should have. It's got my air ticket in it. And my money. All my money."

"So?" The question was reluctant, wary.

"My bank card is there, too. And my check book."

A long pause. A raindrop trickled down my nose. I wiped it away. "So how was I going to buy another ticket if I hadn't a penny with me?"

Then Colum swung around to face me again. "Go on." His tone was shuttered, hard.

"I wasn't heading for the airport, you idiot," I said. "I was going for the cavalry."

"You mean—?"

"For the stouthearted men in blue. The cops."

"Then you're not—oh, my darling girl!"

"And you're not, either," I said simply.

"You mean you thought—?"

"After what I overheard, you bet I thought . . . Fanning and you and that other man. You had gone on so about informers and about people here being so against government regulations, et cetera. Oh, Colum, it was awful."

"Overheard? What do you mean, girl?"

Swiftly, graphically, I summed up as best I could. About the landing and the Libyan end and Moone and Gardiner making their preparations. All of it. "And then there was the tiepin I found in Mainstay on Tuesday. I thought it was Fred's, but it's Mike's, and he wasn't supposed to be in Kilcollery till Wednesday. And you meeting Sheridan in the road that night. He came up to Mainstay and terrified me," I said, somewhat incoherently. "He talked about murder. He warned me. Oh, Colum, is Katrina really dead?"

"Yes."

I swallowed.

"Joanna, all I talked to Sheridan about that night was the money for the camp photos. He wanted more. You didn't think I put him up to anything? You couldn't! Oh, Lord, I forgot—"

He dived for the Triumph, scrambling awkwardly into the front seat. Seconds later, he emerged with a small radio in his hand, pulling the aerial up as he jumped down onto the asphalt again. He touched a switch and spoke into some speakerlike holes on the front of the radio.

"Two-way. Borrowed it from Mike," he said rapidly. The little radio crackled with badly obscured chatter. He fired off a quick string of letters and numbers. There was a lot of indistinct Rogering back and forth, something about everything being safe and sound and about being right all along. He repeated the last phrase twice. Finally he said, "Over and out," and switched off. The crackling died away.

"What was all that about?" I demanded.

"I was just asking them to cancel the general call they put out for you." Colum's eyes were actually dancing. "You were on the wanted list there for a time, girl!"

"The call who put out?"

"Superintendent Brennan and Detective-Inspector Michael Fanning."

"Mike? And the man with him? In the hall at Mainstay? You mean to tell me they're both police? And you let me go through all that!" Words failed me completely.

Colum nodded and grinned. Then his face sombered again.

"Joanna, if you thought Fanning and Brennan and I were gunrunning, why did you turn around and come back here?"

"Because I realized that there had to be an explanation, that you couldn't be involved, that you couldn't be a murderer, that I would trust you with my life . . . that's why I came back. . . . Oh, Colum . . . my love . . ." He was crushing me to him in a rib-shattering embrace.

Then he shifted his grip on my shoulders and held me at arm's length. "You were kissing Moone that night!" he accused.

"He was kissing me! There's quite a difference!" I retorted.

He bent his tall head to mine but paused in mid-motion. "You nearly killed me!" he said, aggrieved.

"I know," I answered, happiness bubbling into laughter. "Now will you shut up and kiss me!"

He was kissing my hair, my eyelids. Warm, searching kisses all over my face. My lips found his throat and slid up to his mouth. He pulled me fiercely to him and his mouth closed hungrily on mine. As if he would draw my whole being into his. To become one in a blaze of joy.

And gladly, ecstatically, I melted with happiness.

We kissed and clung, wordless with the rightness, the completeness of it. . . .

A long time later, a very long time later, we pulled reluctantly apart and stood, hands clasped, somewhat shakily in the middle of the deserted road, beaming blissfully and idiotically at each other.

Colum broke the silence. "I have wanted that since I first saw you alone in the sunshine above this very road."

"Me, too," I said, wonderingly, knowing even as I spoke that it was true. I trailed a finger down his beloved cheek. He turned his head, kissed the finger. Quite naturally, I lifted my head again to meet his kiss. . . .

The world was spinning dizzily and a sweet, infinitely serene contentment was coursing, accelerating, racing through my veins. . . .

Then he gripped my shoulders and pushed me gently away.

"Whoa!" He laughed softly in his throat. "If you keep on at this rate, I won't be answerable for the consequences! And stop smiling at me like that, girl. I might point out," he added, breathlessly, "that we still have some unfinished business back at Mainstay."

I sighed reluctant assent.

"But when that's taken care of, my love, my dearest girl . . ." The blaze was still deep in his gray eyes though his arms held me lightly now. "Takes three weeks, I think. Of course, in the meantime . . ." His eyes were laughing, outrageously, irresistibly.

"Three weeks! What on earth . . . ?"

"To call the banns properly."

"Banns?" I squeaked. Then an answering, joyous laugh broke from me. "I might point out, sir," I teased in my turn, "that you haven't asked me yet!"

"So I haven't. Well—" He dropped on one knee on the wet asphalt.

"You'll get soaked!"

"Well?"

"Yes! Oh yes."

"To love and cherish and all that?"

"Yes! Oh, Colum, you idiot, you're getting mud all over you."

"And obey?"

"There I think I draw the line," I said, laughing.

He stood up and attempted to brush some of the mud from his trouser legs. "It was worth a try." He grinned and reached for me again.

I was just going into his arms when I remembered the key. The key to the front door at Mainstay, the key Mike and the other man had used only a short while ago.

"Sorry, love," Colum answered my quick question ruefully. "I borrowed it from Peggy last night when you were ill with that bash on your head. Had to go and get some things and didn't want to disturb the whole house each time. I gave it to Mike in case you and I had already gone out to dinner tonight. We were supposed to, remember? Brennan said they must have access, to cover off against having to mount a siege or some such thing. Madness, all of it. And when I went rushing off to find Danny, I forgot about the key."

"And why wasn't I at least told the landing was to be tonight? I can understand wanting me out of the way, but, well, it's my house . . ."

"Brennan wouldn't hear of it." To my surprise, Colum shuffled his feet and colored slightly under his tan.

"Why not?" Then I understood. Plainly. "You mean, *all* this time, you've all been suspecting *me?*" I spluttered, and my voice rose in an outraged squawk. "And that's why Mike asked all those odd questions about my holiday in Scotland? And why he seemed to be cross-examining me!"

"But I didn't know then that he suspected you. Honestly!"

"But surely when I was attacked down in the cove . . . they couldn't have thought I did that to myself?"

"Brennan pointed out that you could have slipped, hit your head, and missed the tide, saved yourself in the cave because you already knew about it, and just invented the story of an attack to cover your tracks. You see, you didn't speak of going to the police . . ." he finished apologetically.

"To Sergeant Burke?"

"I see what you mean."

"And why would I tell you, as I tried to this evening?"

"That scared me to death, love, because you hinted at a fortune to be shared. . . . Mike said you might be trying to enlist me in a double-cross, that is, if you were involved."

"If I—*you* didn't think so, Colum, not you?"

"Not until you cut and ran tonight. I didn't know till then that they'd thought so all along. I argued, but there wasn't time, so I said I'd go after you, bring you back, prove them wrong . . . and then you ran me off the road, nearly did for me. And all I could think of was you kissing Fred Moone. . . . Do you know what kind of speed you were doing over this road? . . . I told Brennan you couldn't possibly be mixed up in such a filthy game, not even if you stumbled into the middle of it and they offered you a fortune to keep quiet. Not you, not unless all the laws of judgment had suddenly been turned upside down. . . ." Unconsciously, he echoed my own previous thoughts and I drew in my breath sharply as happiness surged in me again.

I held out my arms to him.

His response was satisfactorily enthusiastic, though suddenly abbreviated.

"Oh, Lord," he exclaimed, pushing me away again, this time turning me toward the Ford. "You're soaked through. What the hell am I thinkin' of, and you only too damn likely to come down with pneumonia or the flu or something after that cave business. You're running a fierce temperature, did you know that? And you still drove that car that way?" He opened the Ford's passenger door. "Come on, I'd better get you back home and dried out, so to speak. Where d'you learn to pull a stunt like that one at the barrier, anyway?"

"Cross-country rallies." I smiled blissfully despite the long shivers that were running through me now.

"In someone else's car, I hope," Colum replied dryly. "Oh, God, don't smile at me like that, sweet, please, or I'll not have the strength to take you home at all tonight!"

Hand in hand we came back to Mainstay. To the library where three people waited. A grave-faced Mike Fanning, an impersonal, efficient Superintendent Brennan, and a skittish, white-faced Danny Sheridan.

The young face was alive with edgy anticipation. I suspected that he was thoroughly enjoying himself. At least he was safe. I didn't have to worry about him now.

Colum performed introductions. The Superintendent and I shook hands.

"She ran me off the road. Wrecked my car for me," Colum said. "Then she came back and we got things straight, didn't we, love?"

"The Dublin girl's dead!" Danny burst out loudly.

"I know," I answered quietly and sat down, pulling off my wet jacket. The fire was almost out. I poked at it, added some turf briquettes and watched the tiny flames flicker and grow. Then I remembered Peggy.

Mike answered my query. "Colum mentioned her before he took off after you. We checked just a while ago. In stable condition. Holding her own. They'll phone the doctor's house if there's any change. They said she'll pull through. It was a stroke." Mike's tone was kinder than I'd heard before. He went on. "Sorry we had to deceive you, Joanna, but you turned up so unexpectedly that we didn't know what to make of you at all. Had to check. Even then we couldn't be sure."

"I explained all that. You should have seen her face. Talk about outrage," Colum interjected, pushing a large brandy into my hands. "Here, love, that'll keep the chills at bay. Super, she really ought to go and get out of those wet things."

"In a moment, Colum," I said. "I want to know about poor Katrina, and what happens next, everything. Who killed her? Do you know yet? And why? Surely she wasn't in on it, too?"

"We don't know." The superintendent offered me a cigarette, lit one himself and drew on it. "We don't know either what she was doing up on the moor. We found her car parked on the main Cork road, on the edge of the village, just where the moor up there starts. There was a fully packed case on the backseat. As if she was leaving Kilcollery and stopped, or was stopped, along the way."

"She was killed up on the moor? Where?" The whisper escaped me slowly.

"On a path up there not far from this house. Could she have been coming here? To see you? Without anyone knowing?"

"I don't know. I only met her once, in the village the other day. I didn't know her at all, really." The brandy was burning its way down my throat and a fiery warmth was chasing away the shudders. They were coming less frequently, at least. . . . But I was once again out on the bog path, in the thin clean evening air, among the wild flowers and golden gorse, where a startled bird was wheeling and darting, where a twig was cracking under a foot sensed but not seen . . . An unseen, lurking presence . . . with murder in his heart, or just obeying orders? The tinker had warned me, spoken of murder. . . . Had that someone later, unexpectedly, come across a girl making her way toward Mainstay in the gathering dusk? And this time completed his fearful business?

Had the murderer mistaken Katrina for me?

And made sure, this time?

"She was so young," the superintendent mused, "too young to die. Alone up there, with a vicious killer, who knew how to use a knife. One easy thrust, Miss Wentworth, under the ribs. Pierced her heart. Bled to death in no time at all."

I shuddered, but not with cold. Colum protested. I stopped him gently. I had to know. All of it.

"Makes you think," the superintendent went on. "Makes you realize what a thin veneer civilization really is. I suppose you wouldn't care to say why you haven't been back here in some years, why your old friend Fred Moone moved his sister in here to look after your grandmother, and why you were apparently satisfied to let them communicate to you only a simple message periodically? Moone, who was using the house, your house, as a cache for smuggled arms?"

Colum started, exclaimed, subsided.

"It's all right, Colum," I said. "Superintendent, it's quite simple. To put it baldly, my parents drowned down in the cove five years ago after an argument with my grandmother. I—well, I blamed her. I hated her. When I got over it a bit, I came to see her. We fought immediately—seems so stupid now—and I said I'd never come back. I wrote a couple of times but when I got no answer I stopped. I came to Kilcollery last Monday because of her death. I didn't know about Nita living here till Colum told me. And as for the notes, Nita simply took it on herself, and maybe Fred kept on with it to keep me away, out of their game."

The superintendent nodded. "Thank you, Miss Wentworth. I appreciate your frankness."

I went on. "I don't know even now how long this game of theirs has been going on, but anything I can do to help stop it before it goes one day further, I'll gladly do. Gladly, Superintendent, because of what they did to my grandmother. And to Peggy and Joe. Poor things, they've both been terrified all along. I can see that now."

"What they did to your grandmother?" Mike's tone was puzzled.

"Yes. I think they murdered her. Or at least caused her death. She wouldn't willingly have gone out that night. Not out there. She only walked along that path when it was dry and fine. And she had arthritis and she hated storms. And I'm not sure, but I think Katrina was killed in mistake for me."

"For you?" Colum exclaimed.

"Yes. I was up there late this afternoon. Looking for Danny, as a matter of fact, and I thought I heard someone behind me. On my way back from the camp. The tinker camp."

Mike Fanning spoke slowly. "And young Danny here tells us that the Big Fella was getting money regularly from the Moones."

"See, I told ye!" put in Danny quickly.

"Piece by piece. Inch by inch," said the superintendent with chillingly quiet emphasis. "Sooner or later. Somebody always knows. Did you know, Miss Wentworth, that there are really no genuinely unsolved murders in a small community like ours where the name of the game is everybody knowing everybody else and his business inside out? Very hard to keep secrets. Of course, we can't always get enough evidence for a conviction. Gossip and laying information are not the same thing. And of course, getting them to stand up in court . . . You did say you'd be glad to help?"

"She can't!" Colum objected instantly. "You can see, she's coming apart with exhaustion and strain now. She needs rest."

"That's just what I want her to do," the superintendent

rejoined blandly. "You see, when the tinker kids found the girl's body, they had the sense for once to go straight to Sergeant Burke. Probably out of fear of one of theirs being accused, who knows? And he in turn had the sense to detain them. So the word isn't out. Yet. We want to keep it that way. Now, if your friends"—the word was heavily sarcastic—"if they've been keeping an eye on this house this evening, what will they have seen? Miss Curran and her brother being taken off to hospital. Yourself and Colum leaving, and coming back. It could be assumed you went to Carnmore Hospital, too. Then we all sat about having a chat. No one here knows who we are. So when we leave, Miss Wentworth retires as usual for the night. Everything *as usual.* You see? Nothing to alarm them. If you'll give the impression nothing's up. Otherwise, months and months of work may go for nothing. We'd like to get every last one of them this time, break this particular group completely."

"How do we know they'll think that way?" The wary question from Colum forestalled my ready agreement.

"They have to, really, you know," Mike answered him. "The message we got from our man in Libya made it clear they've little choice. The stuff's already on its way. And this time it's tied to a schedule. They've added a wrinkle, two birds with one stone, and a bigger profit; this time there's a heroin shipment coming in as well. They've done that once before. Got away with it because we didn't know the landing arrangements. This time we'll be waiting. Our people are already in place." Underlying the precise tone was a curious note. An edge of anticipation.

"I didn't see anyone," I remarked.

"You weren't supposed to. Will you help, Joanna?"

"And keep the boy here with you?" added Superintendent Brennan.

"I just want to know one thing. Who killed Katrina?"

"We don't know yet, but we will. Does it matter just now which of them did it, Miss Wentworth?"

Then I realized that it didn't. Not anymore.

Colum demurred a last time. "We can't leave them here!"

"I said I would help. And I meant it!" I answered.

The superintendent stood up. Suddenly he and Mike

both looked subtly different. Businesslike, I'd have said. And very capable.

"After we leave, Miss Wentworth," the superintendent said briskly, "you lock up, move about, put lights on and off, you know what to do. Everything must look normal. And don't worry. We should have it all wrapped up by one A.M. If they're on time."

"I'll come back when it's all over, love," Colum said.

"I'll keep an eye on him, Joanna," Mike teased with one of his rare smiles. "And not just for you. The super and I don't want to have any explaining to do to his uncle."

"Colum's uncle?"

"He's by way of bein' a cop. That's how I got into this thing in the first place," Colum appended laconically.

"An assistant commissioner is rather more than just a cop," Mike said precisely. "That's how Colum got me down here so fast, because he already knew we were investigating along this stretch of the coast and had the Moones in particular under surveillance."

"Why in particular?" Tired, head aching, I couldn't stop now.

Colum spoke urgently. "Think, love, think of the necessary ingredients. A place big enough to hide the stuff, with no likelihood of being discovered. We were wrong about the hotel itself, but it seemed possible in the off-season. And when the time came, a mode of transport, which no one would suspect, constantly on the road anyway, unremarkable, that could come and go all over the area, or anywhere in the country, roomy and . . ."

". . . big enough. The Kilcollery Crafts van. Of course!"

"Right first time, love." Colum's mouth was set, pressed in a thin line. He looked, somehow, surprisingly dangerous.

I thought of the dark green van that had loomed up in my rearview mirror on Monday, the van that had seemed to be trying to send the Ford over the cliff edge. Four days ago. I shivered.

I left the library light on for a few moments after the three men left Mainstay. I would play my part. But I wasn't in the library. I was doing the rounds, checking clasps, locks, shooting the heavy bolts across the doors. Then I switched out the library light and went upstairs.

Everything must look normal. I discarded my damp clothes, donning not night things but slacks, sweater, warm slippers. Flicked a switch or two. On for a while. Then out. I padded soundlessly downstairs, joined Danny at the library window. Swallowed some aspirin for my aching head. Settled down on the velvety window seat. To wait.

And, in the darkness, Mainstay waited with me.

They were late. Very late.

They came at twenty-five past two in the morning.

It was gloom, not quite dark, faintly luminous, when I spied the movement. Almost imperceptible, then growing clearer. Long, twin shadows cutting silently through the gently rolling night sea.

Disbelieving my eyes, I strained out into the black and silver night. Behind me, curled up in my grandfather's chair, Danny stirred at my whispered exclamation. Noiselessly—every sound would carry for miles over the quiet water—he joined me on the cold window seat, frowning as curiosity fought with sleep, following the line of my pointing finger to where two long black shapes were moving soundlessly in from the open sea. Farther out, I could dimly discern a large opaque lump. About the size of a trawler. Standing to some distance off the end of Mullaghbeg headland. Without lights.

Fiercely I wished I could be out there, a part of it, and no matter about the consequences. I'd done my bit earlier. The aspirin had lowered my temperature and the night was not frosty. But if I did go, what about Danny? And I might inadvertently jeopardize the carefully laid ambush and my grandmother's murderers would get away. No, reluctantly I conceded the point. I had to stay here at Mainstay.

Then I thought of something and sped through the dark house to the kitchen where I stopped with a chuckle of relief. The cellar cupboard was not only locked, but one of the kitchen chairs was wedged under the handle. I tried it, it wouldn't budge. Someone, probably Mike, had been there before me.

From the library, Danny and I saw the two currachs make for the cove, negotiate the currents, slide between the entrance reefs into the still, deserted, narrow inlet. Their strokes were expert, easy, assured. But the tide was already rippling in and Mullaghbeg crouched lower and lower in the rising water. The tiny curl of sand would still be exposed, smooth and clean, but not for long. The currachs glided purposefully, rhythmically, and disappeared under the cliff overhang.

"Upstairs! The end room! We'll see from there, Danny!"

Thus, from my parents' old room, we saw the currachs pull heavily in and the rowers get out, wading through the shallows with large crates. One of the boats drifted a little, and they pulled, three of them, on her bow. In the stillness I distinctly heard the crunch of the hull on sand. I scarcely dared breathe for fear the faintest sound might escape and alert the boatmen to our watchful presence high above them. A cloud obscured the moon and everything else with it. My nails ground into my palm in frustration. But, clearly audible in the carrying air was the rasp of heavy seaboots on sand and rock. Scraping sounds. Vague movements. Then nothing.

Were they in the cave now, deep in the cliff beneath us? The moon peeped out on the deserted boats. Still nothing. Where were Brennan's men? I waited, tension gripping me. Danny pulled at my arm but said nothing. I followed his pointing finger to where, out at sea, the opaque blurred shape, at anchor in the cold predawn gloom, rocked soundlessly.

Another crunch of loose rock. A seaboot incautiously placed. They were leaving! Getting into the currachs. They mustn't leave! They were to be caught tonight. The whole horrible business was to end tonight. Now. Agitated, anxious, I rose. Then the cliffs, the rocks, the path swarmed suddenly with dark shapes running silently and fast. The whole place was alive and moving! The men on the tiny strand stopped, looked up, tried to scramble into the boats, to push off, but it was too late. Dark figures closed on them, surrounded them. One shape broke, ran. A shot rang out. There was some brief scuffling and then they stood about.

Out at sea, a powerful searchlight was blazing a path. The trawler, caught in the beam, tried to gun its motor but it choked, spluttered, died even as a fast, high coast guard cutter sliced through the water toward it. It closed relentlessly on the trawler which wallowed helplessly, taken completely by surprise. The cutter, too, must have been waiting all night, hidden in the lee of a spit or head somewhere down the jagged coast.

So it was over. The silence settled. It was really over.

"I'm going down," I said breathlessly.

Joyous with anticipation and excitement, Danny leaped for the door. "Me, too!" he exclaimed. There was no need for quiet now.

Wondering at my feelings, not so much of triumph or vengeful satisfaction but of letdown, emptiness, I limped hastily down after the boy into the still-night dimness of the kitchen. He snapped on the light and tugged at the heavy bolt that barred the side door. There were sounds outside, slow footsteps. Then a sort of thump rather than a knock.

Could it be Colum, come to tell us it was over? But the silence outside sent a shiver of doubt through me.

"No, Danny! Don't!" I cried, not really knowing why.

But I was too late. He had already wrenched the bolt back. "I want to see!" he was shouting joyfully even as he twisted the key with one swift movement and yanked the door wide open. Then we both cried out as the big man swaying on the threshold took one stumbling step forward and fell.

Sheridan crashed to the floor, one hand extended blindly, the other clutching at his left side.

Danny uttered a low, animal sound and backed to the wall where he stuck, immobile.

Sheridan huddled on the tiled floor, his face ashen, eyes open, staring, glazing. Blood oozed very slowly, then faster, through the filthy shirt. Between the fingers of his clenched hand protruded the handle of a knife. Blood seeped along the wood, dripped from his hand onto the floor.

It's a plain wooden handle, I thought, quite coherently. A fishing knife, quite common around here. The sort everybody has. With the long thin blade for filleting fish. Suddenly I felt sick and had to cast about for something to hang on to.

Sheridan's lips were moving but no sound was coming out. His eyes widened. He moved, emitted a groan, clutched convulsively at his side. Then his lips moved again and a pitiable gurgling emerged. A bubble of blood appeared on his lower lip.

Must *do* something. Can't just wilt here and watch him die.

I crept forward and sank to my knees near the contorted face. Shouldn't I try to stop the bleeding? I didn't want to touch him. But I must.

"A towel, a cloth, Danny! Quickly!"

But the boy didn't move. White-faced, he cowered against the wall, dilated eyes fixed on Sheridan. Shock had immobilized him completely.

I stumbled to the cupboard and pulled out a pile of clean linen. Glass cloths. They would have to do.

Tentatively, then more firmly, I pressed a wad of cloth against the terrible wound, noting with rising fear that the pool of blood on the floor was widening visibly. Sheridan groaned. Then his eyes focused and he saw me, knew me. His strength was ebbing only too obviously but the glint of recognition was unmistakable. One hand crept out to grip mine. He tried to speak. I bent down. I caught only two words.

". . . the doctor . . ." Sheridan grimaced dreadfully and clenched his teeth.

Of course! But could I leave him? I looked around wildly. Could I send poor, terrified Danny?

Sheridan tugged weakly on my hand. Glaring eyes fixed on mine, he took a racking, croaking, rattling breath and tried to speak again. The effort cost him too much and he fell back, shuddering. His eyes glazed, his grip slackened, his hand slid out of mine. It came to rest, bloodied and inert, on my lap.

Must get help. Though as I looked again, I was horribly sickeningly sure that the Big Fellow was dead.

"We must get the doctor, Danny," I said anyway. I lifted the tinker's hand from my lap and placed it gently on the floor.

The boy's eyes flickered dazedly to mine and wandered back to rest in horrified fascination on the body of his stepfather.

I stood up. "Danny! Look at me! We must go." The boy's

attention jerked abruptly to me. He emitted a suppressed scream.

"Your hands! They're all bloody!" His eyes traveled down. "An' your clothes. You're all bloody!" He shrank away from me, looked again at the crumpled body on the floor. "He's dead!"

"Stop it, Danny!" I ordered sharply. "I don't know, he may be still alive." I looked around for something to put under Sheridan's head. The floor was so cold and hard. Then I was easing a makeshift pillow of rolled-up cloths under the tinker's head, talking to Danny, as much to lessen his shock as to calm my thundering heart. "The doctor, Danny. That's what Sheridan said just now. The doctor!"

A voice from the doorway made me whirl in fright.

"A kind touch, the pillow. But it's wasted, I assure you. There's nothing you can do for him now. He's dead, quite dead . . . eh? . . . I'm quite sure." The voice rolled over me in waves, quiet, soothing, nightmarishly ordinary, but his eyes, dead eyes, were terrifying. "I had no choice, of course," he went on mildly. "He'd have bled me dry. First the girl, then him. I couldn't let it happen, spoil everything. He got away from me, somehow, and next thing I spotted him, down here, with you. I underestimated his strength, unfortunately. How much did he tell you?"

"Tell me?" Stupid with shock and bewilderment, I could only reiterate the question.

"Yes," was the impatient rejoinder. "Not that it matters now. You just had to come over from England, didn't you? Ah, well, it's all up now, but I've got a chance at least. Come on, we must get going before that bunch in the cove comes back here. Got to get to my car, up on the main road. Oh, yes, you too. You'll be my insurance. No matter now how much Sheridan told you."

"But all he said—" I stopped as the memory flooded back, cleared, sharpened. "All he said," I repeated slowly, "was 'the doctor' . . ."

"That was all?"

"Yes." My answer came flatly, uselessly. For I understood now. And wished to God I didn't.

"Pity," he remarked briskly. "I mean, it was a pity I didn't know earlier that was all the damned tinker had time to say. For your sake, that is, my dear girl," came the chilling clarification.

Then ice-cold eyes met mine.

"Right. Come along. Both of you," ordered my old friend, Dr. O'Brien.

CHAPTER 18

The light blue eyes were wide and empty.

"He had to go. He tried to blackmail me, the bloody up-start. Forgive the language, my dear. He was following me tonight, waiting for me when I got back from meeting the trawler. I still have my own boat, you know. But Sheridan would have ruined everything, all I'd worked for, all my plans. You see?" The doctor's tone was quiet, even conver-sational, but his eyes were wiped clean of all reason.

"He tried to blackmail you?" I whispered.

"He saw what happened with the model girl, Katrina. She was leaving, going back to Dublin. Fred swore she didn't know anything but I knew better. She'd been nosin' around, talkin' to you. Gardiner and I followed her. Sure enough, just outside the village, she pulled over, got out of the car, and started to walk across the moor toward Main-stay. To put you wise. We couldn't let her do that. She saw us and started to run. Then we knew we had no choice. Gardiner's legs are younger than mine. When I caught up with them, she was already dead. Nobody knew about me, you see. They all think Gardiner is the brains of the opera-tion. They don't know about me." Incredibly, the old voice was clear and proud.

I gasped.

Straight-backed and suddenly arrogant, he continued. "It was through me that Kilcollery was chosen. I put them on to Moone and Gardiner and they paid me a percentage. Not like the old days. Oh, I remember some high old times in the old days when we didn't make a penny out of it. Ah, but they're all dead, everyone's dead now. . . . You see, girl"—the tone dropped, waxed conspiratorial—"there was the crafts van doing all that nice legitimate travelin' up and down the country. And Gardiner only too ready to turn a quick profit and no questions asked, using the dress

200

house for the onward passage. I did a bit of travelin' myself, but there's a limit to the trips you can go on without some infernal, gossipin' so-an'-so noticin'."

"Sooner or later somebody talks?" I quoted the superintendent's words. Surely I was light-headed, wandering in a dream.

"Eh? Yes, yes. Couldn't have put it better myself. That's the crux, secrecy. We put a false floor in the van, installed Nita Moone here at Mainstay, so the van could come and go with no one the wiser when it collected the guns. Foolproof. The hotel's too conspicuous, right down in the middle of town. And, of course, it doesn't have that special feature your ancestor so thoughtfully provided. I daresay he meant the name 'Mainstay' as a delicious, private joke. See, my dear, how perfect it all was?"

"Yes. I am beginning to see." Must keep him talking; play for time. "You always knew about the cellar and the cave, then?" My mind was sending out a silent cry for help.

"Ironically," the doctor replied with a wintry smile, "it was your grandmother herself who told me all about it. Boasting about the Wentworths, she was, the old fool. Your grandfather had the whole thing blocked off when your father was born. Plastered over the door to the second cellar. Afraid the boy would come to some harm down there. Typical Victorian rubbish about protectin' the young from themselves. She even had the gall to liken the old duffer to me—in my untiring efforts to look after the health of the people hereabouts. Especially the children, she said in that damn affected, superior, bloody maddening way of hers. Little runts, what do I care for their snivelin' and their spots! Running myself ragged to take their temperatures and dose them with patent medicines while, before my eyes, my Mary was dying and not a thing could I do about it, except ease her pain with more and more morphia. Oh, God, Mary!"

The doctor gave a great cry and dashed a hand at his eyes. He looked at me. He looked at Danny. And a slow smile spread over his face.

"Tryin' to keep me talking?" He wagged a finger at me in that nightmarishly ordinary way. He was almost playful. "Time to go." His calmness was uncanny.

Danny shook suddenly and whimpered. The doctor's

hand, lined and clawlike, shot out and closed on his arm. "You, too, brat." Still smiling that gentle smile, he pulled Danny with him toward the open door, stepping fastidiously around Sheridan's body.

"Go where!" I stalled.

"I told you already! Now move!"

"He's going to kill us!" Danny cried. He hiccoughed and choked on the words.

The doctor raised quizzical eyebrows. "Not unless you give me trouble. Any trouble," he added significantly. "Now, there's just one little thing I want you to do, Joanna. I'd do it myself but you might try something foolish. Pull out my knife there." He gestured in Sheridan's direction.

I shrank back in horrified disbelief. "No."

"Just one little pull, or I'll deal with the boy. Here and now." He jerked viciously on Danny's arm. The terrified boy cried out softly. "Ah, good. Grasp it tightly. Pull. Pull!"

There was a ghastly sucking sound. The knife came, an inch or so; then it stuck, on bone or muscle or something. I retched and turned away.

"There, there, if you can't . . . Pity, it was my favorite fishing knife. Had it for years. Still, with your fingerprints on it, they may think *you* killed him! Confuse things nicely for a while, who knows? After that scare Fred sent him up here to put into you . . . A head start, that's all I need. People are waiting for tonight's delivery. I must get it to them."

"But the guns are down in the cave and the police are all over the place! You'll never get near—" I shook my head in deepening bewilderment and promptly paid dearly for the sudden movement as the cut on my head throbbed into life.

"Puzzled, dear? I don't mean guns, you know," the doctor answered me briskly. He brought a floppy paper parcel halfway out of his pocket, let me see it briefly, pushed it back down again. He spoke quickly, contemptuously. But I already knew what the small package contained.

"Heroin, Joanna. The stuff the dreams of fools are made of, fools who pay well. Half a kilo. Worth a couple of million or so. Of course my share is a pittance by comparison, but it's enough to get me free of this place, free of everything, for the rest of my life; and it's waiting for me in Switzerland. Ironic, isn't it, that my poor Mary had to have so much of the stuff; oh, all quite legal, of course. And I would sit by her side for hours . . . then one day I realized that she'd really gone from me a long time before. I gave her a little extra, just enough to end the pain forever."

Thus did my old friend, Dr. O'Brien, confess to the murder of his dying wife.

He was mad, raving mad. He had to be.

His eyes were glazing. He was staring far away, into an unseen distance. Seeing something we couldn't, as on that first day in the silent graveyard. Only a few days ago.

Oh, God, where was everyone? Of course! They thought they had them all, down there on the beach and at the hotel. They didn't know about the doctor. Nobody did. Except Danny and me.

A diversion. We must, somehow, manufacture a diversion. If even Danny could get away . . .

The doctor shook himself. Squaring his shoulders in a macabre caricature of the erect, honest, kindly country doctor he had once been, he frowned and barked sudden orders.

"Outside, both of you. Now!"

It was still night, but graying, paling. A soft, gold moon was sinking toward the sea. Puffs of early mist floated in the calm air. The damp underfoot struck a chill through my slippers. But it also instantly sharpened my thoughts. He was gesturing in the direction of the goat track, toward the moor, where Katrina had died. . . . His car waited beyond, on the Cork road. . . .

Summoning all my strength, I said, "Why not go on without us, Doc? You'll get away faster by yourself." I tried to sound very composed, matter-of-fact, but my voice betrayed me, cracking in midsentence.

He didn't even bother to answer but withdrew something from his pocket and pointed it, first at Danny, then at me, then at the boy again. Steadily and purposefully. For all its small size the gun looked deadly. I nodded in defeat.

"We're wasting time. Move!" he said. "Quietly, mind!"

We moved. Across the garden. The wet grass struck

coldly through my fast-sodden slippers. Danny moved like an automaton.

"Let the boy stay here!" I pleaded once.

The gun waved suggestively. Toward the wall and the goat path. . . . He mustn't get us up there. . . .

Danny scrambled awkwardly over the wall, his usual litheness deserting him. I made to follow. Then I jerked my head to one side and whispered sharply, "What's that!" But if I had hoped by this last-ditch maneuver to distract or delay the doctor, I was doomed to dismay. I had underestimated him.

"Nice try, girl." Incredibly, the old man laughed! A rusty sound that made my flesh crawl. Impatiently he jabbed at me with the gun. Obediently, despairingly, painfully, I pulled myself up onto the wall. I started to swing my legs over. Then I realized something. Danny was already *outside!* Maybe we had a chance . . .

I rubbed at my ankle, wincing very obviously. Then I braced myself with my hands, for the jump down on the other side. I let one hand slip on the wet wall, cried out, lost my balance, and fell with all my weight back into the garden. Instinctively the doctor put out his hands to push me back, to break my fall, and dropped the gun in the process. I grabbed for his arms and yelled like a madwoman, "Run! Danny, run!" The doctor and I struggled on the grass in an ungainly muddle of arms and legs, he trying to push me away, to extricate himself, I clinging all the more tightly.

A split second and there was the thud of running footsteps. Mercifully, the boy had understood.

But the doctor had found the gun. And it was pointing dead straight in my face. He struggled to his feet. The gun jabbed painfully at my shoulder, once, twice.

"That was not wise, Joanna," he said heavily. "On your feet. Hurry!"

"You're not still going to try to get away!"

"While I have you, my dear, what do I have to fear? A few country peelers? Pshaw!"

I can't quite explain what came over me then. Exhaustion combined with hysteria, perhaps. Anyway, I laughed. Simply laughed. Stood there and laughed.

"You know," I remarked conversationally, "I've never

before known anyone to use that word. Pshaw! It's quite ridiculous, isn't it? Except in Sherlock Holmes stories. Or was it Watson?" And I chuckled again.

The gun jabbed into my ribs. "Get . . . over . . . that . . . wall!" The look in his eyes was enough to sober a drunk.

"Oh, well," I conceded desperately, "if you're set on ignoring every attempt at civilized, reasonable conversation . . ."

Colum! Mike! Somebody! Please!

"Cease your chattering, girl."

I met his cold, faraway, pale blue eyes and I ceased my chattering.

We were over the wall now and climbing. Clambering, slipping, sliding on the muddy patches, grasping at the grasses on either side of the steep track. The doctor was making better weather of the climb than I was, with my ankle and my throbbing head. He must be incredibly strong. I could scarcely see where I was going, but I went anyway, prodded forward whenever I stopped to catch my breath. "They'll not get me, they'll not get me . . ." The doctor's voice was almost pleading, unreal in the predawn stillness.

Then the queer, spellbound silence around us was shattered. Footsteps thudded below and, with a roar of black rage, Colum came hurtling at top speed up the track. He was yelling with fury as he launched himself at the doctor. At the same instant the doctor turned as though jerked by a string. His gun hand came up. There was a deafening report. The bullet thudded into Colum's thigh. He fell heavily. Someone screamed. The doctor stumbled. Colum was crumpling, sinking to the ground, one hand clutching at his leg, blood welling out in a spreading, ugly stain. And the doctor's gun hand was coming up again!

I was still screaming as I hurled myself blindly at him. I could see nothing but that horrible little weapon. We both fell. The gun clattered down the path. A few precious feet. I sprang toward it. This time I got there first. I turned. I was shaking all over, but I had the gun now. I stood up, steadying the deadly little thing with both hands.

Slowly, the doctor straightened up. He came toward me. He was smiling!

"Not another step, or I fire!" I whispered.

"No! No, girl. Not on your old friend. You wouldn't hurt me! Think of all the years, all the times you came to visit, to listen with my stethoscope, to twirl on my surgery chair until you were a very dizzy little girl. . . . Come along, dear, give it to me." His eyes, his voice, the memories, were mesmerizing me . . .

"Stop! Please stop!" I whispered.

He was coming, right hand extended . . .

"God! Joanna, don't let him take it!" Colum was struggling up.

I backed a few steps. My feet were ice cold. I stumbled, steadied myself again. The doctor inched forward. Too close, he was getting too close! That fixed smile was unnerving me!

Then I saw the gleam in his eye. The tiny, triumphant gleam.

"Not another step, Doctor, my dear old friend." I hardly recognized my own voice. Hard, cold, sarcastic, final.

He didn't believe me. He came on.

My hands tightened, steadied, straightened. And there was another deafening explosion.

I could hardly miss at that range.

They were patching up the gaping hole in his shoulder when he told Superintendent Brennan there was something he must say to me.

We were in the library. Dawn was not far off. Outside, two ambulances were pulling up. Men with stretchers were coming up the path. Propped up with cushions, ashen-faced but tranquil, Colum lay on the window seat, gripping my hand. Neither of us spoke. There was no need.

"I don't want to see Dr. O'Brien," I answered Mike's query. "I just don't want to."

But a few moments later, escorted by Mike and the superintendent, the doctor, gaunt but erect, stood in the library doorway and spoke to me anyway. Around his shoulders, his jacket drooped, torn and bloody. His right arm was caught up in a makeshift sling. Two uniformed policemen stood behind him in the brightly lit hall.

"Before I say anything else, Joanna," the doctor said with remarkable calm, "let me say that we never thought you would be involved."

I didn't answer. I felt drained, empty.

"We didn't mean your grandmother any harm originally. But you see, on Holy Thursday night, she found out what we were doing. We'd always managed to slip her a sedative before. She was furious, ordered everyone out of the house, said she was going for the police. Nita and Gardiner were here with her. They didn't know what to do. Then Gardiner decided we had to go ahead. She'd have to be forcibly sedated, enough to knock her out till the job was over. He came for me. We were on our way back to Mainstay when we saw her coming out. You have to remember it was dark and wet that night."

I found my voice. "You said you were in Dublin."

"I came down for the job. Think I'd miss that? Like as not Moone would have cheated me if I hadn't kept a strict eye on him. I've no doubt he's singing to the high heavens right now, though you won't get a word out of Gardiner, Superintendent."

I remembered the flat reptilian eyes and I shuddered.

"But something went wrong," the doctor continued. "When we called out, she ran. And the next thing I knew, Gardiner was after her. Then they were struggling on the path and she suddenly slipped and went over."

I pressed a hand to my mouth. Tears pricked behind my eyes.

"You murdered her. All of you. You murdered my grandmother!"

"That's what I'm trying to tell you, girl. We didn't! Your grandmother is alive—sedated—down at the hotel! It wasn't your grandmother who fell that night! It was an old tinker woman!"

CHAPTER 19

"It all began to come apart that night," Dr. O'Brien said heavily. "Just one old tinker woman. It seems your grandmother had only a few days before given her some clothes. Then Sheridan and she had a fight—he was probably drunk at the time, he was very violent when he had a drop in him—and he threw her out of the camp. She came to Mainstay for money, saw Nita holding your grandmother at gunpoint, and ran. That's when James and I came back." He slumped into a chair.

The silence fairly prickled with tension.

"It was the chance of the tinker woman being dressed in some of your grandmother's clothes that gave us the idea. They were much of a size, the two women. And nobody questioned Nita's identification of the body a few days later. We had to talk her into that, promise her that no one else was going to get hurt. Everything was under control. Or so it seemed. This was the last job. Fred reported that you were away and not expected back for two weeks. We thought the rest of the shipment would be here long before then. But when it was delayed, Fred got edgy and wrote you the second letter. A damn fool scheme he and Nita cooked up between them. Fred says he thought the way to keep you in England was to take the house off your hands. Left Gardiner and myself no alternative but to go along for the time being. Of course even he only meant the offer as a delaying tactic. We were all leaving after this last shipment. Even the hotel sale had already been arranged. And then you came," he added with leaden finality.

"And then I came." I struggled with a sense of unreality.

"Couldn't leave well enough alone, those two. And, of course, when Moone came upon you down in the cove, he lost his head completely."

"Fred hit me?"

"And when I came to see to you that night, you muttered something about the cave and the door, so I had to shut you up fast. Those pills should have kept you asleep for another twelve hours at least. Odd, that. But I didn't think Fanning or McCarthy had caught what you were saying."

"Colum had," Mike put in impersonally. "It took us a while to figure it out, though."

"And I didn't give Joanna the last of the pills. She asked me not to, so I said there weren't any more." Colum's grip tightened on my hand. "If I'd known what you were up to, you—!"

I spoke unsteadily. "What were you going to do with my grandmother?"

The doctor compressed his lips.

"But you've known her all your life!" I whispered in horror.

"Just like Nita Moone, aren't you, girl? She didn't want to accept that Elizabeth Wentworth couldn't be kept quiet forever. After the landing tonight, Gardiner and I were going to take my boat out. And your grandmother was coming with us."

"But not coming back . . . ?" I shuddered.

The doctor didn't answer. With his good arm he pushed a straggling white lock back out of his eyes. He looked old, worn, defeated. He pressed lightly, then more firmly against the bandage that hid the bullet wound in his shoulder. He winced and shifted the sling, changing its angle on his forearm.

"You'll live," the superintendent said coldly.

"I know. You should have killed me, girl. 'Twould have been kinder. You know I didn't think you would really do it." His tone was weary.

The light blue eyes met mine for a long moment. It was his eyes that fell. Only then did I turn away, to conceal the hard lump that was blocking my throat.

"Superintendent! My grandmother! We must go, at once!"

"Taken care of," the superintendent replied reassuringly. "Mike's gone."

Out at the gate, the maroon Mercedes was already moving.

* * *

Grandmother came home to Mainstay just as the first cold radiance glimmered through the paling night sky.

Between the two burly young policemen as they lifted her out of the superintendent's Mercedes, Grandmother's tiny frame looked doll-like. Her eyes were enormous in the small, pale, old face, pupils large and black. She smiled and nodded regally to the motley assembly at the gate. Her gaze wandered about, light as a butterfly.

"She's been drugged for some time; lucky the stuff didn't kill her. Constitution of an ox," remarked the police surgeon to me. Haled from Carnmore in the middle of the night, he was a grizzled, prosaic man who seemed to take the entire night's extraordinary proceedings quite in his stride.

"She's still pretty high, I'd say. I'd like to check her over in the house first, boys; then probably we'll need to take her on to the hospital." Businesslike, he wasted no words.

"I am not quite as dopey as you think, sir," interrupted a new voice that trembled a little, then grew stronger, more like its old self. "I foxed them, you know. Pretended to be asleep. I didn't drink the stuff they gave me. Poured away every drop. They each thought the other had made sure of me. Neither of them noticed anything amiss. I was very clever. But then none of the Moones was ever noted for brains." Asperity crept back, increasing with every word.

"Oh, Grandmother! Grandmother!" I was laughing and crying at once.

"Joanna! Are you here? Oh, my dear girl! My very dear girl!" Then we were embracing.

"Been a long time, Grandmother," I said unsteadily.

"My fault entirely. An interfering, bossy, stupid old woman, that's what I've been. No, don't try to tell me otherwise. I had a great deal of time to think in that horrid little room they kept me in down at the hotel. I realize so many things, now, my dear, so many things." Then we were embracing again.

"Can you forgive me, Joanna? I should never have allowed the Moones over the threshold of Mainstay. But at least I had the sense to move most of my investments to the care of an old friend in Dublin. Oh, yes, I realized a long time ago that Fred Moone was not entirely reliable. I just had no idea how far he would go."

"Don't think of it, Grandmother. It's all over, and I'm here . . ." I broke off.

"And I'm not asking you to stay. I've learned my lesson. But . . ."

"Friends, Grandmother, a truce. And welcome home. To Mainstay."

At the police doctor's nod, the two uniformed men picked her up again and made for the gate. Then, it seemed, a small crowd erupted from Mainstay. First the superintendent, escorting Dr. O'Brien, bandaged, head erect, haggard in the morning light. Next, Danny, tired, pale, somehow older. And last, two ambulance men carrying the stretcher on which Colum lay. He was white but smiling as he caught sight of the little group standing back at the gate.

"Good morning, Elizabeth." Dr. O'Brien's greeting to my grandmother was calm, unhurried. Her answering snort was not. The doctor got into the front of the first ambulance. The driver started up the motor. The rear doors were closed. Of course. Sheridan. A policeman was following the doctor into the front of the ambulance.

Then it happened.

Someone shouted. There was a thud. And a crash.

I whipped around in fright. I saw the policeman fall from the first ambulance as it started forward. The driver was already sprawled on the road on the other side. And the ambulance was moving!

Dr. O'Brien's arm was out of the sling. He was dragging at the steering wheel. Then he must have put his foot down on the accelerator. Down hard. The ambulance jumped forward, spattering gravel as the wheels spun. Then they gripped. The whole car roared as it turned.

But it was off the gravel, onto the sea grass. The slippery, treacherous sea grass.

And the wheels were locked. It was sliding, sliding . . . There was nothing anyone could do. Unless the doctor himself could pull it around in time. . . .

He might have made it with two good arms.

The ambulance exploded when it hit the rocks. The fireball ballooned, billowed, smoked, dissipated. The flames didn't crackle for long. . . .

A curl of smoke spiraled into the tangy air, swirled lazily and evaporated away to nothing. . . .

Colum was leaning on one elbow. He gripped my hand tightly.

Slowly, then more quickly, Mike Fanning headed for the cliff path. A uniformed policeman followed him. Nobody said anything. There was nothing left to say.

The eastern sky gleamed pale rose and lavender and blue, sending before it the clean fresh scent of a new morning.

It had been only five days.

It seemed like an eternity.

NOVELS FROM BESTSELLING AUTHOR

DAOMA WINSTON

MOORHAVEN   63925-4/$3.50

Daoma Winston's MOORHAVEN tells of the breath-taking passion between the governess and master of a magnificent mansion built at the edge of the sea. Secret love affairs, life-long hatreds and stormy passions wind their way through three generations—until a powerful love unravels the mystery of MOORHAVEN.

EMERALD STATION   63933-5/$3.50

When a young bride discovers the terrifying curse that surrounds her new home, she is forced to place her trust in the man she has come to fear most—her new husband—and learns that only love can overcome the violence, betrayal and death that will curse three generations of his family.

AVON Original Paperbacks

Available wherever paperbacks are sold or directly from the publisher. Include 50¢ per copy for postage and handling: allow 6-8 weeks for delivery. Avon Books, Mail Order Dept., 224 W. 57th St., N.Y., N.Y. 10019

Winston 7-83

FROM *NEW YORK TIMES* BESTSELLING AUTHOR
Patricia Hagan

GOLDEN ROSES is the vivid, romantic novel, set in colorful Mexico, of a Southern belle who, torn between two passions, is forced to fight for a man's love with a woman's courage.

An AVON Original Paperback   **84178-9/$3.95**

Also by Patricia Hagan:
LOVE AND WAR	**80044-6/$3.50**
THE RAGING HEARTS	**80085-3/$3.50**
LOVE AND GLORY	**79665-1/$3.50**
PASSION'S FURY	**81497-8/$3.50**
SOULS AFLAME	**79988-X/$3.50**